Date Due			
AUG 4 1983			
OCT 2 0 1995			

DARK STRANGER

Books by the Author

Breakthrough
The Storms of Summer
The Clouded Sky
Dark Stranger

DARK STRANGER

by John Iggulden

McGraw-Hill Book Company
New York   Toronto   London

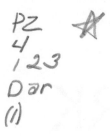
DARK STRANGER

LES CLARK   ED WILLIS   DAVID UNIAPON
Were these living, they might discover in this
book some faint echoes of their lives

1 When James Duncan began to recover his senses it had
been dark for several hours. Had this rebirth of consciousness
been a first experience of human life he might not have been
more confused, or more distressed.

Where there had been nothing, now something was.

What was it?

The blind dark of night pressed on his eyes. Darkness, and
space, and nothing . . . and yet? Yes. There was something.

What was it?

Awareness. A feeling. The awareness and the feeling of fear.

A voice shouted.

That was me, he told himself. I made a noise. I did it. There
is something I can do.

He shouted again.

A voice answered.

His voice?

No.

Another.

He seemed to know that other voice.

They had been in the boat since afternoon. Peter stared into
the night and wondered what was to become of them. And
without warning the long hours of silence were shattered by the
white man's crazy shout.

He cried out, badly startled. "What is it?"

He calmed his voice. "Mr. Duncan? We're safe. Listen, we're
all *right!*"

The white man groaned and muttered. Peter reached out. At the touch of his hand, James Duncan yelled again and tried to climb from the boat. Mouthing his obscure despairs, one leg out of the boat and one leg in, not knowing which way he must go to elude those unutterable fears, he wrestled with Peter. The lurching boat shipped water.

He lost balance and fell back.

"Mr. Duncan!" Peter shouted, holding him, turning his face from the water in the bottom of the boat, so that he ceased spluttering, "Mr. Duncan . . . Mr. Duncan . . ."

He said it again and again, hoping that this best-known sound—this name, identity, this vital clue, whatever it might be—might help. As perhaps it did. Or perhaps James Duncan, the bitter water of the sea choking in his gullet, found in this a more acute first point of reality and sense.

For he knew what it was, that salty draught; that simple first identifying fact of this new life into which he had been delivered by the womb of insensibility and night. He knew. He knew the harshness of that taste. He knew that one real fact.

His fears seemed less. He decided to abide the grip of those hands which held him. He would let himself be held. He let his limbs relax, testing the flavor of existence. Water. The sea . . .

He found the words and, with an effort, said them.

"The sea . . ."

"Yes," said Peter. "We are in the boat."

"Boat . . . ?"

One of the shadows of darkness had been the shadow of this other man. He accepted the shadow of the man. He accepted the man; his hands; those strong holding hands which were part of the man's dark shape. His fear had not been a fear of men. He accepted men. Men and darkness.

"You feel better? Mr. Duncan? Better now?"

"Duncan? *My* name? Me?"

"Yes. Don't you remember?"

Remember. The word made pictures pour into his mind. Flash flash. Flash flash. Too fast. Too fast to see. Remember set new fears leaping in his heart. Remember   remember

remember. Remember rolled in his mind like thunder. A sound like thunder . . . ree—mem—berrr!

Like thunder.

"Yes," said darkness. "James Duncan. It is your name. We are in the boat."

James Duncan? Jimmy? *Hey!* Jimmy Duncan! *Yes!* Jimmy bloody Duncan!

Oh *Christ! Help* me! Christ help Jimmy Duncan . . .

"Don't *cry*, Mr. Duncan," said the soft voice of darkness. "Listen, we are in the boat. The sea is calm. Daylight's coming. We'll soon see where we are. Go ashore. We are safe. Are you listening?"

"Listening? Who are you?"

"I am Peter. Don't you remember?"

"Must I remember? Do I *have* to?"

"No. No need. I'll look after you. Believe me."

"Cold . . ."

"You're in water. In the boat. You fell. Hit your head. You don't remember?"

"I don't have to. You said . . ."

"Not unless you want to."

"I *don't* want to."

"I'll bail the boat. You can sleep till daylight. You'll be better then."

"Better? Am I sick?"

"Not sick, no. Sit up now, while I bail."

Bailing the boat, Peter supposed that he must be nearly all of James Duncan's present diminished world. In that world only shadows would exist, shadows hardly more substantial than the dark of night. The shadow of the boat. Beyond the boat, a running wave, an instant ghostly crest appearing, for a moment curling white. One sound, the lapping monologue of waves, the splash of bailing. Water, the only sound. Faint smells; the salted fishy timbers of the boat, and the sea's cool breath. And the smell of an abo, thought Peter wryly, with one of his sorrowful ironies, the smell of another kind of darkness.

By all the signs of the few words spoken, that would be the entire domain of the white man's awareness on this black night. Bereft of memory, robbed of sense, what wider horizons could he know?

Hard to believe, that was. A man slipped in a boat, and fell. In the fall, somehow, the man you'd known became a stranger. Wits knocked sideways. Transformed. That worldly man, unusual in his certainty and shrewdness, became as helpless as a child. Hard to believe, certainly. But, for all that, it had happened.

He'll recover, Peter assured himself. He must. He is needed. I can't do that thing on my own. His qualities are needed. He *must* recover.

"Lie down again," he said. "And sleep." He crawled to the bow and found his jacket, lying where he'd left it.

"Put this across you."

James Duncan was weeping.

"Why are you crying?"

"Frightened . . ."

"Of being here?"

"Don't know. Of something else . . . ?"

"Tell me," said Peter.

"Could it be . . . I don't know . . . of sadness?"

"Are you thinking of something sad? Is it Jinben, perhaps? Are you thinking of him?"

"Of my friend. My friend Rob Maxwell. Of him."

"That is sad?"

"Why should it be? He is my best friend. I told you."

"Mr. Duncan. Wouldn't it be best if you went to sleep?"

"Why do you call me *mister?* Jimmy is my name. Call me that."

"Yes," said Peter. "But you should sleep."

"What was your name? Did you tell me?"

"Peter."

"That's right. Peter? How big are you?"

"Medium size, I guess."

"Smaller than me?"

"A little. I'm lighter built than you."

"Do you know Rob Maxwell?"

"Don't think so."

"That's stupid. Everyone knows Rob."

"Tell me then. What's he like?"

"Well, he's big and he's strong. Always smiling at something. They all want to be his friend. But I'm his *best* friend."

With a shock of comprehension, Peter interpreted the halting restraint of the white man's voice. He said, uncertainly, "Is he in your grade at school, Jimmy?"

"Of course. That's how I met him."

"Stop it!" cried Peter. "You must! Mr. Duncan, you are not a child! You are a *man!*"

"I will tell you how I met him . . ." James Duncan stopped. Belatedly, the meaning of Peter's words stirred in his mind. His mind seemed to slip over to another level.

He was in this boat. Talking to someone . . . and it seemed that Rob had been there for a moment. But this chap wasn't Rob. Someone else. Didn't know him. No wonder he was frightened. That mess of pictures and thoughts and feeling that came and went. Nothing fixed. Nothing solid. The feeling of time slipping around all over the place so that, at one moment, the time in which the happenings of his thoughts occurred was now, and at another moment it was yesterday, or a time so little removed from his existence now that it seemed like yesterday, and yet, in every thought it was as if all this had happened some dim long time ago.

Would that not worry anyone? Would not anyone be afraid to find, under every other thought, the deeper knowledge that time had somehow slipped, that present life could not be what it seemed, that what seemed present life had been, somehow, lived out and forgotten—who could tell how long ago? That present life, by some awesome trick of time, was lost?

Now Peter said, "Well then, tell me about your friend. How did you meet him?" . . . and it was all right. Still like a dream, but a dream that wouldn't hurt you.

"You know about the farm?" he said. "We had to leave it. I don't know. We had to leave . . ."

He had spoken slowly, and oh the farm was very real, like

being there again. Down by the creek the feet of drinking cows struck hollow on the boulders of the crossing, and from the lofty trees the silver voices of the magpies chortled songs of joy. Busy at nothing the dogs pranced barking in the stream, and every small certainty of his child's life was there around him.

"When we went, I *hated* it," he said. "We should have stayed, no matter what. Forever and forever. But we're going back, you know. My father says so. Some day . . .

"I was scared when we come down here to live, when I started going to this big school with a million other kids. And we had this horrible, horrible bastard for a teacher. I think it was last year, then, when I started. Would it be last year?"

"Longer than that, I think," said darkness, the name of whose voice was Peter. "But I don't suppose it matters. Go on."

"Well, anyway. I did a very silly thing, straight off. Said something . . . I didn't mean it the way he took it . . . and that *bloody* teacher, that Swanno, he thought I was cheeking him. He makes me into the big joke of the class. You know? The mug for all the class? The one they laugh at? And if a teacher does that, what can you *do*? Straight off, all the kids are in it. They hate you, anyway, that's common sense. They're city kids, and you're a kid from the bush, see? So naturally they hate you. That's right, isn't it?"

"Hate needs no reasons," said the reflective voice of Peter. "Any little thing will do. It doesn't go by reason."

"I hated *them,* anyway. I had to. There was so many of them. And when Swanno does me like that all the city kids laugh themselves sick. They roll around and stick their elbows in each other and scream like crows. Then Swanno calls me Duncan and somehow he makes it sound like dunny-can, and that kills them. They roll around so much that Swanno has to go round hitting with a ruler, to shut them up.

"And I'd only been there a couple of days. Then, at dinnertime, I'm out in the yard trying to get a kick at the ball. I thought I'd show them how I could kick, and it would be all right. But they keep pushing me over every time I get near the ball and one time I get pushed over, and I stand up, and I get the ball right in the face. That *really* hurt, I can tell you.

"I look up and see this big kid that kicked it standing there, grinning. And that was Rob. He was going to be my friend, but I didn't know. I was so wild I didn't care what happened. I chucked myself at him, and he grabbed my arms to stop me hitting, and we swayed around, sort of wrestling. Listen, he said, that was an accident, you better cut that out, squirt, he said, before I dong you.

"And he shoved me away and I swung one and got him in the nose. So he tripped me up and he pounced, and he got his knees on my arms and ground my muscles. That hurt bad and I couldn't get away, he was too big, and I started crying and I had to give in. I didn't want to cry, you know, but all the other kids were crowding around and they were singing out . . . good old Maxwell, do him Rob, come on Maxwell, kick the shit out of the dunny-can . . . they were shouting things like that.

"They *wanted* him to go on hurting me. They wanted to see me crying. Every one of them city bastards wanted to see me tortured or killed or something. And I bet you don't know how that feels . . ."

"You might as well go on," said the voice of whoever it was he was telling. "You might as well."

"There's not much else. A funny thing happened. Rob changed his mind, you see. Suddenly he got mad at all the other kids. He got up off me and helped me up, and he took the ball from the kid who had it, and he handed me the ball, and he said . . . all right, snow, have a kick. And after that it was all right.

"After that, Rob's always been my friend. He wants to be a farmer, and we talk about the farm. I tell him everything, and it's all right. We have to fight some of the other kids when they call me names, but we fight them together, the both of us, and it's all right. Nobody's got such a good friend as I've got . . ."

He stopped talking to think about Rob Maxwell, and there were words he hadn't known he knew to think with. He thought about Rob Maxwell's hard, fair virtue that made him like a man while other boys were merely boys. He could not understand why these thoughts should make him want to weep.

"You have no more to tell?" said the soft voice that had been there to speak whenever it was needed. "That's all?"

"I'm tired now. You told me your name, didn't you?"

"Peter is my name."

"That's right. I don't want to talk any more, Peter. Can I go to sleep?"

"Yes," said Peter. "I'll look after things."

Peter heard the white man sigh, and stretch himself, and turn. What if he stays like this, he wondered. What will I do? Can I do what must be done, without his help?

We must get back to land tomorrow. We have no time to lose. Somehow we must get ashore and find the mission. It can't be far. And then we'll see. But it isn't good. How will it be if Mr. Duncan stays this way, thinking he's a kid? Not going to be so good. But, maybe . . . after he's had a sleep . . .

What in the name of heaven am I doing out here, he asked himself in sudden disbelief. Away out here! Lost somewhere on the ocean, in a battered boat never meant to venture near the sea, no oars, no sail or engine; with nothing; and here I am out here, guardian to a man who thinks himself a child.

And yet, it could have been far worse than this. We could have been drowned, when the flood came tearing down the river. I gave up hope when I saw that wall of water come rolling around the bend. But we came through, he and I. We were lucky, sure enough.

The sea was quiet. The clouds had opened, and a few stars shone.

Riding the sway of the boat, Peter leaned back and thought about his life.

It was strange to be here, yes, but what was life but the passage of one strangeness following another? His life, anyway, had been like that. Strange always.

As if the life that came to him, and moved around him, and took him with it, didn't always fit the man he knew he was, or sometimes imagined he might be.

2

Dawn began opaquely, through a mist. At first obscured, the sun became a narrowing source of light. The foggy vapors of the sea, in stronger light, receded.

Peter did not doubt that land was close.

He waited, while all around the boat distances of gleaming sea grew wide. No sign of land. With appalling suddenness his certainty was gone. Land would not be seen. He was, instantly, as sure of that as he had been before that land would meet his sight at any moment.

He looked at James Duncan, asleep in the wet bottom of the boat with his feet under one seat and his head under the other, and he didn't know whether to be afraid or angry.

He would be angry. Someone must be blamed for what might happen to them now. Perhaps at a time like this being angry was better than being frightened.

He gazed on the sleeping man. You fool, he said in his mind. You fool. *You* told the man with the boat that he had to cross the river.

He was worried, that man, he knew the flood was coming down. I saw that, and I talked to him about it. He told me, and I told you. But you wouldn't listen. No. You, with your white man's absoluteness, *you* told him he had to cross. I'd have waited. But I couldn't argue. In case you thought I was a coward.

You're a fool.

When the outboard came off the boat, and the man fell over, *you* threw the oar. We needed that oar more than he did. It

9

could have saved us. Wasn't he swimming well without it, nearly safe? We could have been swimming, too. But you lay there unconscious. I couldn't leave you. Standing like that to throw the oar, with the boat riding the flood like a rearing horse, couldn't you see how certain you were to fall?

Well, I hope the oar helped to save him. I hope for our sake he got ashore. He'll go for help, and a search will start. But it's going to be hard to find us. Wake up and look around you! We are nothing but a speck on the ocean.

The mist had cleared. He could see the horizon right around, the boundaries of a world of sea, and nothing else.

He wanted to wake James Duncan. Shake him, show him where the folly of his arrogance had led.

You see? See that? We've drifted right away from land. How do you think we're getting back? Have we an oar to row with? Have we anything? No. *You* saw to that. Wait until you wake. You'll get a piece of my mind, white man or not!

Ah, what's the use, he muttered, anger's lively pulse fading to dejection as he scanned the empty sea once more. What's the use of blaming him? We were committed to this the moment we boarded that plane. I suppose it is part of God's design that it should happen in this way.

I must resign myself.

Yet, resignation wasn't easy. Surely God must know delay was dangerous? It was all in the open now and anything could happen. Perhaps the police would come, asking questions, and get the old man's story, twisting it then to suit their case. Had God allowed for that?

God moved in mysterious ways, they said. His wonders to perform.

But did He, always, perform wonders?

You dared not ask yourself that question.

"Who are you?" said a small, sharp voice.

James Duncan was awake. He had bumped his head on the seat as he sat up. With doubt, as he rubbed his head, he stared at

Peter. With more than doubt. With a kind of furious alarm.

"I've told you. I am Peter."

"Then who am I?"

"Your name is James Duncan," said Peter wearily. "Jimmy Duncan, if you like."

"I knew that."

"Then why did you ask?"

"To see if *you* knew. Listen, you're a blackfeller, aren't you?"

"Yes."

"But I'm not?"

"No. I'm the only blackfeller in this boat."

"Look, Peter," said James Duncan more trustingly. "I'd like a drink. Water will do. Will you get me a drink of water, please?"

"Can you wait a while?"

"I suppose so. But I'm getting thirsty."

"Do your best not to think about it," said Peter. "We might have to wait a little while for water."

"How do I *know* I'm not a blackfeller?" said James Duncan. "You might be only saying it. How do I *know?*"

"Look at yourself if you don't believe me. Look at your hands."

"Jeeze, they're *big!*" said James Duncan, studying his hands. "Look, will you? They're bloody *enormous!* Jeeze . . . what's happened?"

"Don't worry about it," said Peter uneasily. "At least they aren't black. What I told you was the truth."

"They're not my hands, that's why!" James Duncan shouted. "What have you been *doing* to me?"

He threw the jacket clear and ran his hands along his legs, wildly, as if his legs could not be real. He passed a hand across his face.

"Tell me what I look like," he whispered, facing Peter with haunted eyes.

Peter licked his lips, and looked away.

"You're a man," he said at last. "A man of fifty, or a little less.

Your face is sort of square. Your hair is dark, and going gray."

"And how big?" whispered James Duncan. "How big?"

"Five foot nine or ten. Heavy built."

"It isn't true!" James Duncan cried, in rage. "Listen, what's going on? You have to *tell* me!"

"You had an accident. Yesterday. You banged your head. It's made you so you can't remember."

"Remember? Oh Jesus! Don't *say* that! Stop *talking* about it! Please, is there any food? I'm getting hungry. What about some breakfast?"

"Would you like a sweet?"

"Are there any?"

"Should be a little packet in my coat. Look in the pockets."

Sitting up, James Duncan for the first time saw beyond the boat.

"Shit!" he cried, with a boy's intensity of voice. "Where's the friggin' land? Jeez-us . . . where *are* we?"

"We drifted out."

"How they going to get us back?"

He need not know the truth, Peter told himself. Now is the time for a lie to be invented. But how find the words of a lie when only the words of blame and the words of fear were in his mind?

It is his fault, and I am frightened, too. Why spare *him,* whose fault it is? Let him share my fear, my fear of dying, and dying in one of the cruelest ways. Dying of blazing sun and of salt windless sea, and of heat and thirst and madness. *He's* to blame. He made us cross the river. He threw the oar. He fell unconscious, so I couldn't leave him and save myself. So why should he not be frightened too?

"Well? How they going to get us back?" said James Duncan. "How?"

"I do not know," said Peter.

"You mean they don't know where we are? They won't come here and get us?"

"Who?"

"Mum and Dad. No. No, I . . . I mean, *people*. Doesn't anyone know where we are? Won't they come and get us?"

"I don't know."

"Well, never mind it now," said James Duncan. "Here are the sweets, a whole new packet. You want one?"

"Not just now."

"How many can I have?"

"A couple, I suppose. We'd better leave the rest. It's all we have."

"Nothing else for breakfast?"

"No."

"No water?"

"Not until it rains."

"When will that be?"

"Not today."

"That's a pity," said James Duncan calmly, chewing.

"I think I will have one of those," said Peter, swallowing saliva in a dry mouth.

"Have two. The same as me. I know about this. We have to go on rations until we're rescued. It isn't much, though, is it?"

"Better than nothing."

"But blackfellers always have tricks for getting food when they're in a boat . . . don't they? You'll know some tricks? We'll get more food, won't we?"

"I guess you'd call me a city blackfeller," said Peter, surprised by a moment of amusement. "It's been a long time since I was a proper abo, Jimmy. When I left the bush I was only a little boy." Like you, he nearly added, I was only a little boy like you. But the white man's delusions must not be encouraged, incredibly easy though it was to believe this aging man a boy.

"Now look, you don't *forget* things like that," said James Duncan. "Tell me one good trick to get food when you're cast away at sea."

"One thing they do," said Peter, "I've seen them, is lie in a boat and wait for a bird to settle, and grab his legs."

"There's birds out there," said James Duncan, shading his

eyes, and scanning the sea. "So why don't we have a go at that?"

"Because it isn't as easy as it sounds. It could take all day. You'd have to lie absolutely still, perhaps for hours. That's hard to do."

"What's so hard about lying down? Come on, why don't we start? It could be fun."

It will keep him occupied, thought Peter, though not for long. Let him find out. Let him find out it's one of the hardest things a man can do.

"We could try," he said, putting his legs under the seat and getting down beside the white man.

"Why must we keep so still?" James Duncan whispered.

"If a bird comes close, the slightest movement will scare him off," said Peter. "Birds watch everything from far away, so far sometimes that a man can't see them. But the bird sees. He sees everything from far away, even a little fish, smaller than your finger, swimming in the sea."

"Yes," said James Duncan. "What else?"

"Suppose a bird is watching this boat. What's that thing, he asks himself. Is it something a bird can stand on? Is there something in it a bird can eat? A bird is a thing that must come flying to see what everything is, you know. And if he thinks it might be something bad, he'll wait. He doesn't care if he has to wait all day. And while he waits he flies around and watches, and if we move he will see us, and he will never come to the boat so we can jump on him and grab his legs. That is why we must keep so still that no bird will see us move."

He saw the white man's face so close to his that it was slightly blurred in focus. Studying that jowled, tired face, with its stubble of middle-aged whiskers, Peter felt it strangely sad that he should be talking to this man as if he were a child. It moved him strongly now, for the first time, that in that face, graven with the lines of long, hard-lived experience, two blue eyes, flecked with brown, should shine with the candor, and the keen expectance, and even the innocence, of youth.

"How will we cook him?" said James Duncan.

"We can't."

"We'll eat him raw?"

"Yes" said Peter, growing a little tired of having to treat as a game this matter which before long might be grim. "That's what we'd have to do. Eat him raw. And drink his blood to quench our thirst."

"Is that all right?"

"If you're hungry enough, it is."

"I don't know," said James Duncan, with considerable doubt. "I don't know about *that*."

He lapsed into silence. Because it had been his idea to do this, he felt obliged to see it through. Peter had said it would be hard, and it was, lying still against the lurching movements of the boat. And it was hot. The sun was climbing into a clear sky, a concentrated sun, clear and sharp and fierce. Beneath his damp clothes, his skin began to itch. His clothes were steaming, it was as hot in the sun as that.

After a while he could not bear it. He had to sit up, or scream. He raised himself.

"That was a mad idea!" he shouted. His mouth trembled. He was close to tears. "It isn't fair!"

"Don't get upset," said Peter mildly, getting up. "That's a real hard way to catch a bird."

But beyond the boat he saw the birds, birds as dark as soot resting on the water, and gulls above drifting in the air, and the pert heads of all the birds were turned to watch the boat. In this short time the birds had come so close. A little longer and it might have worked.

"Look at the birds," he said. "You should have waited. It's bad luck."

"I don't *care!*" said James Duncan. "I bet you don't know any more about catching birds than I do!"

Still faintly annoyed, Peter smiled. But the smile was a mistake.

"Don't laugh at me, you black bugger!" said James Duncan, and at once his voice was that of a man. At once the pettiness of his child's temper became a man's controlled ferocity. His eyes met Peter's with the forceful glare of an angry man.

How should he be handled now? Peter weighed this astonishing reversion, staring at James Duncan with a kind of horror, as at a changeling found where some other person was expected. Seeing the man's face where the man who thought himself a boy had been, he fancied the change as one from good to evil, a change supernatural and alarming.

Not knowing what to say, he said nothing. He turned away, and watched the birds, and from long practice digested the white man's rough contempt. Swallowing his resentment, he thought how sadly lonely it might be for them to die in this boat, together, now that his companion's manhood was recovered.

He thought of the boy, Jimmy Duncan, the acted creation of this crazy man, banished and farewelled with a thoughtless smile, and he thought of him as someone real. A friend, recently discovered, a friend to be encouraged and protected. A friend, now lost.

Sadly, he watched the birds, and the birds watched him.

Turning his head at last he found the white man changed again. Staring across the sea, he sat in an attitude of desolation, his mouth squared in an ugly grimace of unhappiness that made him look rather like a frog.

"Are you all right?" said Peter.

"Leave me," said James Duncan, grinding his brow with knuckled hands, turning his head from side to side, groaning. "Leave me alone. Oh Christ! What's this about? What's going on? Who the hell are you?"

Ah, God, thought Peter, not that *again!*

"My name is Peter," he said. "I am your friend." Though he said this with diffidence.

"What the *hell* are we doing in this boat!" cried James Duncan. "Who are you? One of the kriegies? I can't remember. Did we have any black men there? Where you from? West Indies or somewhere? What's happened . . . did we crash out? Jesus, I never meant to be mixed up in anything like that. I never meant to crash out. I'd have stayed. What's *happening?* You'd better tell me."

"Mr. Duncan, I don't know what you're talking about. Listen, you and me were going to the mission at Ben-gingin to see that old man, Binben Freddie. Do you remember that? The one who was there when the girl was murdered?"

"Christ, man, you're raving. You better get a grip on yourself. Just you tell me what I asked you. Did we crash out? Did we go over the wire? How did we get out? What happened?"

"We were crossing the river," said Peter desperately. "In this boat. And a flood came down. We were swept out to sea. There was an accident. You were hurt. Mr. Duncan, you're sick."

"What d'you mean, I'm sick?"

"You fell and knocked your head. You were unconscious. You seem to have lost your memory."

"Well, bugger me. That's fair enough. Yes, that could be the gen. I know I've got this bump right here, and it's bloody sore. Could be, you know. You say I couldn't remember anything?"

"Only things about your childhood."

"Like what?"

"You told me about your friend."

"Which friend?"

"You called him Rob. Rob Maxwell."

"Bloody old Rob, eh? Told you about him, did I? Poor bugger. That was a bastard the way he bought it, wasn't it?"

"Did something happen to him?"

"*Happen* to him? Did it ever! That was a couple of years ago ... early forty-three, when Maxwell got the chop. He was in Beauforts, see? Torpedoes. How's that for asking for it? What else could he expect? I mean ... *Beauforts!* Bloody torpedoes! What sort of lark is that?"

"Was that in the war?"

"Shit yes. What the Christ you think we're talking about? We're *all* in the bloody war! Why do you keep on talking like a stupid bloody twat?"

"But ... Mr. Duncan ..." Peter said, but he held back from what he had meant to say. For a moment it had seemed best to tell James Duncan the truth, and see what he made of it, but he pulled back at the last moment from taking such a risk.

For a dreadful risk it well might be. To believe yourself a man, a young man, still to reach your prime, engaged in war, and to be told that your war had been over many years, that a new generation had grown to the age you thought was yours, that no more were you young ... that might be enough to push a man right past the edge. Far better let him reach that truth himself.

"Well?" said James Duncan, at this delay. "You got something to say?"

"How much do you remember?"

"What d'you mean, how much? I remember everything. Except how we got here ... I'm lost on that. But get off my back, sport, I'm tired. I'm bloody tired. I think I'll have a sleep."

3

Of course he could remember. But when he folded the jacket for a pillow, and lay down and closed his eyes, the task of recollection seemed beyond him.

It wasn't fair.

All was mystery. This crazy boat, pitching and swaying in uneasy motion. The silent darky, that stranger with the worried eyes. The clothes he was wearing. How the hell did civvie clothes come into it?

He could find no sense in anything, no slightest fact of memory to tie it all together.

Well, then, he'd have to work at it. Do what he meant to do, work it out and show the darky he was wrong.

As if it was any other forthright job of work that needed to be done he set himself the task of finding memory, and memory at once offered a sequence of disconnected pictures and sensations.

In a leap of recall, as convincing and urgent as something happening now, he was falling weightless through yielding pressures of wind and darkness, screwing his neck to see that the canopy above had opened clean and hadn't candled.

He was following with outraged eyes the flaring tail of fire the poor old Lanc dragged out behind as it spun down to the lurid ground.

He was listening to the fighter, still on the job, hacking away at some other luckless shit trying to catch up in the returning stream.

He was blinded by the hot arcing glare of searchlights leaping across the sky to cone.

And it all vanished. He was there no longer.

Suddenly, there was that kid in Nazi uniform the Russians caught.

He was watching the way the kid was kicking. He was listening to his screams with prickling horror as they strung him by the feet and hung him from a tree and doused him with petrol and lit him like a bonfire. He was sweating and retching at the smell of burning, and trembling to hear those screams you would hear forever, the screams that seemed to continue long after the Nazi kid had died.

And, suddenly, somewhere else. Where? It was dark. He had been sleeping, awakened by a nightmare shout.

He was hearing men breathe tiredly, sighing, muttering in their sleep, and his mind was clogged with the timeless drag of endless physical restriction, that gloomy stalag feeling, that boredom, that constant need to hide from others your own hysterical demand for freedom. That panic need, always on the edge of uncontrollability. That feeling sometimes very close to madness.

Madness? Had he given way? Had he taken that way out? Was he mad?

His heart moved in a plunge of terror. That German kid . . . the Russians . . . that was near the end! The war was over. The time of his mind had slipped.

Madness!

He scrambled to his feet and the boat rocked dangerously as he jumped to the seat to examine the convincing illusions of his lunacy.

There sat the black man, staring, startled. There the boat, so old and gray and weathered. There burned from a metal sky the furious eye of the fiery sun.

And there was the sea. All around, the oily rolling sea. And a few birds. Nothing else.

Birds? Would he have bothered to imagine birds?

"You better sit down," said the black man, with studied calm. "Go on. Sit down. You'll have us over."

"Those birds . . ." said James Duncan haltingly.

"Those are the birds we tried to catch."

"I . . . I hadn't forgotten."

He stepped from the seat. He sat down. He put his head in his hands.

He remembered the birds. He remembered lying still to lure them close and catch them. He seemed to remember the black man's name.

"Peter?"

"Yes?"

"Nothing . . ."

He seemed to remember Peter's voice at another time. In darkness. Something about Rob Maxwell. He had told Peter something . . .

His thought seemed to take a straight line through all the times of his life, his mind seemed to wing lightly through time like a bird flying home. To that day when he had Rob's letter.

Not merely to the day. To the very moment when the envelope was opened and he saw that sketch of the sharp-nosed little man with flying hair. The sketch they had practiced during dreary lessons so it could be done in seconds with a dozen strokes, a secret sign between them.

"I'll tell you something," he said to Peter. "When I left school I didn't see Rob any more. Not for a long time. We moved away. My dad got another job, and we had to move. And I went to work. With a printer."

Mr. Ransom came into his mind, and he saw him with affection. How lucky he had been to find a boss like Mr. Ransom.

Mr. Ransom, standing with his back against the sloping racks of type looking as he always looked when he was talking. A thin man with a stoop, as if he leaned your way to bring you closer. A kind, slow man with faded eyes and a fading, drooped moustache.

"You don't want to be a printer, boy," said Mr. Ransom's voice. "Hand setting's going out. It's a slow thing to learn and it's going out of date. You're a smart kid, Jimmy. I'm going to put you on the paper."

Of all the things that Mr. Ransom ever said, that was the best remembered. For that was the starting point of something most important. Manhood, perhaps. A job that seemed to have real meaning.

Big deal. Tapping out social notes and club activities and council doings for an antique, suburban paper. Print run, four thousand. A losing proposition.

Was he laughing at himself? Laughing at one of the best things in his life?

"God, I loved that job," he said. "I'd have liked to stay there all my life. I wasn't on the printing side, you know. I was helping to run a paper, and I was good at it. Right from the start, a kid come straight from school, I was pretty bloody good."

"You left it?" said Peter.

"Not straight away. I was there for several years. And I'd have stayed. Only, that letter came from Rob."

He could feel the letter in his hand. He could see it. The sketch at the top of the page. Where was he then?

A place with willow trees along the side. The drains were always blocked with roots. Under the willow trees, standing at the letter box, coming home from work.

Jubilee Street. That's where we were living. That dank old house. We were poor. What sort of wage could the old man get for grinding castings in a foundry? Bloody job for a bloke of sixty, a man who'd been a farmer. But in those years it was a miracle to be in work. Even work that made men ill. Dad was always coughing, and no damn wonder. Did it kill him, all that dust? Maybe. Maybe they just gave up. Mum gave up, that's bloody certain, when he died. Hospitals. Oh Jesus, hospitals.

"What letter was that?" Peter's voice reminded him. Reminded him to come out of those thoughts where, in any case, he didn't want to be.

"From Rob," he said, "to tell me he was going bush. He couldn't stand accountancy. That's what his old man was, accountant. Maybe it would have worked, but Rob was a clot at sums. He stuck it for a year or so and then he made his break. Put in for that land scheme out in Timbillico mountains. You got the land for bugger-all and, the next hundred years or something, paid for it.

"That was all in Rob's letter I got that time when we lived in Jubilee Street and I was working on the paper for old Ransom. Did I tell you that? Never mind. The thing was, he couldn't get into the scheme without me. You went before a board. You had to show you'd done some farming. He sent a paper for me to sign to make us partners. Undulating country, they said it was. Light to medium timber."

Undulating country. Some might call them mountains and bloody steep at that, but the soil was good.

Applegums and stringybarks. He stood beneath the trees kicking with a toe to check the soil, and Rob was there, rifle in hand, tickled pink because they'd seen a thousand rabbits. We can live on rabbits, Rob had said. We can trap them and sell the skins.

Rob would come to curse the rabbits, but that first day he itched for animals to shoot. Farming was a glorious lark to Rob that day, but I guess he had to learn. Yes. And so he did. Rob could learn as quick as anyone.

"And what did you do?" said Peter. "Did you leave your job?"

"Well, you see," James Duncan said, "I felt I had to. He couldn't get in the scheme without me. But, Jesus, I hated to leave my job with Mr. Ransom. How do you reckon Ransom felt when I told him I was leaving? I waited as long as I could, thinking perhaps we wouldn't draw a block. It was several months before we heard and I kept hoping the answer would let me out of it. Then we heard. We'd drawn one of the best blocks in the mountains. Ah, wouldn't you know it. I guess the best way to get something good is not to want it.

"So there we were. We put in nearly three years on that place and we hardly ever saw another soul. We had this bark hut with a roof of tin. Rabbit stew. Jesus, when I think of it. For those three years we lived like bloody boongs."

It had caught him now, he was absorbed, he spoke with animation, watching Peter as he talked, and he saw Peter's changed expression at these words. For a moment he wondered why, and belatedly recalled the thing he'd said. He didn't know whether to go on, pretending not to realize he'd said this most offensive thing, or whether to face it and explain.

"Now, wait," he said. "It wasn't meant that way. I'm sorry."

He would have welcomed some clear guide to Peter's feelings. Even anger, openly expressed, would help. But the change of expression which had caught his attention had been a change like sunset, where light vanishes, and life, and only the unresponsive dark is left.

"It wasn't my choice to be a bloody boong," said Peter, very softly. "I'm not at all sure I like it. I'd as soon be white."

"You've got it wrong . . ."

"Forget it. Mr. Duncan, I think it's time we worked out what to do."

James Duncan felt like saying . . . but what about my story? Listen, I could tell you so much more, so much that I'm coming to remember . . . but to say this would expose him, surely, to a sharp rebuff.

"What to do? How do you mean?"

"I mean we have to do something. I don't know what. I think we're drifting further out to sea. That wind, it hasn't changed direction."

"Is it the wrong way, or something, the wind? Are you worried?"

"Yes."

"What about?"

"About dying, mainly," said Peter, with an immediate flash of anger in his eyes. "About dying like a bloody boong. Dying thirsty, and hungry, and mad from the sun."

"We've got those sweets," said James Duncan childishly. "Perhaps you've forgotten that?"

4 In restless inventory of their scant possessions, Peter wandered from stern to bow, touching things, weighing their uselessness, putting them down.

With the sour smile of the skeptic, James Duncan watched, believing one short glance enough. One glance that discovered in the boat two men, their jackets, their bags, a bailing tin almost rusted through, a chunk of scrap iron tied to a seat by a faded rope of many knotted pieces, a pair of rowlocks, an old spark plug, a spanner with one end broken; and nothing else.

He said, not kindly, "Looking for something?"

Peter refused to hear. He held up a bulging leather briefcase. "What's in this?"

"Should I know?"

"It's yours."

"Look inside. I wouldn't know."

Peter slipped buckles free and laid on the seat a cardigan, a towel, pajamas, an ink-stained folder of papers, a spectacle case, and a spongebag. From the spongebag he took a safety razor in a plastic case.

"There," he said. "Razor blades. We have something to cut with."

"You're going to cut something?"

"We needed something sharp. A knife, or something."

"I have a knife," said James Duncan. "Why didn't you ask?" He felt in a pocket and held out a pocket knife. "Here."

Peter opened the single blade and thumbed the edge. "That's

very good," he said, with what seemed disproportionate approval.

"You worry me," said James Duncan. "You really do. A knife's not *that* important. And a while back ... talking about dying ... what did that mean? You were angry. I suppose you were getting at me. Having a hit. Well, that's all right, as long as you didn't mean it."

Peter gave no answer.

"You didn't mean it, did you?"

"What am I supposed to say?" said Peter, his eyes leaping away from the white man's harassed appraisal. "Can't you see things for yourself?"

"See? See what?"

"Can you see anything to drink? Aren't you thirsty?"

"But there'll be water where we're going," said James Duncan reasonably. "We can wait, can't we?"

"Where *are* we going?" said Peter, the taste of fear in his mouth putting aside his duty to protect from this very fear this man so shaken in his mind.

"Would I know that? Now listen, boy. You put me in this boat, and I've had enough of your nonsense. I want to know where you're taking me. I will not have any more of this bullshit! I want to know."

"You put *yourself* in this boat!" cried Peter. "I was dead *against* going on that river. That was your idea, entirely."

"What river?"

"The Gingin river. The one we had to cross to reach the mission."

"Never heard of it," said James Duncan brusquely, in a voice he had not used before, the voice of a man masterful and short-tempered. A man accustomed to his own authority; to using short answers, and finding them enough. This new voice had an unaccountable effect on Peter. His resentments vanished.

"All this stuff ... arguing ... that's enough of that," said James Duncan. "Let's get on with the job. What were you looking for? What was in your mind?"

"If we could catch a fish . . ." said Peter . . . "if we had something to fish with . . ."

"Fish? Isn't water our problem?"

"Raw fish have a kind of water in their flesh. It would be better than nothing."

"Fair enough. Let's have another look. A proper look. You were only picking things up and putting them down again. Most likely they used this boat for fishing. Right? Supposing someone dropped a hook, where would it go? Under the boards is where we have to look. Get it? I'll take the knife, you take my toothbrush. Scrape under every board."

Their patient search found nothing.

"That's it, then," said James Duncan. "It was just a thought."

"A hook wouldn't have been much use, anyway," said Peter. "We have no line."

"We have laces in our shoes. A bit of colored cloth from my pajamas. I've seen barracuda caught on colored rag. Yes, I'd have liked a hook. You'd have seen. Well, bugger it. What's next?"

"I could make a spear. That's how we boongs catch fish," said Peter.

"Listen, drop that boong stuff," said James Duncan. "You've had your money's worth on that. So give it up. Suppose you had a spear? What would you do? Dive over, and go down after them?"

"We'd have to bring the fish up to the boat."

"How do you do that? Sing a special bloody abo song, or something?" He sounded more scathing than he intended. He expected a hurt glance from those easily wounded eyes, at least.

But Peter said, "The scent of blood would bring them."

"What d'y mean?" James Duncan was startled. "Whose blood?"

"Not yours," said Peter. "Some of mine."

"Christ. Where you going to get this blood?"

"From my toe."

"Ah . . . your toe. Why didn't you say so?"

"Did you think I was going to cut my throat? Make myself a martyr?"

"I didn't know. Listen, if that's all it is you can have a bit of mine."

"What's the difference? My blood will do."

"That's why you were looking for something to cut with? To make a spear? You'll use one of the floorboards?"

"That's right," said Peter. "But it will be a long job."

As they took turns to cut the wood for the spear the sea smoothed to an incredible calm, without ripple or wave or swell. In these windless hours the heat of the sun became insufferable.

While one worked, tapping the flimsy blade along the mark with careful strokes of a rowlock, the other lay resting, covered by a towel dipped often in the sea.

"Wake up," said Peter, at last putting the rowlock down. "You work it smooth. I'll make some bait."

James Duncan pushed the towel from his face and took the crude strip of wood from Peter. He was dazed by the blinding sun, so confused for the moment that he could not recall the object of their work.

"Smooth it?"

"Cut the corners off. Like this."

"All right. I can do it."

From the corner of a nauseous eye, James Duncan saw Peter slicing at his toe. Blood came, seeming on Peter's dark flesh an alien fluid, not blood of the familiar hue which oozed on a white skin, but darker, as if from an exotic creature whose veins ran with an unknown juice.

Peter tore a handkerchief, and wrapped the toe, and a stain of normal scarlet, like a white man's blood, grew sodden on the rag.

"I'll finish her off," said Peter, and while he worked James Duncan knotted laces and trailed the bloody rag behind the boat.

Peter squeezed his toe to start new bleeding, and placed another rag.

He worked steadily until the spear was finished.

"That's terribly good," said James Duncan, taking the slim stick which some innate artistry, descended with that strange dark blood, had changed to a primitive and deadly weapon. It tapered to a narrow blade in which flat barbs were carved. If Peter was any good with a spear, this thing might work. The skepticism he had hidden from himself; because it was better to work at something, even uselessly, than to do nothing; turned to a faint hope, and to admiration.

"It's really good," he said. "The real thing."

Peter moved to the stern and sat there, still and silent, with the spear poised in his hand.

With the wet towel cooling his head, James Duncan lay watching him, a dark statue shining in the sun, but after a while lost interest, for nothing happened.

Nothing happened until sunset, when the sharks came.

Running in with the intent, blundering stupidity of a giant beast, the first shark hit the boat a mighty blow. Peter saw it as a fast, deep swirl in the water, and then it hit.

The boat shivered in every board, and heaved, and splashed down again as if it had been bodily lifted from the sea.

James Duncan had been dozing. He scrambled to his knees, and grabbed the side of the boat, staring, a man awakened to sounds of an unknown danger, a man afraid, and utterly confused.

He saw the shark cruising in a circle, surfaced enough for a fin to show, cutting the water with a kind of emotionless, surgical certainty. Further away, other fins appeared.

He turned, looking for reassurance from Peter, and saw in a glance that Peter trembled, equally afraid.

"Get down," Peter whispered. "They'll see us moving. If they get the idea to give us another hit like that we're gone."

James Duncan rolled away and slid his feet beneath the seat

so that he could lie on the bottom at full length. Crawling to join him, Peter brushed a rowlock from the seat. It fell with a sound which to the tautness of their senses sounded like the falling of a tree. Peter raised himself by inches to watch the sea, and froze.

"Watch out," he muttered urgently. "The big one's coming back."

James Duncan closed his eyes and waited.

The shark nudged against the boat as if to feel it out, as if to find at leisure the best way to open up this thing that trailed behind the appetizing scent of blood.

A spine-freezing picture, of rows of fearsome teeth gaping in cavernous jaws no more than inches from where his body touched the planks, filled James Duncan's mind.

The shark worried at the boat as a dog worries a bone too big to take in a single bite. James Duncan could feel the rake of monstrous teeth rasping on the flimsy boards. It was then that he recognized these happenings for nightmare. A nightmare so ludicrously frightening that it was funny. So vastly overdone. He closed his eyes to seek, without distraction, a more agreeable reality. The truth, preferably; the real life which had been lost in this alarming dream.

His thoughts wandered, and yet the feeling of the dream persisted. He decided to wake up, to break this dream and start again.

He opened his eyes.

In that unmeasured interval between sundown and night, twilight had passed, for it was full night now.

He searched the night for a window, for anything that would tell him where he slept and dreamed. In what room. In what house. At what time of his life.

He heard the sounds of a gentle sea sucking at the drifting boat. He saw stars. Something scraped against the boat. It seemed that he was still caught in that confounded dream.

"Garry? That you there?" he said, loudly.

"Be quiet," came a whisper. "Oh please, don't make a noise."

In the dream the shark went on playing with the boat, bumping it, rubbing against it with an abrading tremor of vibration. Going away, sometimes so quiet that he began to think it had gone for good. Each time returning.

"Are you all right, Garry?" James Duncan said. "Is everything all right? Shouldn't you be asleep?"

The shark seemed to hear his voice and rushed the boat more savagely, so that it rocked and shivered and seemed on the point of taking water, or coming to pieces, and Peter drew a shuddering breath, and trembled, and reached for the white man's hand and squeezed it in a grip that fear made painful.

"All right, Garry," whispered James Duncan. "Be a brave boy. I'll look after you."

The shark leaped beside the boat and slapped the sea with a brutal tail, and then for a while was quiet.

"We've got the rest of those sweets somewhere," the whisper said. "Will we eat them?"

"That's a good idea," said James Duncan.

He wished he could sort this out. The way they seemed to be in this boat, hungry and thirsty, sharks around them, could only be a dream. A dream had the same absurd illogic. And he could conceive no possible sequence of events which would have put Garry and himself in such a plight.

Yet, though it was, quite surely, a dream or nightmare—the kind that dramatized, in the unguarded hours of sleep, secret doubtings of your competence to safeguard the son you loved from the manifold threats of childhood—though reason said that this was nothing but a dream, there had never been a dream as real as this.

Knowing it to be a dream, he was still compelled to act, by some force that required his blind obedience, as if the dream were real.

"Here they are," said the whisper of Garry's voice. "You share them out."

"Just give me one," said James Duncan. "You have the rest."

"We must take half each."

Good boy, thought James Duncan. He must be allowed this manly gesture.

"There were eight left," said Garry. "I've taken four. Will we eat them all?"

"Might as well." James Duncan took the sweets in their paper tube and picked off the top one and slipped it to his mouth. He crimped the paper over and put the small roll in the pocket of his shirt, to give to Garry later. Garry would need them.

He chewed the sticky jelly, making it last as long as possible, and when he went to swallow it from habit, he brought it back, hastily, before it went down too far. He chewed until nothing solid was left, and slowly swallowed the liquid, and then it was gone. Nothing was left. Only the memory of the taste, the sweetness, the way each cell of his body had seemed to pounce on this frivolous scrap of food, and the illusion that the sparse saliva running in his mouth had, for a moment, quenched his aching thirst.

He fingered his pocket. In his thoughts his fingers found their way and took another sweet and put it in his mouth, and with a kind of horror at his greed, he knew that the taste in his mouth was not imagined. He took the jelly from his mouth and put it with the others, and he lay beside Garry listening to the tiny sound of sucking Garry made, licking his own lips to catch the last faint taste of sweetness.

The shark had been so quiet that he had almost forgotten why they had to lie so still and quiet. For some time he had not been frightened. And now the shark made another run, high in the water. He heard it coming.

It hit the boat where his buttocks touched the boards. He felt the impact through the wood, like a kick from an evil-tempered man.

The planks strained with a fibrous, cracking sound. With a piercing feeling of alarm, he felt a rush of dampness where he lay against the boat, and it occurred to him that if the shark had hit anywhere else but at this point where he was lying, where the weight of his body acted as a dead-stop, it would have come right through.

He said nothing to Garry, who had stopped sucking and lay rigid beside him. His hand searched for the leak and found it. He scratched his fingers across the surface of the boards, but they seemed unbroken. Water was trickling slowly in between.

Garry was muttering to himself.

"Are you saying your prayers, son?"

"Yes."

"That's a good boy. Say your prayers and see if you can go to sleep. Goodnight, Garry. You needn't worry. I'll look after you."

"Mr. Duncan! Please don't call me Garry. I'm scared enough without that kind of thing. Please stop."

Why did Garry call him Mr. Duncan? Something about Garry was very odd indeed. His mind swooped on the passing thought that the boy in the boat was someone else. It seemed to pick up the thought and throw it into the night as far as it would go. So far that it would stay out there and not come back.

"All right," he said, humoring him. "What if I call you Rob? It's your mother's idea to call you Garry. I wanted to call you Rob, after my best friend."

"No," said Garry. "Call me Peter."

Something rubbed against the keel. Quite gently. Perhaps a smaller shark had come in for a try. Perhaps the big one had given up.

"Rob was very brave," said James Duncan. "He was killed in the war. before you were born."

"God help me," said Garry. "I give up."

"Finish your prayers and go to sleep. I'll talk to you until you fall asleep. Did I ever tell you about our farm? Rob and I had a sheep farm. Did I ever tell you?"

"Oh God yes, you told me."

"Out in Timbillico mountains. Real wild bush. You'd have loved it. Wild country, never touched before. Two sheep to the acre if you worked it properly. If you poisoned most of the trees and cleared up the dead stuff and burnt it, and cut back the suckers every year until the trees were dead. Then you could put down super and sow it and you had good pasture. Jesus, we worked. But we were carrying a thousand sheep when the war came. Mind you, that was a good year around Timbillico. We could have been caught.

"You know, that war was bloody silly when it started. You wouldn't remember. How could you? For a long time nothing happened. Months and months. They dropped leaflets on each other, that was all. Like two kids who've got themselves into a fight by talking big and everyone's standing around wanting to see them have a go, and they can't make up their minds who's going to lash out first. Like that. But Rob wanted to get into it. I mean, right from the very first day. And by Christmas he was gone."

5

He looked up to a soft sky, luminous with stars. It was so calm that the boat in which he lay seemed adrift on some more tranquil medium than the sea. He could have enjoyed this sleepless night had other things been different. Had those hallucinations of thirst and hunger and danger seemed less real, and had he not been so strangely impelled to go along with this dream as if it were, in fact, no dream, but dreadful truth.

Yet, even in the strength of this compulsion, reason told him, some possibility must be accepted that the real delusion lay in believing this a dream.

For a few long moments he examined their condition from this other aspect, this possibility that all was real. That the sharks were truly there, the signs of their constant presence not imagined. In calm analysis he studied their sounds, the sly touches of their rasping bodies on the boat's thin shell, the taut ripples of emerging fins, the splashing of a tail.

He decided with reluctance that the physical presence of these creatures could hardly be denied. They were there. Their first bold attacks had ceased, but they would not leave off. The seeming restraint of these vicious beasts was but a cruel kind of patience that waited on the light of day.

With an effort like taking something resistant in his hands and making it go the way he wanted, James Duncan forced his mind to the continuation of the story he had begun to tell to Garry.

Meaning to whisper it all, in case Garry was still awake and needed someone whispering of other things to give him reassurance, he thought much of it silently and spoke only occasionally.

Catching at a broken thread of memory, he found a thought that put him at the wheel of the old car driving back from Bowanowa the night he said goodbye to Rob. Driving the car, he was laughing.

Why? Why was he laughing when he should have been so sad? He was laughing because he was so fantastically drunk he couldn't drive. He couldn't see a thing, and yet he drove. Somehow, by fleeting glimpses of road and trees, he was steering the car through that irresponsible fog of drunkenness. Even when he hit the tree, even as he struggled back from floor to seat, he laughed. He laughed like a moron, and went to sleep, and woke in the frosty mountain dawn.

"I shouldn't have let Rob go like that," he said. "On his own. We should have gone off to the war together."

The boy was awake. "I guess it's all my fault," he said. "Putting blood over the side. I should have thought of sharks. It's all my fault. I'm sorry."

"Don't worry, son. Go to sleep."

"Can't you hear them? Don't they worry you?"

"I wasn't listening," said James Duncan. "I was thinking of something else."

I was thinking about how I got so drunk. We'd been drinking all the afternoon. We went to the station and Rob bought his ticket for the early morning train, and we went to the pub and started drinking. We had dinner there, and when we went back to the bar it was all locked up. But the old girl let us in.

We were the only ones. Rob and me and the old girl who owned the pub, and her daughter.

The daughter served us. The old girl sat on a high stool, knitting, listening to all we said. Watching like a damn old hawk squatting on a fence. And while her mother watched and listened the daughter gave us the eye, and we tried to say things the old woman wouldn't hear. We put the hard word on the daughter without her mother guessing what was going on, and the girl winked and batted her eyes so that we didn't know whether it was on, or not.

I looked at the clock and it was ten o'clock and I couldn't drink another drop. I put down my glass. I walked to the door and tried to work the bolt and Rob came and did it for me and without a word to the woman or her daughter we went outside. As soon as I was out I opened my mouth and let some go. I wasn't sick or anything, I'd just drunk so much I couldn't hold another drop.

We hunted about and found the car, and went around a couple of times to find the door, and at last I got in and started the engine and waited for Rob to get in and Rob said . . . sorry mate, I'm not coming . . . not this time. So we shook hands, and laughed, and I drove off.

After that, sometimes I had letters, and with each letter Rob went further away from me. It was like watching someone going away down a long tunnel into another life. Getting smaller and smaller, more and more unreal.

He went to Canada, and pranged a Harvard there, and the letter about that was like something in a book. To me, I mean.

All I knew was suckering trees and crutching sheep and working from dawn to dark. How could I know then what it was like losing your oil pressure and having the donk pack up with miles of dicy country under? What would I know about the joy of getting her down, wheels up, in a field so small that everyone was absolutely shattered when they saw it?

Then letters came from England, and then they stopped. And I waited.

"But, Jesus, I never thought that he was *dead!*" he said, protesting something in a loud voice, something that wasn't easy to explain. "It never crossed my *mind!*"

"Oh please," said the boy. "Please don't make a noise. If you have to talk, please whisper."

Well. That was a bloody fine way to talk to your father. For a moment he was hurt, and then he realized that the boy was frightened. Poor little bugger. Best go on, keep his mind on something else. But quietly, remembering not to let his voice get loud. Humor the kid.

"After a couple of months I telephoned his mother to see if she'd heard anything. Oh man, had she heard! Rob was dead. I talked for a while and the three minutes was up and I put down the phone and after that I was like a robot.

"You know? Like a mechanical man? I packed my things and I drew all my money from the bank in Bowanowa and I got on the train and I took a last look at Timbillico mountains standing up against the sky and I never laid my eyes on them again.

"Rob was on Beauforts, I found out later. Bloody *torpedoes!* Look, he wouldn't have made it through the war, in any case, doing that. Nobody did. I don't know, he must have thought he was fireproof or something, taking that on. He'd gone in against one of those Nazi ships and they set him on fire, but he went in all the way. Scored a hit, they thought.

"I got that gen from his parents, and it was bloody grim to see them trying to believe it was nearly as good that Rob had been a hero, as having him alive. But, you ask me, I think they really wished he'd been a sort of lazy coward, like me, and still alive."

"I wouldn't call you a coward," said the boy.

"I was hoping you were asleep," said James Duncan. "I was more or less talking to myself."

"Asleep? I don't dare close my eyes."

"Now, Garry. I told you. I'll look after you. There's no need to be afraid."

"Listen, Mr. Duncan. *I am not Garry!* My name is Peter. Peter Jirapon. An abo. A bloody *boong!* Will you listen? My name is Peter. Don't call me anything else!"

"Why do you go on like that? Is it a game or something?"

"No. It is not a game."

"And you're an aborigine?"

"Yes."

"A little blackfeller?"

"A man!"

"Now, listen," said James Duncan reasonably. "I only asked. If we're going to play this game I want to get it right."

"Mr. Duncan, I can't believe it's good for your state of mind to go on with this pretending."

"You're the one who's pretending," said James Duncan, but

he said this without conviction, in the way a man will continue to maintain something he has begun to doubt.

"You're beginning to believe me," said Peter.

"I don't want to talk about it. If you only knew . . ."

"Knew what?"

"If you only knew how happy I am to have you here. My own boy," said James Duncan. "If only you knew."

"Be glad I'm not your boy," said Peter. "Be glad I'm not someone you care about, out here in this boat. With the sharks."

"The sharks have gone away."

"I wish you were right. They haven't gone. They'll never go. They never do."

"It's a long night," said James Duncan. "I doubt it's much past midnight. Hours yet. You should think about something else, or go to sleep."

"I can't sleep. Why tell me to sleep? You can't sleep, either."

"I don't want to sleep," said James Duncan, quiet with these words, but with his next breaking thickly into anguished protest. "God damn it, I don't *want* to sleep. I want to remember! I want to be myself again. How the hell can you know what it's like!"

"The sharks," hissed Peter. "You must stop shouting. Oh, *listen!*"

Close to the boat came a wallowing splash, and silence. They waited for the shark to hit the boat. They waited in silence, but nothing happened.

"That was a stupid frigging idea putting that blood overboard," said James Duncan peevishly. "Things were bad enough without that contribution."

"It's easy to say that now. You could have . . ." Peter stopped as his mind leaped on implications. "Mr. Duncan! You remember? You remember that?"

"This afternoon. Making the spear, waiting for the fish. Yes, I . . . and then the sharks came . . . it was dark . . . it was all . . ."

"Who am I?" asked Peter quietly. "Mr. Duncan, what is my name?"

In the protracted silence Peter longed to put his question again, to hurry an answer, but he forced himself to wait.

"Peter," said James Duncan at last, in a voice strained out of shape by sadness. "Your name is Peter."

"You have been calling me Garry."

"I thought . . . when it was dark . . . when I . . . when you were there beside me, I thought you were Garry. My boy."

"And now you remember who I am. It happened suddenly?"

"Yes. There was a noise. My heart jumped with fear. Yes, it was sudden. Suddenly I remembered."

"How much?"

"Today. I remember that. I remember the things I have been telling you about."

"Are you remembering more and more?"

"I . . . there's something in my mind. A thought, I mean a thought about why I can't remember. It might be because I don't want to. I've been sort of fighting against remembering. I feel sick in the guts when I think of having to remember. Listen, Peter. Do you think I could be forgetting some awful thing on purpose? Could there be something bad that I must not let myself remember?"

"I wouldn't have thought so," said Peter cautiously.

"How well do you know me?"

"Not well. For a week or so, that's all. But, Mr. Duncan, I wouldn't imagine you a man with a secret of that kind."

"If it was a secret you wouldn't know about it, would you?"

"No, but I wouldn't . . ."

"Where did you meet me?"

"In your office."

"Where is that?"

"In Queen Street. One of those old buildings. You're on the third floor. You get out of the lift at the third floor and it's quite wide in front of the lift, but narrower passages go each way. It's left you turn, I think. Yes. To the left. And yours is the first door."

"And that's my office?"

"Yes. It says on the door, J. B. Duncan, and then . . . Public

Relations Consultant. Something like that. Can you remember that?"

"I thought I was a farmer. How can this be? Well, I don't know, it does seem I could be doing a thing like that. It seems familiar. Doesn't worry me. That's not so bad. Not bad at all."

"Your office gives an impression of success," said Peter, anxious to encourage him.

"Tell me."

"There's this very . . . I suppose you'd call her pretty . . . there's this girl at the desk as you walk in. She looks rather proud. Haughty, I don't know, is that the word? She looks at you without smiling as if she belongs in this flash office, and you don't."

"What's her name?"

"I wasn't told."

"Don't you like her?"

"Yes, I like her. But, I don't think she liked me much. Made me feel like a proper blackfeller every time she looked at me. I was sorry about that."

"Sounds a thorough bitch, the way you put it. What does she look like?"

"She's very pretty, I suppose. Even though you can see she only likes herself. The way she holds her mouth, as if she's sulking about something."

"She doesn't mean a thing to me. Tell me more."

"She kept us waiting for a while, and then she took us to your office. There's a big desk of brown wood, so polished it looks like glass, and that's where you sit with your glasses on, looking very serious and important."

"Good for me," said James Duncan, amused. "Where are my glasses now?"

"You don't wear them. Only in the office. I believe you think they make you look important."

"I'm not sure that's fair. I can't believe that I'm a fake. I need them for reading, perhaps. But never mind. What were you doing in my office?"

"Eddie Samson and I went there."

"Who's Eddie Samson?"

"An aborigine. Not as black as me. One of those Victorian abos, a half-caste, I don't know, maybe his grandfather was white or something. Look, Mr. Duncan, we're not getting anywhere with this, are we? You haven't remembered anything."

"What's it matter? It's a way to pass the time. Or have you decided you'd prefer to sleep?"

"If the sharks would go away, and I knew we'd get a drink tomorrow, and some food before we starve, maybe I'd feel like sleeping."

"I guess we'd better deal with the sharks in the morning when we can see what we are doing."

"We'll *deal* with them?" said Peter in disbelief. "How?"

"We'll think of something."

"And what about water? What about being lost out here at sea?"

"If one wind can drift us out another wind can drift us back. Listen, boy, one thing at a time. I'm going to come through this, I'm telling you. I'm going to come through this and get my memory back and find out all about my life. But you think we're going to die, don't you?"

"I hope not," said Peter. "But I'm frightened I might be wrong."

"Well, hell," said James Duncan. "There's better ways than this to pass the time. Why did you come to my office. Go on with that. Who's this Samson feller?"

"There's a thing called Aboriginal Assimilation League. He's president."

"And you?"

"I'm their legal man."

"Their *what?*"

"I'm their solicitor."

"You mean you're a lawyer? With a degree?"

"I realize that might surprise you."

"It might, at that," said James Duncan. "But it was rude of me to sound like that. I guess there's no good reason why you shouldn't be a lawyer."

"Excepting for the fact that I'm a boong, of course."

"Ah Christ, get off that, will you," said James Duncan in disgust. "You going to rub my nose in that forever? How many abo lawyers are there, anyway? Why shouldn't I be surprised?"

"Only me," said Peter. "I guess you'd call me a star exhibit. I think that's why the league employs me. So they can show me off. Proves their point that abos can live like whites. That's what they want. Every abo living like a white. And a lot of whites think that. It's the big new word. Assimilation. Get rid of the boongs by turning them into whites."

"All right. So what's wrong with that?"

"Everything's wrong with it. I guess you think the same as Eddie Samson does. As far as Eddie is concerned, only one little thing is wrong in the whole wide world. He's black. That's all. He's one of those people who think that every problem in the world would disappear if we all woke up one morning and found the color of our skins had all become the same."

"It might help . . ." James Duncan began, but Peter broke in with words that, by their earnestness, were deeply pondered.

"It *wouldn't* help," he cried. "It would destroy something that men have never valued. The thing they should value, I believe, almost above all other things. It would go against God's intentions. God *meant* us to have these differences. He meant this to be one of the great joys of our life here on this world. Isn't it a miracle to know that you will never find one single person who is not unique? That there can only ever be one of you, and one of me?"

"Perhaps it would have been harder to make us all identical," said James Duncan. "Snowflakes. Look at them. No two ever found alike. Perhaps that was the easy way to make a world."

"Which is the better world? A world of ants, not to be distinguished from each other by any means? Or the human world we have with all its inconceivable variety? God could have made a world of either kind. And yet, He made this one. You must concede that this was His intention."

"Oh, I'll concede that all right. But mainly because you're so steamed up about it."

"Perhaps I didn't go far enough with what I said. God's design, in creating these limitless differences, is that we should *cherish* them. See them as a blessing, and not a curse. We should see that as one of God's greatest gifts to man. For it is. What is human love if it isn't the cherishing of another being's individual uniqueness? That is the way men and women love."

"Perhaps," said James Duncan, a little sourly.

"Could we not love other races in the same way, for the same reason? Because of their God-given difference from ourselves? If God made these differences for us to cherish and enjoy, to be the source of our love for others, should we not enjoy what God has given us? It's so *simple!*" Peter cried, forgetting the need for quietness. "The love I'm talking of is the love that would let others be what they are. A love that would at last bring peace. Wanting to change others, to make them like yourself, can be a kind of hatred. There are people who would rather have you dead, who would rather kill you, than have you stay unchanged. It's a kind of hatred that is sometimes thought of as a kind of love. It is sometimes called Christian love. I have had sometimes to endure it."

"I'm afraid I'd have to chew that over before I could agree with you." A mood of awful depression and hopelessness had swept James Duncan, and from no obvious cause. All he wanted was that this talking should be ended.

"I see I've failed to convince you," said Peter, not caring that his voice trembled and perhaps revealed to the white man the enormity of this failure. "I've been worrying out these thoughts for years, thinking in my conceit that I was finding my way to truths of which the world had need. And the first time I attempt to put them into words I merely cause annoyance. For I've annoyed you, haven't I? You think I'm talking rot."

"I have troubles of my own," said James Duncan. "This Goddamned boat is leaking in on me and I'm wet all through. I'm cold and I'm frightened and I don't think I can go another day without a drink. So don't expect me to be worrying about philosophy. Just now, I doubt I would listen very patiently to Jesus Christ Himself. So don't take it personally."

To Peter he sounded unbelievably brutal.

"No," he said. "I'm sorry I was upset."

"But listen to me, boy," said James Duncan, still in a casually brutal voice. "You want to sell these ideas of yours, you better get them sharpened up a bit. I guess they're clear enough to you. But what the hell's the use of that, if you find they won't go over? You got to make it simple, boy. You got to hit them hard with one thing at a time. Bang! And if you get through with that . . . Bang! Hit them with another. That's the way you do it."

"Yes," said Peter meekly. "I can see I'll have to . . ."

"I'm lying deep in water," said James Duncan, breaking in. "We really ought to bail her out."

"We can't risk it."

"I guess you're right. We don't want to see this old tub stop another wallop like the last. *Jesus,* it's a long night! If it wasn't for this God-damned water coming in I think I could sleep a while. Could you?"

"If they left us alone. Yes. I could sleep."

They said no more. Shortly, Peter seemed to fall asleep, and James Duncan envied him, certain that in his own case not even exhaustion would be enough to bring on sleep. He imagined how it would be if the blessed shades of sleep would fall on everything that had changed life to a nightmare. He might wake to a new day, finding the dreadful lapses of his mind all healed by sleep. This new day might bring gifts of courage and re-source, and better happenings. He imagined miracles; waking, lifting his head, looking across the sea, spying land, drifted near them by the vagrant airs of night. He imagined these saving things that sleep might bring.

But instead of seeking sleep his mind grew sharp in a fever of pointless activity. The depression, which had descended so forcefully when Peter was talking, now deepened. He was physically affected, as by a real sickness of the body. Suddenly he knew that only in violent bodily release would he find deliverance. He must get up and run.

Run? Yes. He must.

Running far enough, and fast enough, he might escape. But I must lie here, he told himself, still and patient. I must lie still and quiet, for many hours. For there is nowhere to go; nowhere to run. Even if I can't bear it, can't endure the frantic torture of lying cramped and helpless, when every nerve demands that I start my body moving, and keep it moving, I must lie here.

Must I?

The thought of running is beyond any joy, any salvation, I have ever known.

But where can I go?

Nowhere. Only the sea.

He decided he would bear it as long as he could and if he could not bear it long enough he would go over, into the sea.

It was a pity, but there was no other way. Only the sea.

What would it be like to slip over the side?

Sinking down, down. What would it be like?

Why, it seemed very good in the sea.

The way he saw it now, when the torment of staying where he was increased like a scream with every moment, the sea was any wise man's choice. The reasonable way. Strange that he had not seen this before. The sea was *all right!*

He ran it through his mind to see how it would be.

Moving his feet from under the seat. Sitting up, careful not to waken Peter. Standing.

Going over.

Nothing to it.

The sea was warm. Sinking into this enveloping warmth, having it close around you as warm and soft as a mother's arms, was like falling into the peaceful dark of sleep.

A deeper, more satisfying sleep that would be forever.

In this dark warm peace the sharks came, and to the sharks, willingly, he gave up the body with which he was forever finished. He did not feel their wide-jawed blows as with scavenging neatness they disposed of this body that, wrongly, as he saw now, he had thought he would always need.

He came to his senses with Peter's strong arms about his chest, and Peter shouting. He opened his eyes. He was kneeling, clutching the side of the boat in a grip of such power that it would have taken him off balance, and over into the sea, without Peter to hold him back.

"Let go," he said, defeated, coming wide awake. "Let me go."

"Come back," said Peter.

"I'm coming back. Let go. I wasn't going to do it. I was dreaming."

But Peter still clutched him, and trembling now, weak, he allowed himself to be guided away from the side and moved to the seat, where he sat with bowed head, with arms hanging strengthless between his legs.

That arm of Peter's, sure in its youth and strength, held him comforted as they sat together on the seat.

The boat began to move more actively on a sea which was coming to life in a freshening breeze.

At times the boat struck waves at an angle and showered them with spray. They were cold and wet in the wind but they stayed where they were, huddled together on the seat.

Waiting for day to come.

6 "I can smell land," Peter said, but saw no sign that he was heard. Gazing from the vacancy of tired eyes, James Duncan appeared unconscious of existing time. It was as if, in secret escape, he had removed himself into some unfathomed distance of the mind.

Peter stared upwind, awaiting day.

Moments ago the wind had brought a complex of odors so clear and sharp that he had raised his head with a startled movement and sniffed the air. It had been almost dark, dawn's first moment, when the development of day begins by soft changes of imperceptible degree.

Now Peter stood erect, in stoic patience, passing each breath through nostrils which ached with a kind of wishful effort of confirmation, knowing that, for all this sudden hope, his skillful, analytic senses could not be trusted, now that they knew what was so ardently desired.

Warm sand, and sun-baked mud, still hot from yesterday. Grasses drying, giving their dying sweetness to the wind. Trees breathing a spiced distillate of saps and bitter oils.

To satisfy a fervent hope, all these a willing nose might forge, to please its master.

Unable to believe, not daring to doubt, Peter waited.

Sighing, James Duncan mumbled confusedly and leaned his head on Peter's knee.

The highest clouds showed golden edges. Near things developed sharply into sight. The boat was seen in every detail; and the gray sea, the freshening sea chopped by the steady wind.

Morning flowed, as if light had been spilled on the sea in a pool which must adjust itself by the natural laws of flowing liquids, and Peter saw the ghostly line of land, and doubted, and rubbed night from his eyes, and looked again, and then was sure.

"It was true," he said, with a kind of prayerful and submissive quietness. "It was land I smelled. It was true. Look there."

James Duncan, still not listening, answered with a heavy sigh.

Peter's false calm erupted.

"Land!" he cried. "You see? Land!"

"Ah . . . tired," James Duncan mumbled. "Le' me 'lone."

"You must stand up!" Peter was shaking with impatience. It was as if, for full belief, they both must see. There must be another witness. "Stand up and look!"

"Chris' sake stop y'r fuss. Chris' sake stop it. Le' me 'lone."

Peter tried to make the white man stand. They swayed. The boat rocked, and James Duncan ceased resistance as he took a step for balance.

"What's the matter?" he said, in an aggrieved but more awakened voice.

"Look! In the night. We drifted. There's land."

"Over there," said James Duncan. "Yes. That's land. Sure enough. There it is."

"Hills and trees. Can you see? Can you see the trees?"

"How long will it take? When will we be there?"

"With this wind . . ." Peter began, but stopped, dismayed, as he recognized the adverse direction of the wind.

He should have thought of that. A wind that carried land smells out to sea . . . how could such a wind drive a boat to land? He should have known immediately. He felt like crying, with disappointment and fear, with a fear which had been faced yesterday, and somehow accepted, and which now seemed new.

"Are you off your head?" said James Duncan. "Don't you see which way this wind is blowing?" He raised a hand and turned, so that he pointed out to sea. "That's where this wind will blow . . ." But he, too, stopped.

"It's there as well," said Peter, awed by the unbelievable. "Land on both sides. How can that be?"

"Islands? Could they be islands? No. We're going across a bay. Isn't that more likely?"

"It doesn't matter. There's land ahead, and land behind, and almost any wind will do the trick."

"Good boy," said James Duncan vaguely. "You're a good boy, Peter. You've done damn well. There will be water. Food. People, maybe."

Peter wondered, studying that scrubby headland, or island, or whatever it was. Even from far off it looked an arid coast. No rule dictated that where land was there must be water. Yet, to doubt so quickly would be shameful ingratitude in a man who recognized a miracle in what he saw. Was one miracle never sufficient for a man? Must there be always another miracle to follow?

"I must have water, you know," said James Duncan, quite reasonably. "I couldn't last another day. Did you say? When will we be ashore?"

Peter dropped to his knees in sudden fright, and crouched, holding the seat.

"Get down," he whispered. "We forgot about the sharks."

"Ah, bugger the sharks."

"You must," hissed Peter. "Oh get down, please. I saw the big one. Right beside us."

"Never *mind* about those frigging sharks. You hear? Stop going on about them. What you have to do is get us ashore and find some water. Don't you realize that, you fool? Water! I must have water! Don't you understand?"

Peter tried to calm this wild man, who sat on the seat, staring around with violent eyes, looking, with his tangled hair, like a madman, whiskered, crazy, burnt by the sun.

God help me, I'm all alone, he told himself. Alone. His two bad nights and that dreadful yesterday have been too much for him. Yet, by myself I could last for many days. Oh God, I'd be better off without this white man. Oh yes. It would be better with an abo like myself.

A heavy body, moving lazily, hit the boat and backed off, and hit again. The big shark seemed to have begun all over again, in an experimental way, to discover the best way of dealing with the boat. He would go on, all day, until he succeeded. Nothing would stop him.

Peter raised himself enough to see. The shark, almost as long as the boat, rolled in the waves close by. Now, as he watched the shark, hatred poured into Peter's limbs in a sensual flood. Hatred that was a tremor in the limbs, a prickling of the spine, a lust, a killing lust.

Kill! he shouted in his mind. Kill! Kill! The word had a vibrant fervor which captured him entirely, so that he was aware of nothing else.

He pushed James Duncan aside and wrenched at the floor, not knowing what he was doing or why he did it, and a plank began to yield. He did not care that this might harm the ancient boat. He did not care for anything but finding himself a weapon, any weapon, something for his hands to use against the bestial arrogance of the shark.

"Stop!" James Duncan shouted. "What the hell y' doing? Silly bastard! Want to rip the arse right out of her? Now stop it, or I'll crack you!"

Peter released the board, recovering at once his normal senses. *He* isn't mad, he thought, not now. *I'm* the one who's mad. Why can't we just go mad together, and get it over with, instead of taking turns?

"You think of something better," he said, angry that his killing fever had been so easily frustrated, resenting the loss of that fearless rage.

"Ripping the guts out of the bloody boat won't help," said James Duncan.

"I've stopped. Can't you see I've stopped? Don't go on about it."

"What did you think you were doing?"

"I wanted a board. I was going to use it for a spear or something. A weapon."

"You got a one-track mind," said James Duncan. "You made

that other spear, and where the hell that got us I wouldn't know. What say we forget spears for a while?"

Peter sulked.

"You leave those bloody sharks alone," said James Duncan. "You listening? They haven't hurt us yet. Maybe they'll get tired of it and go away. You start to poke at them with sticks you're only going to make them mad."

"We have to get in first," said Peter. "We have to do something."

"I listened to one of your smart ideas before, and look what happened. You're going to hear me for a change. Things are going pretty well. We're going to lie quiet in the bottom of this boat until we drift ashore and then we're going to find some water. We're doing nothing to upset the bloody apple cart. You hear?"

"But . . ."

"Shut up a while. That's all we're going to say. I've got a throat like dog's meat. I've finished talking, and so have you. You're going to get down here with me and shut up for a while."

"We're going to have to bail this boat," said Peter sullenly, sliding over the seat and letting himself down to the bottom where water washed around as the boat moved pitching in the swell.

James Duncan refused to answer.

"I can't see why you have to lie right in it," said Peter. "You could sit with your back against the seat the way I am."

"I don't care whether I lie in it or not. It's all the same to me. I can lie here all day without the slightest fret now I know we're going to get some water."

I wish he wouldn't go on about water and be so confident, thought Peter. He can't imagine how wrong he very likely is. This wind will have to blow all day, that's how long it's going to take to reach the shore. And in spite of what he says the big shark's going to jump us. I bet he's never even *seen* a shark before. And if we get ashore, if we get through the surf without being tipped out and drowned, or taken by the sharks, who's to say there will be water?

But still . . . the sight of land has made another man of him. He wouldn't have lasted through the day without something like that to give him hope.

For the first time the shark threw itself against the boat with all its weight. By chance it hit where the boat was strongest, at the bow, where the boards curved in a solid arc of timber.

The boat went right around and crashed against a wave.

Peter leaped to his feet.

"All right! Will you listen to me *now?*"

James Duncan crouched wordless.

Peter's eyes raked the boat in desperate search for the weapon he had sought before and hadn't found. The old rope tangled in the bow stopped his eyes. Frantic, his mind worked on the thought of making rope into a weapon. A noose? No. The problem of using rope defeated him. The rope was tied to an iron weight, the coils of the rope led his eye right to the weight. His thoughts seemed to wrap themselves about the weight. At once he knew that the weight could be a weapon.

He crawled to the bow and pushed the rope aside. He hefted the weight to get the feel of it. He studied it. It was the kind of makeshift anchor sometimes used in quiet waters, an old cylinder head, jagged, broken in half.

He lifted the weight to the forward seat, and coiled the rope.

He looked for the shark, first at one side of the boat and then at the other, staring down as far as he could see, through clear water to the green that lay above the darkness of the un-plumbed ocean. He saw nothing.

He turned. James Duncan was leaning against the seat, watching him with doubtful and frightened eyes.

"You'll have to help," said Peter. "We will have to hurt that shark or he will smash us open. And you will have to help."

"What can we do?"

"You'll have to hit him with this weight. There's nothing else. It's solid enough to hurt him if we hit him right."

"What will you be doing?"

"I'll bring him right up close so you can hit him."

"How?"

"I'll show you how," said Peter, grim of countenance and voice, stripping off his shirt. "This will bring him. You be ready."

James Duncan raised the weight and turned it in his hands, so that the jagged end was pointing down. He tried to lift the weight above his head in readiness to throw.

"*No!*" he cried. "It's too heavy. Can't lift it. And the rope catches. We'll have to work this out. Oh Peter . . . stop! Don't bring him yet!"

Peter pulled his arm back from the water, seeing the shark move in its green world, seeing its lithe shadow rising from the depths, gliding into clearer water, looking even larger than it was as the lens of a wave swept by with magnifying light.

The shark moved beneath the boat and Peter stepped across to see the fin as it tipped up through a rise of water and sliced along in leisured circling. He showed his teeth in a grin that quite lacked humor.

"I'll have the weight, then. Take off your shirt. You can be the bait."

"Undo the rope." James Duncan worked at the buttons of his shirt with trembling fingers.

"Leave the rope on," said Peter. "We might need another go."

He took up the frayed rope until it was tight against its ring. He coiled the rope at his feet and made several swings for practice with the weight.

"What do I do?" asked James Duncan helplessly, clutching himself with his arms as if to keep the wind from his shivering body. "Tell me what to do."

"Do nothing until I tell you," said Peter. "I'll bring him around behind so he makes his run along the boat. If he comes straight in he'll sink us."

He studied the shark's position, and his teeth showed that

fixed grin that had nothing to do with humor. His teeth were very white.

Oh Christ, he's a savage all right, thought James Duncan. He's *enjoying* it. The only thing in his mind is how to kill the shark. All he cares about. He doesn't care what happens to him and he doesn't care what happens to me.

He felt sick.

The shark rolled in the swell, sitting there, poised on a wave, as high as it could float.

"Watch him now," said Peter. "Don't take your eyes off him. Tell me what he does. I have to watch down here in case the smaller ones are hanging round."

"He's coming. Moving closer."

"Fast?"

"Not very. Taking his time about it."

Peter turned to see. The shark stopped moving.

Peter leaped to the stern and leaned out to stir the water with his arm.

"Watch him," he cried. "Don't look at me. I know what I'm doing."

"Careful. He's coming behind."

"Right behind yet?"

"Nearly. Watch it. He's going faster."

"All right," said Peter. "I can see him." He let his arm lie in the water, not moving it now, trying to judge how long to leave it there so that the shark would be tempted, but not tempted too greatly.

The shark cruised around to the right place.

"Your turn," said Peter. "Put your arm in. Don't take it out too soon or he'll turn into the boat after you. Leave it as late as you can. Then throw yourself out of the way."

He glanced at the rope to be sure it was clear and stood in the middle of the boat with the weight balanced on his shoulder.

"Now," he said softly, dropping into a pose so tense that it quivered the knotted muscles of his legs.

James Duncan thought he would vomit. His heart was beating in his throat. He looked around, but the shark was hidden behind the stern. All he saw was Peter's perfect sparkling grin.

"Wave that white meat," shouted Peter. "Splash it around. Keep it going; he's coming in."

James Duncan saw the shovel nose of the shark surging around the stern. For the fraction of a heartbeat he forced himself to wait, and then, even as the shark rolled with yawning jaws to strike, he threw himself back from the stern.

The chilling scream from Peter shocked him. Peter plunged down with the weight, hurling it at the shark with the whole force of his body, so that he finished up half across the side of the boat, kicking his legs wildly to regain his balance.

The boat rocked, the rope ran tight. Each sought the eyes of the other as if this must be the first thing done, find the other's hopes and share them. So, at first glance, each found uncertainty.

"I hit him," gasped Peter. "Got him right in the head with the sharp end."

He pulled the rope and the weight came dripping in.

"Did you kill him?"

"Oh no," said Peter. "You'd never kill a shark like that. But I hurt him, I'm sure. He'll think twice about coming back for more."

"I was frightened as hell," said James Duncan. "Jesus, I was frightened."

"Nobody could have done it better," said Peter. "You did it perfectly."

They looked for the shark, shading their eyes, for in the short time since dawn the sun had leaped up into morning. From a clear sky it flashed a thousand mirrored beams as they scanned the sea around.

Not far away they saw the shark, lying motionless below the surface.

"He looks the same," said James Duncan. "As if nothing's happened."

"I hit him," said Peter. "I swear I did. I hit him hard."

"Perhaps he didn't notice. Perhaps he had his mind on something else."

The drift of the wind took them closer to the shark.

"He's bleeding," said Peter, and his defensive voice grew strong with triumph and vindication. "Look! That's blood. You see? He's hurt. Now do you believe me?"

A slow brown stain trailed from the shark's jaws.

"Blood, you say?" said James Duncan. "It could be, I suppose."

"*They* think it's blood," said Peter, and James Duncan followed Peter's gesture.

Rising now, green from the green depths, came the smaller sharks in a weaving interchange of movement that made them difficult to count; four of them, or five—it was difficult to tell.

In the sparkling silence of the sea their fluent motion was deadly and controlled. They approached the big shark as if in play, coming close, rolling and turning away, coming back.

The first to attack came from behind in gliding stealth. It slowed, and nudged against the big shark, which did not move. It turned away and curved around, seemingly without physical effort gathering speed, and it came in on the flank, jaws agape, hitting the big shark heavily, so heavily that it rolled, and rolling came to life, while the attacker hung on, and then came free and dived away.

The big shark hurled to the surface and came partly into the air, near the boat. It fell back in the sea, tail thrashing, cavernous jaws opening and smashing closed. And now the pack came, tracing the rippling waves with a pattern of cutting fins, rushing and feinting about their massive victim, while the two men watched absorbed, with not a word, leaning far out to see all details of this cannibal display of fury in the sea beside them.

As they watched, the big shark lost its very substance in lumps and strips, ripped flesh trailed as its consorts came darting in from every side, no longer stealthy, rushing bold and hungry to have their share, while their huge prey, thrown this way and that by the weight of uncounted blows, released an enormous and senseless energy, to no avail.

It rose again and again to the surface, as if safety might be found in the air above. It foamed the sea for yards around. Snapping the water with giant's bites it hurled showers of spray with frantic exertions of tail and body, only to be pulled down, until it rose no more, and slowly sank, still being torn to pieces, still writhing and snapping, until only ghostly movements could be seen. And in the end, nothing.

The men in the boat sighed, and turned away.

"He's finished, that one," said Peter, with a growling edge to his voice, that same primordial note of triumph. "That's the end of *him*."

Wearily, James Duncan picked up the bailing tin. "I guess we can bail out now."

He kneeled at the stern where the floorboards ended. The depth of water surprised him. To lift the tin to the side and pour it over required a tiring effort.

"You'd better take a turn," he said weakly. "I'm shot."

Peter turned. James Duncan, having poured water over, rested the empty tin on the side, as if the effort to put it down might be beyond him.

He looked at Peter with a curious expression of apology. He sighed, and lowered the tin, and filled it, and lifted again. But he fell back against the seat and the tin dropped, spilling.

"Are you all right?" Peter was alarmed.

"I've had it. Something's wrong. Just now. You'd better . . . do the bailing, boy. I think . . . think she's leaking more. Up at the bow . . . where the shark . . . have a look."

"Lie down," said Peter. "Leave it all to me."

He helped James Duncan to lift himself, feeling his own weakness as he guided the white man down between the seats. James Duncan lay with closed eyes, sighing and breathing heavily.

Peter went to the stern and started bailing, and as he dipped, and bailed, and emptied, as this simple task became mechanical, his thoughts were freed to probe among his many worries.

When we get ashore . . . *if* we get ashore . . . he won't be any use. I'll have to look after him. And I'll be weaker, too. I've gone as long as he; with thirst and sun, and hunger; and it's having its effect. Yet, I'll have to find food and water, and get a fire going, I suppose. I'll have to remember how to do that with a stick, and it's so long since I saw that done. And we're not ashore yet, not by a long way.

He stopped bailing to look at the land. He couldn't tell if it was any closer than when dawn revealed it first. In the strong light he saw low country with a bit of a ridge inland, wooded, the heads of mean-looking trees making a rippled skyline. It was close enough to be seen in reasonable color and detail. How close? Five miles? Ten? He couldn't tell.

It was a long way. At first it had been enough to see the land. No need to think past that. No reason to expect that they might drift close enough to see land clearly and still not reach it.

He held a wet finger to the wind, and the heavy thought he was refusing to think lay hard in the pit of his stomach, as if there was a nervous center there where bad thoughts came from. He decided for his peace of mind that the wind was blowing as strongly as before, and that they were drifting in the right direction. They *must* be. They *had* to be.

He went on bailing until the boat was as dry as he could get it.

He took the towels and dipped them, and spread one over James Duncan and took the other for himself. He lay down to rest, and fell asleep.

At noon, as he judged it by the sun, the water had risen far enough to wake him as it swirled around. As soon as he opened his eyes he sat up to see the land.

They were closer, no doubt about it now. The nearest land was a point of yellow rock, washed by a light, quick surf. Listening intently, he could hear the distant mutter of this modest sea as it ran across a reef and up the wedge of rock and broke in flashing arrowheads of foam.

Beyond the point the shoreline curved around the bay, and in the bay, far around the curve, the heavy green gloss of mangroves showed.

Again he measured the wind with his finger and tried to decide exactly where they would be taken. He couldn't tell. They might be taken to the point, or past the point, along the coast. Or the wind might favor them and drift the boat into the bay, and that would be, by far, the best. It would be calmer there.

He imagined coming ashore so vividly that he felt it happening. He felt the hard packed sand on the soles of his feet as he jumped over in the shallows to pull the boat ashore. The loose hot sand of the yellow beach. The trees behind the beach. Their shade. Their coolness.

I'll weep for joy, he thought, with a pricking of the eyes. And then I'll kneel on that beach and give my thanks.

He bailed the boat. He wet the towels again. He covered James Duncan, who didn't move, who breathed through a slack mouth, who lapped the air with a swollen tongue as a dog laps water, whose skin beneath the stubble was scaled and red, whose lips were cracked and purple.

Bailing again, Peter thought about James Duncan dying. He adjusted himself to this thought, calmly, as he dipped and bailed. Looking at James Duncan now, it could not be denied that he had taken, on the way to death, a long, quick step. To-morrow it could happen. Or today. Without fuss, he would die, and he would look very much the way he looked right now.

Peter finished bailing and lay again to rest.

I will not die, he said to himself, moving his dry lips over the silent words, *I* will not die. Over and over he said this to himself, until the sound of the words in his mind lost meaning, and he fell asleep.

Again he was awakened by water in the boat. He knew as soon as he opened his eyes, before he sat up, in that instant moment of perception that tells a suddenly awakened man where he is and why he is there, and provides the facts of what has happened—in this instant he knew that the wind had died.

Sitting up, he saw the sea flat calm, felt the dead air, listened for the sea washing on those dingo-colored rocks, now not a mile away, and he did not catch the slightest sound.

The sun was low, and darkness soon to come. Something must be done.

We must swim, he decided. In this calm sea we could surely get as far as that. We can't stay with the boat and let it take us out again.

He lifted the towel from the white man's face. "Wake up," he said. "Wake up."

He shook James Duncan, but saw at once that this would not arouse him. Nothing would. This was something more than ordinary sleep.

If he was dead I could leave him, he thought.

"If he was dead," he muttered aloud, to hear how this would sound.

Why didn't he die while I was still asleep? Then I could leave him, and swim ashore.

Poor man; he's going to die. Oh, but why doesn't he get it *over* with! Then I could leave him. Now, even if I could wake him, he wouldn't come. Not after he's seen what sharks can do. He wouldn't take the chance.

I'll have to leave him. *I* will not die.

He said this to himself, but it lacked conviction. He gave up the thought of swimming.

He must find some way to move the boat. That would need a paddle. One of the floorboards would make a sort of paddle. But the white man had been right. Ripping a floorboard up might do great damage to the boat. Sink it, maybe.

Well?

If the boat sank, then they'd *have* to swim.

He couldn't do it to the sleeping man. He looked at him and he couldn't do it. He must remove a board in a way which left the boat undamaged. Unclinching the copper nails would be the way, but that was a job that would take too long, even with proper tools.

A rowlock might make a tool. He found one of the rowlocks and rested the curved end on the rib at one end of a floorboard. Using the pin of the rowlock as a handle and the curved tongue as a lever he pushed down hard, watching to see if the bottom planks would move. But instead of that the floorboard came up with surprising ease, right off its nail, leaving a small, slotlike hole.

He worked along each rib until the board was free. It was long and thin, three or four inches wide. It would do for a paddle. It would have to be used carefully, or it would break, but it would do.

It wasn't very hard to turn the boat in the right direction. He paddled on one side until the bow came around and pointed at the yellow reef. He paddled furiously on that side until he was sure the boat was moving, and leaped to the other side and paddled there, and the thin board bent in his hands, so that he had to ease up, afraid that it would snap.

Glancing back he saw the ripples of a modest wake, the only indication that the boat was moving. The land stayed in the same relationship, any lessening of distance unmeasured by the eye. This trail of ripples at the stern was the only product of his ceaseless and tiring efforts. Yet, what else could be done? Even if these efforts were quite useless, he must maintain them until his strength had been expended.

Jumping from one side of the boat to the other, he flailed the water with the flimsy board. He kept going long after his body issued its first warnings that he should stop, and when he did give in, when at last he fell to his knees in the bottom of the boat, and let the paddle lie, his state of exhaustion was extreme enough to be alarming.

He sobbed for breath, and each breath was like the ripping of a knife inside him. He could not see. His vision was lost in a lurid fog, in which white streaks and pinpoints whirled and vanished.

Gradually, normal sight returned. He breathed more easily, and it hurt him less to draw each breath. And now that he could see clearly, and measure how far it was to land, he could not assure himself that the distance had been reduced. The land appeared no closer. He could pretend it was, but there was no way of being sure.

When he had recovered he tried again to wake James Duncan. He shook him and shouted in his ear. If only the white man would revive! Two of us would have a chance; I could do all the work, thought Peter, and he could keep her straight. I wouldn't have to keep jumping from one side to the other.

"Wake up, Mr. Duncan," he pleaded. "Oh please, wake up."

Then if you won't wake up, why don't you die? You're going to die anyway; why won't you please die now? So I can swim ashore?

James Duncan was ugly. There was something piglike about him; in the swollen face, the protruding tongue, the broken lips. It was hard to pity him as he should be pitied.

Couldn't I leave him, Peter wondered, mightn't that be the proper thing to do? There's that other life ... the thing we came to do ... what about that? Doesn't the other life have equal rights? Oh, I wish there was something to tell me what to do!

And if I stay here with him, to die with him, what will become of my dreams about the future of my life? It will all be wrong. And I cannot bear that thought. If death came and I saw that my dreams were nothing but delusion? No. I could not bear it.

And yet ... ? If I leave him? Just as wrong. I would have to live with that. I could bear that no better. Someone ... something ... tell me what to do!

You must stay, and if you must, you must die.

These words came into his mind as if they had been said aloud, a thought he had not constructed. A thought that might not be his own. That, surely, was not his own.

I must stay, and if I must, I must die.

Courage was in these words. Acceptance. For several moments he bowed his head.

He took the paddle and with a kind of determined calmness worked the water on each side until the boat resumed its sluggish progress.

He continued to paddle until the rhythm of the paddling was the only thing he knew. He fell into a trance of effort.

The sun sank out of sight behind a somber bank of clouds, and in the briefness of twilight a different wind arose. Coming from land, the first squall darkened the waters of the bay in a ruffled line. The sea became disturbed. The strengthening wind carried the boat away from land. The headland disappeared. Night fell.

In darkness it was hopeless to continue. The boat moved sharply and the paddle at times struck the full depth of a wave, and on the next stroke encountered no resistance. He could not keep his balance. He did not know which way the boat should head.

He put down the paddle. In the distant clouds lightning danced. A feeling of imminent storm was in the air.

Peter hardly noticed. He did not care.

He gave up.

7

The hellish glare of day had gone. On his closed eyes James Duncan felt the gentle weight of night, on his face the cool of an evening wind. The sense of time and of real things, lost in the parched fevers of the day, now returned in tentative perception of himself, his body, the physical world around him.

He flinched from recollection of those lost, febrile hours, that wild, inward life his mind had led, when in long continued fantasy he had seen paraded all that the buried layers of his mind contained.

He had found memory; seen his life.

In the disordered flow of time and memory he had at last found order, a continuity of past experience raised on a scaffold of regret, a history for himself, a life, a life he would not care to live again.

Now, in darkness, finding again some parts of that real world of here and now—that world in which, moment by moment the future came, turned to present, immediately changed to past—he was at first relieved.

He knew about the boat, and remembered that it leaked. For he was wet, and that was why.

He heard the rising wind. He felt the leaping of the boat in lively motion, and pictured the restless sea.

In difficult words, questions formed:

Peter? Are you there?

What has happened?

When will we be ashore?

He would have said these things, he tried to form the words, but no words came.

Peter? I have found my memory. I have remembered everything. I am myself again.

That, most of all, he would have liked to say.

He could make sounds in his throat, insect sounds, frog's sounds, but he could not speak.

He moved his hand. At least he thought it moved. Perhaps the hand stayed where it was, sending back the false feeling that it had obeyed the order? An illusion?

No. His hand had moved. It had discovered Peter. His leg. He closed his fingers on Peter's leg.

"Oh!" said Peter. "What is it? Are you awake?"

"Yes." Could Peter understand that only noise at his command? Insect noise? Frog's croak?

"Don't try to talk," said Peter. "Your mouth is swollen. Listen, I can't talk very much, either. Listen, I saw lightning, a while ago."

What about the land! Why aren't we ashore?

"It might rain," said Peter.

What about the land!

"We drifted near that headland. Then night came. Don't know where we are. See in the morning. I tried to get ashore, Mr. Duncan. Really tried. But tired now, too tired to talk."

Peter's fingers moved on James Duncan's arm, and found his hand.

"Go to sleep," said Peter. "I'll look after you."

Yes. Look after me.

The boat rolled his slack body and he had no strength to resist.

Wonder what Wendy is doing tonight?

Wendy? The question arose from no connecting thought. Came out of nowhere, the sick stab of jealousy as painful and as mixed with perverse dislike as ever.

Was he to be like that again, a prey to any random thought? Wasn't that over, now that memory had strung itself together? He could not decide when that had been. First the sharks and then the bailing, and then the sudden loss of all his strength. That nightmare day. His life a dream of teeming images. But, waking in the dark, it had all been there.

And now, wondering about Wendy. Wendy, back now with all the rest of it.

Someone said—Peter had said—she looked as if she only liked herself.

Here I am, Wendy. Far away. Far away as a man could go. I guess I'm dying.

And you are my only thought.

Dying?

Yes. That shocked you, if you'd never used this word so certainly about yourself before. That shocked you, now it was happening, and real.

How cunningly you taught yourself to forget that all men died! All men. No exceptions. That one will die, and so will he, that's natural. Ah, but so will I!

You never admitted that before; never believed it, did you? You'd be the one exception. For you, a special dispensation. Death would stay his hand.

Not forever, no. But until you were ready. And you weren't ready, were you?

No. Not ready. You never would be. And because you wouldn't be, ever, truly ready, the hand of death, when at last it came, touched your living heart with the tips of icy fingers. Death had a cold hand when, as now, by all the signs, he would not be cheated any longer and must be faced, not as vague concept, but as inescapable fact.

I must now reconcile myself to the fact, James Duncan told himself. I must take this surprising gift of clearheadedness to face the facts of my life, which are about to be brought to conclusion by the fact of my death.

Well said!

And all that is in my mind is my lust for the body of Wendy Bracker, my secretary, and my part-time mistress.

My lust? Please, on this sad and important occasion, which happens but once to any man, might I not call my feeling for

Wendy Bracker by a better name? Not love, perhaps, I hesitate to ... but still (it only happens once), on this special occasion ... ? Give it any name, the plain fact is I'd have been better off without it.

Oh? You mean that? Really mean it?

Oh come, where's the audience? You're dying, man. Only fooling yourself; who else hears you? Hypocrisy looks no better when it's called repentance.

That's true. I am relieved to hear it.

Well, then, the truth is, if I had every single moment of my time with Wendy Bracker now at my disposal, to live again, or live through in a different way, there's not a moment I would change.

Now I will be in my office. I will see Wendy.

"Alec thinks you're a dirty old man," says Wendy. "I have to get another job, Alec says."

His own voice speaks in natural answer. "What does he know?"

"Nothing, really. The way you look at me, that's all. He doesn't like it. But you *are* a dirty old man, aren't you? Aren't you, darling? Even dirtier than Alec thinks?"

That had happened. Had been said. And he had laughed.

What's the time of this night? What's this night of the week? Who is she with? Alec's night, perhaps. Or that one I've never seen? Someone new?

I'll never know. All the things I'll never know. Never see or hear or feel again.

Why can't there be a miracle? Why can't I have another year? Six months? A week? One more weekend with Wendy?

His mind made a leap to another kind of thinking, to a dreaming state where some of the dream came under his control; though he tried to control it all. Feet on the desk, telephone in hand, leaning back. George Baxter's whisky voice guttural in his ear.

"Favor? Anything for you, old boy. *You* know that."

George ... what about the shack? Were you going down there this weekend? Did you want the shack?

"Aha! What's on? Another piece of grommet? Hey? How do you find 'em?"

George . . . what about the shack? This weekend?

"I never like to be a prawn, Jimmy. But *you* know how it is. Some of the boys . . . Sammy and his mob, Jimmy . . . talking about going down to try for salmon off the beach. *You* know how it is, Jimmy."

Come on, George. What about it? (Don't make me remind you, George. All the stuff I put your way. Don't make me, George.)

"Guess we can work it, Jimmy. Seeing it's for you. But I'm going out of my way, old man. I'm really putting myself out for you. I'm doing it in the way of business, Jimmy, and you won't forget it, eh? It's up to you to see it's worth my while. What about that, old man? Hey? What about it?"

Yes, George. Yes, George. As long as I can have the shack. I'm dying, George. That's all that matters. Two sweet nights with Wendy Bracker. Then death. Death's here, impatient. I must die.

It's a dream, he reminded himself. I made it. Why do I make it so much harder than it really was? Why must I abase myself?

The only point of the dream is to get there. To be in bed with naked Wendy Bracker. Leave out the obstacles.

He started the dream again. It had to be in the office, where Wendy was, so that he could ask her. So she would come with him. There wasn't much time. He was at his desk.

Silverman was there.

Oh God, not Silverman!

"Five grand a year we're putting your way," said Silverman. "Who else pays as much as that?"

It's a big account, I know. But a lot of work, Sir Philip.

"Five grand on top of all the costs. How about answering the question? Who pays you more?"

Nobody does.

"We're your biggest client?"

Yes, Sir Philip.

"Value for money. That's all I want."

That's what we want to give you, Sir Philip.

"Don't feed me that. Listen, Duncan. They got this National Credit Corporation deal spread on every paper in the country. Listen, you're on the payroll, what in hell you going to do about it? Making us look like a bunch of cheap crooks and what the hell you doing? What about our side of the story, when's that going to . . ."

You'll have to excuse me, Sir Philip. My secretary . . . I must . . .

"It's time I was going, Mr. Duncan," Wendy said. "Was there anything else?" She was ready to leave.

Wait. Wait. You can't go. Something I must ask you.

Silverman disappeared.

Silverman will never forgive me. All that gone for nothing. I should call him back.

But I am dying, he remembered. It doesn't matter now.

He imagined he went from desk to door, weak all through, shaking with a boy's first love. Or lust. That shameful sickness, lust: only disease that asks no cure.

Wendy. So young. Must not tell her he was dying. She would be afraid. It would put her off. To be asked to sleep with a dying man would frighten her.

Wendy. This weekend. I have the shack. Down there on the beach. Sand blowing in the wind. Spray misting through the valleys of the dunes. I have the shack. George said. You must.

"Not this weekend," said Wendy, moving away, fading. A voice now, only a voice. "Can't Jimmy, sorry. Not this weekend. It's all arranged. Alec. He's getting very serious. I didn't want to tell you."

Come with me. You must. I will give you anything.

"Alec is very serious."

I am dying. You must.

"I am so young," said Wendy. "It is wrong to talk of death."

I didn't mean to say it.

"It was very wrong. You must say that you are sorry."

I am sorry.

"I am going now," said Wendy. "It was very wrong."

He could see her now. His arms could reach her.

"You have no right," said Wendy. "It meant nothing to me. I was never serious."

He kissed her cold, wet mouth. Her cold hands touched his face. Her cold hands turned his head.

She was weeping.

"Open your mouth," said Wendy. "Do not die."

Her tears fell in his mouth like rain.

He awoke.

"Open your mouth," said Peter. "It's raining."

Those were Peter's hands; Peter's cold hands; turning his head.

"Wake up!" cried Peter. "Get all you can!"

He shook his head to be rid of Peter's hands, so that he could tip his head back all the way. So little water. He would go mad if there weren't more. It would stop at any moment.

His swollen tongue stopped up his mouth. He pushed out his tongue as far as it would go, lapping at the fat drops, the melting, scattered drops, rubbing his face with his hands to guide the wetness to his mouth. But sounds now recognized, the hissing of rain on sea and boat, became fainter, and soon could not be heard at all.

"It's stopped," he sobbed, finding his voice again. "Must have . . . oh, more!"

"Hurry," said Peter. "Drink it before it leaks away."

"What? Oh what? More?"

"Your briefcase. I emptied it, held it open. It doesn't hold it very well. But wait. I'll drink mine first. Then I can help you."

"Give it to me now!"

"Shut up," said Peter savagely. "You'll only spill it."

In a moment he was holding the sodden end of the briefcase and a thin flow of water, tasting of leather and ink and salt, ran into James Duncan's mouth. He swallowed and choked. The larger quantity of water, the three or four mouthfuls, gave him an immediate spurious vitality.

"I need more," he said. "Christ Almighty! I must have more!"

"If it rains again," said Peter. "We'll be ready to catch it next time. I was sleeping when it started. It was like a miracle."

A miracle? Were there miracles? So suddenly, when you had agreed to die, did the thing that saved you become a miracle?

Rain is not a miracle, James Duncan decided. Rain is a natural event. Seeming now a miracle only because it has countered death. Death, that most awesome of natural events. Thus, rain is greater than death. Rain is a miracle.

He stared into the night, now so dark that nothing could be seen. Yet, seeing nothing, he was sharp in his consciousness of the world around him.

The sea was very rough. The rain had added to the product of the leaks and in the boat water rushed from side to side with a most disconcerting sound. So high in mighty clouds that only reflections of the flashes could be seen, erratic lightning glowed. He could hear the thick, far roll of thunder.

For all the roughness of the sea, and all the signs of storm, the feeling of the night was one of mildness. The air was warm and hardly moving.

"That storm can't miss us," said Peter. "We're going to have to bail her out."

"I'll do some," said James Duncan, moving his right arm painfully, wondering whether it could lift more than its own weight, and doubting.

"Sit there. Mind these." Peter handed him the satchels. "If it rains again we must be ready. Get ourselves a proper drink."

"Will it rain?"

"I hope it doesn't. Another storm, that's the only reason it would rain. And, another storm, we could be in trouble."

"Trouble? That would be something new."

Peter laughed. Had it not been dark he might have smiled and let it go at that, but the laugh was needed to let the white man know it was conceded he had made a joke. To thank him.

For when Peter laughed, courage helped his heart. He was, for a moment, less afraid of what he guessed was coming now across this moody sea, disguised so far by the mildness of the air, its violence hidden by clouds so dense and dark that even lightning was obscured.

"Yes," said Peter. "I guess we should be in the habit of trouble by now."

"God bless you, boy," said James Duncan weakly. "God bless you."

Peter splashed around and found the bailing tin.

The storm moved close and thick. Flickering dragon's tongues of lightning pierced the clouds, spitting blue fire across the sky with crashing roars of sound. He bailed faster, disturbed to find as much water in the boat as when he started.

"Do you think it's going down?"

There was no answer.

"Mr. Duncan!"

"What's that? What's that?" James Duncan had fallen into real dreamless sleep and now awoke reluctant and confused, to the sound of his name.

"Is the water going down?"

Peter heard a hand splashed around in water.

"I think so," said James Duncan obligingly. "Oh, yes."

Right above, the sky split wide in a blinding discharge of frozen light so that for an instant, in a snapshot of sight, they saw each other blackly shadowed. They saw the gray boat, the frightening sea writhing and pulsing as if beasts below fought savagely and in their struggle pushed from underneath against a pliant skin laid on the sea, a skin so dark and tough and oily that it gave to every movement without breaking, stretching and recovering itself in a thousand places at once.

In sudden complete darkness, in an inconceivable thickening of night, thunder roared across the sky. As this sound retreated, as if it was something intact and indestructible, retreating rather than dying out—while their bellies still vibrated to this sound, the noise of wind and rain beat plainly on the sea.

Peter came from the stern, and they sat close, listening to the rush of the storm across the noisy sea.

"We need another miracle," said Peter and his voice trembled. "If we get through this we will get through anything."

"Oh Christ," said James Duncan, believing it was not storm alone he heard approaching, second by second nearer, but his own immediate death, the death he had been ready to meet and had been saved from by that dubious miracle of rain, and was now, again, unready and loath to face.

In the last moment of relative calm, he decided that fear might be the real, and perhaps the only, pain of death. Yet fear was a pain as terrible as any. Waiting for death like this, hearing it come, made him so afraid. And it was too late now to look for courage.

A wave curled along the side of the boat and splashed in his face. Gasping, he spat salt water.

"Where is your knife!" screamed Peter in his ear. "We must cut the rope! Tie us in!"

"No," he groaned, knowing Peter could not hear him. "Why not die? Give up. Give up."

"Knife!" shouted Peter, hitting him. "Knife!"

"Don't know," he muttered. "Give up."

The wind leaped, howling into the boat, thick with rain and spray.

Every sense was choked by motion and noise and water. So much water in the air that it was hard to find sufficient air to breathe. They gagged on salt water, retching. They held to each other while the boat lurched sluggishly against the brutal sea. Leaping from the clouds, lightning brought a semblance of sight to their half-closed eyes. The boat was almost full, and more sea rolled in with every wave.

"Damn you!" cried James Duncan. "You had the knife. You had it last."

"I gave it back," said Peter.

"You didn't."

"It doesn't matter," said Peter. "Too late now."

A wave foamed all around, and the boat made a heavy, settling movement.

"How long have we got?" cried James Duncan, gasping for breath, but Peter didn't answer.

The front of the squall swept on, going away as speedily as it had come, taking with it most of the noise and violence.

Gusts plucked the sea, but between the gusts it was almost calm, as calm as it had been before the squall.

It was as if a hammer blow had been needed to bring them to their knees and, this blow delivered, they could be finished off by quieter means. For the boat was full beyond the slightest hope of bailing. To the two men it was no longer a boat, but something to grasp, something to support them in the water, something they would hold to with their remaining strength until a wave broke their grip and they were washed away, or until it sank and left them drowning.

Up to his waist in water, Peter kneeled on the floor, one arm locked around the seat, trying with the other arm to keep James Duncan in the boat, for he rolled with each wave, in and out. He rolled out as each wave lifted across, and he rolled back as they sank into the trough.

He's drowning now, thought Peter, might as well let him go. Perhaps he's drowned already. I must do something about him, or I might as well let him go.

He braced himself for effort as he waited for the boat to cant across a wave. A wave rose up, and out James Duncan went across the side. The boat paused, and tipped. Peter crouched higher, and raised a leg, and dropped it across the white man's body, so that he was held, nearly upright, jammed into the corner of the seat, with his face clear of the water in the boat. Perhaps it was too late. He pushed against James Duncan's chest with his shoulder and heard him gag, and while he strained his ears for other sounds of life he recognized and understood the newest noise the sea was making.

Then God has decided, he told himself. This surely must be the sign that I awaited. For I did not quite despair. Some faith held me. His heart filled with the calm of humility.

He listened to the sound of surf, breaking on the land. He

measured the feel of the land swell of the waves, as they gathered, stirring the wallowing boat with a regular lift and send, as the boat was taken, wave by wave, to the last danger they must pass before they could escape the sea.

I did not doubt You. No, I did not doubt You. I bowed my head and waited for Your sign. But I did not doubt You.

He shouldered James Duncan again. He heard him grunt, and weakly spew. The white man was still alive.

He did not know how he was going to get him through the surf.

How much must he do? How much could he leave to God?

He knew that he must do everything he could.

But what was ahead? Sand? A sloping beach? Reefs? A rocky shore?

The breakers were loud now, very close. He studied the heavy rumble of their breaking.

"Please, I do not doubt You," he whispered, for it seemed shameful that the forceful roar of the breakers should make him so afraid.

A larger wave lifted up behind. The boat faltered before it decided, once again, to rise. The wave came apart and water seethed around, but the wave went on, leaving the boat sagging in its wake.

It will be the next one, Peter told himself, and he heard the next one coming, breaking early, curling up and cracking open; and letting the boat go, grabbing James Duncan by the belt, turning his head, he saw the smother of surf, pale in darkness, looming above his head.

The boat plunged, down and away, and he kicked his legs free of the seat as it caught him for a moment going down, and then they were rolling together underwater. He was trying to hold his last breath as long as he could.

The wave slammed them hard against the bottom, and Peter's breath went out with the force of the blow. He swallowed water, thick with sand. He tried to let James Duncan go, to save himself, and rise, and breathe again, but his fingers were tangled in the belt in a grip that held him down.

Then he was breathing air, not knowing how this could be. He was standing, up to his neck in water, and another wave was on him. Under they went again.

Rolling, bumping on the bottom.

He was standing, waist deep. He was running backward down the slope of the beach, being dragged back into the sea by the force of the retreating wave.

He was kneeling on the sand, and the wave was streaming past.

He was crawling up the slope, dragging James Duncan.

He was covered by water.

He was crawling.

They were lying on sand, water rushing past.

The water went away, and washed back, and went away. He was crawling again.

He was alone.

He rose to his feet, and stumbled down into the sea.

He staggered around. He fell over James Duncan.

He lay beside him in the water.

He gripped the belt again, and crawled a few yards, and gave up. Though he knew he could not rest. Not yet. But he was too tired and sick to move, and he could not remember what he had to do.

He muttered the prayer that God had taught him. Not God. The prayer his father had taught him. No. Not his father . . .

The prayer that someone had taught him.

Now I lay me down to sleep . . .

Was that it? Was that what he had to do?

Is that what I have to do?

The words of the prayer cleared his mind.

He kneeled across James Duncan and turned his body over. He pushed on the white man's back, with both hands flat, and heard a small sound of water rushing from his mouth.

He tried to do it exactly right, but it seemed so useless. Forward, weight on hands. Pause. Forward again. He had little faith in this.

But when he leaned to listen, he heard James Duncan breathing.

He had done all he could. All that God, in fairness, could require of him.

James Duncan was breathing. It was the white man's task, or God's perhaps, to make of that breath continued life.

They could do it between them.

He knew that he could do no more.

8

Something was hurting Peter's ear. He opened his eyes and he saw the birds, close up. So close that at first he wondered what they were. His blurred eyes focused. His frightened waking stare was met by beaded eyes, the cold eyes of a giant gull, inches from his face. He was too shocked to move.

The gull was ugly and gray and arrogant. Horny growths lumped the rapacious beak that made Peter flinchingly aware of that precious jelly of his eyes, that soft, always protected jelly, now so vulnerable.

He shuddered, and uttered a sound of outrage, and at this sound the many birds moved back and screamed in anger. Peter raised his arm, and they rose in a scolding cloud and swung out on the wind, robbed, yet still expectant, staying close, crying to each other their fury of disappointment.

Peter sat up. Face down on the sand beside him, James Duncan sprawled, limbs lifeless, legs and arms spread wide in slack abandon, lying as death, in its first rigor, might well have posed him. The birds had been busy with James Duncan. All around, the fussing of their nimble feet had arrow-marked the sand. Their droppings streaked his shirt. The lobe of his ear was bleeding.

Peter rolled the white man over, to see his face, his eyes, to see if he was dead.

Powerful emotions surprised him when he saw James Duncan breathing, and saw his eyes intact, unmarked. He realized then that he had given the white man up. Last night he had done what he could, and he had left the rest to God, but he had done this without the unquestioned trust in God he should have had. He would not have thought it mattered so much to him that he would weep about it.

For now he wept, weakly. Now, in a fashion, he prayed, not sure whether his prayers sought to excuse his lack of faith, or whether they were tribute to God's mighty powers of arbitration in the matter of each man's death. Standing, bracing himself to a stronger mood, he decided that his tears had been, as well, an expression of fervent thanks for a decision made so clear.

He swore to himself that he would never lose his faith again. God had decided. He was sure of that. They were both to live.

He looked around him at this place of miraculous salvation from the sea. They had come to land not far from the end of a sandy shore. Further along, rocks began, and the coast continued in rocky points, and reefs, and stony cliffs.

The tide was out, so that the hissing run of a gentle surf ended on shining sand at the bottom of the beach. Inland, the powdered sand ran in long white dunes until, far back, they lost themselves in vegetation. Distantly, across the somber scrub, Peter saw low hills. He examined them but found no smoke or other sign of life or habitation.

He wondered then what was to be done about James Duncan. There was nothing here, nothing on this barren beach which had served its purpose well enough in letting them ashore alive.

He must leave James Duncan, Peter decided. He must go to the rocks to look for water.

But the birds still soared the dunes, still passed along the crescent of the beach, calling down their cries, waiting.

Waiting for me to go, Peter thought, so they can come down and have the rest of his ear, and find their courage, and go to his face, and see what the eyes of a man taste like to creatures that eat fish and rubbish, anything they can find. He watched the birds fly past on graceful wings, hating them, and the birds looked down.

On the closest dune several bushes grew. Close enough. If the birds descended he could run back and chase them all away. He went to the bushes as quickly as he could. He ripped the bushes from their roots and hurried back.

He shoved the stems deep in the sand around James Duncan's head and took off his own shirt and made a small tent from the bushes and the shirt, heaping sand around the edges, and when he had finished he was fairly sure the birds would not be strong or smart enough to break it open.

It was the best he could do; he could think of no way to improve it.

He turned away and walked along the beach, keeping to the hard sand near the water's edge, aware now of alarming weakness, pushing his feet along, head down, not looking where he was going. His lurching steps took him far off course. He was plowing through a dying wave, water to his knees. He turned away. Soon he was toiling through a drift of sand banked deep above the tide mark, and again he changed direction.

At last his downcast eyes saw stones. His feet stirred heaps of broken shells. He raised his eyes, and there were the rocks, and behind the rocks an eroded bank, and behind the bank a cliff of pebbled yellow clay.

He was stupefied by tiredness. Squatting on his heels with his back against a rock, he waited for his mind to clear. Slowly he recalled what it was he had come to do. He had come to find water. And to find water in a place like this you didn't run from rock to rock sniffing like a dog. You thought about it for a while, and you worked out where to look.

He forced his mind into an elementary logic.

Last night, brief storms of rain had come and gone. Either they had passed this way, or they had not. But no real choosing of alternatives entered into this. If a storm had come, there might be water here. If not, there would be none. Not here. Further along the coast, perhaps. Not here. One glance sufficed to make that clear.

Which gave a first assumption, a starting point.

During the night, rain had fallen on this coast. That hope must be accepted as a certainty.

Falling, what did rain do?

It ran in certain paths, according to how the land was formed.

Some would soak into the ground. Some, falling near the edges of the sea, would trickle into tidal pools that salt would spoil. Some, finding its way to a catchment of sorts, a pool, well back from the sea, might still remain. As sweet, maybe, as pure as rain. And that thought contained a kind of agony.

He was trembling at this idea of water as sweet and cold as rain. He calmed himself, finding again the powers of mind that had been scattered by this thought.

Somehow he must find that catchment, that pool in the rocks the spoiling sea could not come far enough to reach. He must go to the top of the cliff, look down from there, and work it out.

There had been in his mind the hope that there might be an easier way.

He rose to his feet, so giddy from the sudden change of attitude that he almost fell.

Studied now by one who had to find the easiest way to climb it, the cliff was seen to be the eroded edge of a hill of modest contours.

He went back to the beach and struck inland to the scrub. He followed the curve of the hill, pulling at the scrub to drag himself along. The scrub became so tangled that he had to crawl. At last the bushes thinned, and he came out at the top. He kept his tired legs going until he reached the edge of the cliff. He looked down.

Soon he saw where water must be, if it was anywhere. Close by, the cliff was not so steep, and on this gentler slope the clay was marked with runnels, and there at the bottom, where the runnels ended, a table of rock lay flat against the slope.

He could not see water on this rock. He could not, at this distance, see the pools he sought, but he was sure that if rain had fallen on this cliff last night the runnels would have gathered it and, gathered, the water would be taken to the rock. All that was needed now was the slightest hollow on that slab of rock, and there'd be water.

He went around the cliff and started down. It was steeper than it looked. The clay was slippery. He lost his footing, and rolled, bumping heavily, but even as he fell he said to himself with joy . . . it *has* been raining, or it wouldn't be so greasy.

Lying on the boulders where he finished at the bottom, hurt and sick, winded, he felt his heart lift at this evidence of God's saving intention. Not just for him, for both of them. For the other man as well.

His shambling stagger across the rocks to reach the water seemed free of any effort. He seemed to rise above the impeding boulders and float across. He was not aware that he sobbed from the painful fall. He could think only of water, and of the certainty of water as a further sign from God.

He reached the rocky platform and scrambled up the side.

For a moment he saw no water, and in this moment he felt the flickering warning of the secret anger that might be waiting in his heart, ready to explode in blasphemy, if God should choose this time to change His mind.

Almost before he could realize the tremendousness of this ingratitude, he saw the water, not seen at first because the pool was the muddied yellow color of the cliff and lay on the rock like part of the rock itself, a flat, discolored patch.

He saw the different texture of the glistening pool, and knelt, and fell flat, and began to drink, sobbing and spluttering, unable to stop even had the water been as salty as the sea. It wasn't salty. It was fresh, agonizingly sweet to drink; sweet even in its earthy taste of clay.

He drank until he hawked and gulped, like an animal about to vomit. Holding a hand across his mouth, keeping the water down, he lay on his back beside the pool, rubbing his swollen belly, and as soon as he felt better he rolled across and drank again.

And then he paused, and looked at the water, and saw there was plenty left, enough for a day at least. As if it were some novel thought, a sudden revelation of common sense, he realized he didn't have to drink it all at once.

For a time he dozed, or fell asleep, or became unconscious. Waking slowly he thought of James Duncan, almost dead of thirst and drowning and exhaustion, while selfishly he lay here beside the water that could save him. He made himself think of moving, and he moved. He stood, and wondered what was next to do.

And that was a problem.

He could take water to James Duncan, or he could bring him to the place where the water was.

But he couldn't drag an unconscious man for half a mile along that beach, and he couldn't take him water without something in which it could be carried.

He realized the stupidity of the first things he thought of:

Carrying water in his mouth.

Carrying it in his cupped hands.

Finding a tin or bottle washed up by the sea. It might take days to find a thing like that.

The thought of using seashells seemed at first as foolish. All the shells he had seen were small or broken, but then, he hadn't been particularly concerned with shells.

It would have to be shells. He could think of no other way to do it.

Going back across the rocks he wondered again at the phenomenal reviving effects of water.

You were dying. As the white man had been last night before the rain, you were far along that steep descending curve that intersected death; and water came. You drank. At once you were going in the opposite direction, back up that curve, to life. And there was something more to this than chemistry. It was not the body alone which changed. When man's body was renewed, so was his spirit.

He had seen that, a plain truth which had some deeper meaning.

Coming to shells and pebbles piled where rocks came to an end and beach began, raking a searching foot in this debris of innumerable storms, Peter decided to leave these thoughts for another time. Deep buried, he saw the volute point of a larger shell and in haste knelt down, digging with his fingers.

The shell was full of sand, but when he washed it in the sea he saw it was intact. Four or five such shells, he supposed, would hold enough to fill a cup. Less than he had hoped, but it would have to be enough. He set the shell aside and renewed his search for others.

A crab scuttled from the cover of a shifted stone, and Peter grabbed. He crushed the crab in his hands, which trembled with a lust for food as they separated shattered shell from a jelly of meat and guts.

Eaten, the crab seemed very small. When he had swallowed the salty fragments, saliva flowed aching in his cheeks.

Now he watched more for crabs than he did for shells, but he found another shell.

Repressed because of duty, released now in an anguished flood by the taste of that scrap of food, hunger became intolerable. He grabbed a stone and ran into the sea beside a reef, bashing at limpets, stuffing his mouth with gritty, tantalizing morsels.

Wading deeper he came to mussels, big and blue, bunched thick like wedge-shaped grapes on the rocks below the tideline, and he went into the mussels with his stone, chewing the colored flesh, spitting pieces of shell.

Returning guiltily, the thought of James Duncan began to weigh itself against the fantastic joy of eating.

It's right for me to eat, he assured himself. I'll be stronger. More able to help him. I'll walk back so much faster; in fact, I'll run. I'll save the time I'm losing now.

No.

I can tell myself these lies, but I must not believe them. I'll eat more later.

He waded ashore, and went on looking for shells until he found another of a different kind, longer, more pointed, slender and screwlike in shape. The wall of this new shell was very thin, and he found it would hold more water than the heavier shells.

Soon he found another of this type. He fitted the four shells in his hand and saw that he could carry six without much risk of spilling, but there wasn't time for six.

He washed the shells, and took them to the water. He couldn't fill them from the shallow pool. A ladle was needed, a flatter shell, the halved shell of a mussel. He went back and found one, and filled the shells and held them in his hands like ice-cream cones. Stepping carefully, he went to the beach and started back.

Now he saw the birds around James Duncan, and wondered why he had not looked before in this direction.

Peter began to run, found water spilling, and walked again. He was appalled.

He didn't know how long he'd been away. Hours, for sure. All morning at least. The sun showed some time after noon.

He looked at the restless birds gathered about that log or stone, that shape that could never be imagined as the body of a man unless you knew that your companion had been left deserted there while you frittered time away and slept and dreamed instead of dedicating everything to saving him.

If anything had happened to him . . .

If the birds . . .

It was terrible not to be able to run.

The birds saw him coming and leaped into the air on a ragged, collective impulse. They settled again, they hopped around, watching him and, thinly, their scolding voices reached his ears.

Stooping, he pushed the points of the shells into the sand so that they stood upright, holding their water, and then he ran.

The birds rose up and he saw the frantic movement of James Duncan's arm. Peter shouted, and the birds lifted on their wings above the beach, rising higher, cutting down across the waves, climbing away again on pointed wings.

Then he could hear the dreadful sounds James Duncan made.

He reached him, and kneeled, wondering sickly what he might see. The white man's face was still unmarked. His eyes still whole. These eyes were opened wide, as wide as they would go, and they contained an expression of such wild despair that Peter's heart was chilled.

James Duncan did not seem to know or care who Peter was.

"Help," he cried piteously, raising a feeble imploring hand. "Oh . . . help . . ."

"I had to go," said Peter, taking the hand in his. "I had to leave you. I had to look for water."

James Duncan opened and closed his mouth. His dry lips worked on his swollen tongue, his eyes began to blink, his whole face contracted like the face of a stuttering man choked by an impossible word.

But Peter knew. "Water" was the word.

Running to the shells, Peter heard behind James Duncan's awful wordless protests at being left again.

Coming back, he saw across the sea the flash of wings. At the birds he sent cursing thoughts of hatred, wishing on each bird a dreadful end. He would hate sea birds as long as he lived.

Who would have thought birds would ever frighten you? Birds were so much admired for their grace of flight, their pleasing appearance, their beauty to the eye; always, the icy cruelty of their tiny hearts was quite forgotten.

But he would not forget.

"Water?" James Duncan had mastered that most terrible of words, that nearly always harmless word that could, sometimes, become the only word of life or death.

And Peter smiled with the joy of being able to bring to any man so great a gift, at being allowed to bring back in an outstretched hand the life of another man.

He arranged the shells securely in the sand where the white man could not reach them.

"Lie down," he said, pushing with firm hand.

"Aah . . ." said James Duncan. "Aah . . ."

Lying on his back he opened his mouth. For a moment his face looked up to Peter's with something of the dependent, loving, and receptive expression of a baby being fed by its mother.

Peter trickled water drop by drop, and at the first taste James Duncan seemed to go right off his head.

His arm swept up for the shell to bring it close and drain it at a gulp. His mad eyes glared at Peter, who fought with one arm while he tried to save the shell from spilling with the other.

Peter yelled, and held the white man cruelly so he couldn't move, while water dribbled to his mouth, and in this way the shells were emptied.

"More?" James Duncan gasped.

"Along the beach," said Peter.

"No more?"

"Not here. That was all the water I could carry."

"Thank you," said James Duncan. "I'm sorry . . . sorry I was so . . ."

"I was the same," said Peter. "I couldn't stop."

Yes, he thought. I was the same. Wrestling with this man . . . I had to do that or he would have split it . . . I was appalled at how like a beast a man can be. I was so superior about it; disgusted.

But now I remember.

Why should it be shameful?

I was exactly the same.

9

Lying beside the fire, head pillowed on an arm, seeing through the fire's thin smoke Peter on the other side, James Duncan heard a bigger wave roll in with crashing force against the outer reef. In rapid declension, the powerful sound ran far into the night along the sinuous line of beach and coast.

He pictured the break of this wave ripping along the shore, a shooting white tear in the fabric of the sea, covering in seconds the course of their arduous journey to the rocks, passing in an instant the scene of that morning ordeal of cruel birds, flashing through the night, on, on, on along the coast, going so far and fast that it would come at last, perhaps, to a place where other men might be.

Picturing the wave in this way, with its movement and its far-reaching, continued line of breaking, he conceived it as a tenuous connection with the life of other men, with civilization, with that other life of his that now had been suspended, the life that, for all its disappointments and regrets, had yet been so peopled and so familiar, so completely known, that it held few fears.

A lifeless kind of life, it might be thought, a life of much dissatisfaction and little joy, where an active worm of disillusion chewed on the core of each success, but it was a life that had lost the power to frighten him, as he was frightened now, by a fear most difficult to understand.

He had been trying to understand this fear when the enlarged sound of the sea, the breaking, traveling echo of the wave, had come to his ears and made its momentary change in the substance of his thoughts.

He seemed stuck in this mood of fear, which no power of logic could affect. He was afraid of everything. He was afraid of the sea, even though the sea had let them go. They had escaped to the land, man's natural field of action, where he could move around, could do things of his own will to save himself, instead of being taken, as they had been, cramped and helpless in a flimsy shell of wood, wherever the wayward moods of the dangerous seas decided. He was afraid . . . afraid . . .

"What is it now?" said Peter suddenly. "What's the trouble?"

"Trouble?"

"You were making noises. Groaning."

"I am afraid," James Duncan said, without thinking, and then felt it would have been better not said.

"Not now," said Peter. "There's no reason to be frightened now. I promise you, we'll get out of this. I know we will."

"Yes. I've been telling myself. But it does no good."

"What are you afraid of?"

"I can't tell you," said James Duncan, "because I don't know."

Peter came around the fire and squatted beside him, pushing a charred branch across the fire.

"Tell me about it."

"I don't know how to."

"Talk about it. Start with anything."

"How is it you saw nothing of the boat washed up? Not a stick, or a piece of wood. Not anything?"

"It went out on the tide. Are you frightened because we've lost the boat?"

"God, no. I never want to see a boat again."

"Do you want to talk about the boat?"

"Not particularly."

"Then talk about something else. Anything."

"I meant to tell you," said James Duncan. "I thought you were very clever to start a fire. I didn't believe you could. I thought you were wasting your time."

"I began to think that myself," said Peter. "It took so long. I wasn't sure I knew how. So long since I saw it done."

"When I saw it was beginning to smoke, I had the feeling I'd done it all myself," said James Duncan with a slight smile. "I shoved down on the top of the stick with all my might, and the more I pushed, the more it smoked. I felt I was doing it all. The thought of having a fire was so wonderful I forgot how weak I was."

"Talk about the birds," said Peter.

"Oh no," said James Duncan hastily.

"Is that it?"

"It's hard for me to talk. My mouth is sore and swollen. You know that."

"Is it the birds?"

"Being left." His hoarse voice broke into a sob, and he held his mouth with a hand, and waited until he could talk again. "Being left again. But this time being left to die. Alone."

"Who else has left you?"

"Everyone I needed," said James Duncan, crying now, and now not caring. "I've lost them all."

"How much do you remember? How much has come back?"

"Everything. All of it. Oh, but believe me, it was better not to know."

"Tell me."

"About my wife?"

"About anything."

"She was no good," said James Duncan. "I knew it all the time. I knew she'd slept with half the air force. But what did it matter, I was sure that I was going to get the chop. Tell you why. Rob bought it, didn't he? And Rob was the sort of chap who *doesn't* die, you can't imagine it. So you see, if they killed him so easily, they'd get me too. I knew that when I took it on."

Words and thoughts and memories raced across his mind. He wanted to talk; suddenly, he wanted to tell it all.

"Most of them wanted fighters. Not me. I didn't care. I guess I had myself typed or something ... I knew the sort of chap they put on heavies. Chaps like me. I thought I was so bloody clever to work a posting to Rob's old mob. Went there from final training, and Jesus, I was raw.

"They had the hell beat out of them when they were on those torpedo ops with Beauforts. The number of the squadron was damn near all they had . . . and half a dozen blokes, chaps who somehow survived the Beaufort stuff. They reformed the squadron with Lancs. I knew about that before I worked the posting. I wouldn't have come at Beauforts. Not with torpedoes.

"This pub . . . we always used to go to the same pub when we were off, and most of the time I'd see Lilian there, hanging around with someone from the squadron. And I was tipped off. She was the one to go to if you wanted it. She was mad about Australians.

"I heard a lot about her. Chaps would take her seriously, and then they'd find out about the others, and there'd be fearful rows. But somehow, when you looked at her, you never would have thought it. She seemed so bloody nice. When I was new there I used to watch her from the corner of my eye. All the time.

"Then I decided to try my luck, and it was so much easier than I'd expected. And it was good, too. She was kind. I liked her very much. From then on I was the only one and, God, I don't know, that made me proud. It wasn't so bad going out at night on ops when someone was waiting at home for me to make it back . . ."

Going out at night . . . he wanted to say more of that, so that not only the words and the ideas, but the actual emotion of those times would be communicated, but he found he could not revive the emotion even for himself. He could not, or would not, live it again.

Incredibly, what came back to him was a feeling of that time, not then identified. A feeling that countered fear.

He had come to believe that every instant of that time of war had been marked, for him, by fear. Looking back, all his memories of war seemed to have been memories of fear. But now he saw that fear was only a part of it, and even, perhaps, the lesser part.

The feeling remembered now, and so clearly that he was tempted to wish for that stretch of life to live again, was the feeling of being part of something truly great that was happening at that time. Something so much larger than common life, so much more dramatic, that in yourself you felt enlarged, a theatrical figure enormously more significant than the ordinary man of common life you'd been before.

But it had a price, that dramatic feeling; and the price was high. Danger was the essence of the drama, and the essence of danger was being frightened.

Being afraid was the price you paid. But the price was not too high. For the first time he saw that now.

He wanted to say all this, and it was clear in his mind, but his tongue fumbled when he tried to think of words, so he left that out.

"It was so good to have someone back there waiting," he said, "that I made up my mind to marry her. Not because I loved her; I didn't, not then. I married her to keep her for myself until I got the chop. Listen, some of the things about Lilian were very good. She was honest . . . she didn't say she loved me. And she never made the least excuse. She was kind too, and she looked so clean and fresh. She was most attractive. The main thing wrong with Lilian was that she didn't ever care much who she slept with.

"Well, suppose I'd got back every time? How would it have been, I wonder? Sometimes I think it would have turned out well. Because she tried, take my word for it. She did do well. As long as I was there. But I went out one night on one of those big jobs and a fighter jumped us and we went on fire. You think nothing will ever make you jump. But when it comes . . . oh man, when you see those flames . . .

"Got back nearly to Paris, I did. Hid in a barn the first night, and this Jew came in with a yellow star on his jacket. A Pole or something, with a pitchfork on his shoulder. Passed me to the underground, but I knew I wasn't going to make it. Those underground buggers, you had to go along with them. Just when I was beginning to think they had the game sewn up and

I might be going to make it, I find myself in the middle of a raid on the brothel where I was being hidden. Jesus, a deadly lot, those Gestapo bastards. Right on to you."

"Are you sure you're strong enough to talk as much as this?" said Peter. "I didn't mean . . ."

"It's boring you, I guess. Sorry. Suddenly I want to talk. Don't know why . . ."

"Not boring me. Oh no. It's just that . . ."

"No. It doesn't make me tired. I feel I want to get it off my chest." James Duncan was quiet, studying the fire.

"More than a year I spent before it ended," he said at last. "A whole year, getting used to the idea that I might have fallen in love with Lilian. I was safe. I wasn't flying any more, and I thought that surely I'd come through. And then I'd make our marriage into something good. I'd bring her home from England with me and nobody would know a thing about it. It would all be changed. Permanent. For I wasn't going to die. That was all I had to think about, you see. Though it appears she didn't think for very long of me. She went back to sleeping with the squadron. But I didn't know that, at the time."

Again he was silent. He remembered the long march through the snow when the Russians were breaking through. The chaps who fell out, never to be seen again. Dysentery. Blood on the snow when you stood up to go. The Nazi kid the Russians caught. They hung him by the feet with wire and burned him alive with petrol. What was the use of going into that? He need not talk much more.

"Well, it had to end. You could see it coming for several months. I nearly went mad, suddenly, so crazy about Lilian, wanting her so much. It was good that I went back with that feeling, because she had to know that someone really loved her. I did, you know; I really did. They shipped us home at last and she liked it here. Soon she was pregnant, and that seemed right. A new start, and a child seemed just exactly right.

"I'd gone into advertising with a chap I'd come to know in Germany. He was a good bloke. Knew all the ropes. We cracked it lucky from the start, and we came good. We did very well. Then Garry came along. My boy, you know. My son."

I won't tell him much about Garry, he decided. I won't tell him much about my boy. He wouldn't understand. As always when he thought of Garry he had that old wish for death—that automatic, unbearably weary, tired old wish, as if to wish for death was as natural to life as breathing.

"Garry died when he was five," he said stolidly. "He was drowned at the beach. Lilian was supposed to be looking after him.We split up over that. She went off with a chap. Back to England. I think the chap she went off with was on the beach with her the day that Garry . . . well, never mind. I can't prove that. I don't know that for sure."

Some distance back in this account he had turned his mind right off. He could talk this part of the story through to the end without thinking about it, without wanting to think about it. Without being able to think about it.

He let silence develop so that Peter would know he had said all that was going to be said.

Peter put wood on the fire. He sat down again, and though James Duncan waited, he didn't speak.

"Well?" James Duncan said eventually. "That's some of the life I'm so afraid of losing. You'd think I'd be glad to see it over."

"Are you afraid of that?"

"What else is a man afraid of?"

"I suppose a man might be afraid of having to live, as much as he might fear having to die," said Peter. "Which do you fear?"

"Both, perhaps," said James Duncan. "I'm not sure I know. But perhaps that would be the worst of all. To fear both life and death. To be caught between two fears that can't be reconciled."

"You shouldn't have talked so much," said Peter. "Your throat sounds so sore my own throat hurts to hear you. That's enough, I think. Now we should sleep."

"I want more food and water," said James Duncan. "I suppose I should say ... please. Maybe tomorrow I'll be strong enough to fend for myself a bit."

Peter went to the rock.

"Not much left," he said, when he returned. "I'll have to find some more tomorrow."

"Will there be more?"

"Oh yes," said Peter. "I'll find it somewhere."

But, he thought ... I hope saying a thing like that doesn't damage our luck.

He raked the fire to make a shallow bed of coals. Before dark, he had gathered mussels in the rising tide while the waves pushed him around against the rocks, and now he spread some on the coals and watched them flop wide open, steaming, filling the air with a cooking smell. They fed.

"Not too much," said Peter. "It could make us sick."

"You were right," said James Duncan. "You were right. It isn't death, it's life that I'm afraid of. Going back. Coming so close to death that I was sure I was going to die, and having to come back to my life. In a short time, if we're lucky, now that we're ashore, I'll start my old life again, just where I left it off. With nothing changed."

"It's only a mood," said Peter. "There'll be plenty of time to talk about it when you're stronger."

"And it was losing my memory, too. I'm seeing my life more as someone else might see it, now I've found my memory one fragment at a time. And it's a mess, Peter. A senseless mess. A thing without the slightest sense or meaning. I don't much want to persevere with it. And yet, I could never give it up. Not willingly."

"We must sleep," said Peter, rising. "We'll talk another time."

He built up the fire with the last of the wood, and settled himself for sleep. He lay on the sand, and scraped a hip-hole, and relaxed his limbs; it was as simple as that, but it seemed as comfortable as any bed in which he'd ever slept. James Duncan said something. I know I should be listening, thought Peter, and it might be good for him to talk, but I simply can't. His eyes closed themselves and there was nothing he could do to keep them open.

He awoke, shivering, before dawn. He rolled over and touched the ashes of the fire. The ashes were dusty and warm. He scraped around until he found a spark of fire. Groping for twigs and the ends of sticks which hadn't burned, he put them around the spark and began to blow. He breathed on the glowing spark until a dry leaf gave a chancy flame, and flared, and suddenly it all burned strongly. He could see other unburned sticks, and he built on the fire, and hurried away to find more wood, wishing he had thrown more from the hill while it was light. But there had been so much to do last night, he couldn't have done everything that needed doing.

Away from the fire his eyes adjusted to the night. He went up the small cliff, crawling, scrabbling with his hands, and gathered branches in the scrub, small stuff that would burn away in minutes.

Crouching, looking at the dark sky's starry glow, he found leafless branches attesting the darkness of a sapling. He pushed against this dead wood, which gave way slowly in the sandy ground. It released its rotten roots with a creak of protest, and went down with a satisfying thump.

At this, a rhythmic thudding sounded in the scrub.

"Wallaby," Peter whispered, following the leaps of sound as the startled beast crashed down a slope into a gully and was silent, so that Peter could picture it timid and alert, turning cocked ears for further sounds, standing in the gully listening, smoothly furred and gentle, a creature with tiny, pointed face, useless forepaws held in front like shrunken hands in that attitude of seeming intercession he had seen so often.

It was a sign of life, a sign that the country here might not be quite as arid as it looked. Dragging the dead wood for the fire, hearing the wallaby start again, Peter was grateful.

His faith should stand on its own, he knew. That it should need support by signs and omens indicated reservations that should shame him.

In that shivering awakening by the dead fire he had recalled at once that this day, in an hour or two the dawn, was the day in which more water would be needed. In sleep, faith had vanished. Waking, he no longer believed that water would be found. Waking to night's dark solitude he imagined them both, himself and the white man, after this false, saving recovery, thirsting their way to death. Wandering away to their deaths, when the water on the rock had gone. And now, here was a sign that other creatures lived behind this barren coast.

He took the firewood down the cliff and stoked the fire. James Duncan was awake, leaning on an elbow.

"Did you sleep?" asked Peter.

"Water," said James Duncan. "Need more water."

Peter brought water and went back to the rock to drink. He sucked water with his lips against the rock. He wished dawn would hurry over night's horizon and let his search begin.

"I hardly slept at all," said James Duncan. "I hardly slept for worrying—about starting my life again, changing it, living a better life. But that's a long way off, isn't it? A waste of time, I think. I've come again to one of those times when I know we won't get through."

"I heard a wallaby," said Peter. "When I was getting wood."

"How can that help?"

"It makes it better. If a wallaby can live on this coast, perhaps we can."

"Is it too late for me to start again?" said James Duncan. "*Can* I start again? In a better way?"

"Why are you asking me? Haven't you been thinking about it? All night? Didn't you come to any answers?"

"Why won't you tell me?"

"What is your question?"

"I told you. Can I start again? Or is it now too late?"

"Maybe it's too late," said Peter.

"No!" said James Duncan. "I'm damned if it is! Why should you say that?"

Impatiently, he turned. The fire was burning high. On Peter's face he found a hidden smile, a downcast look, an expression of irony. Knowing Peter, by now, to be a young man of unnatural seriousness, he found his growing respect for this serious Peter, his growing dependence, warmed to surprising affection by this smile.

"Ah, Peter. You were provoking me. You teased me into giving myself the answer I wanted to hear from you. It's true. It might be possible, to start afresh. But what is the secret?"

"What secret?"

"How does one put meaning into life? How trite that sounds! Yet, that is the secret, isn't it—the only secret?"

"And I'm supposed to know it?"

"Some of it, yes. I think you have it."

"Why should you think that?" said Peter wonderingly.

"You talked. When we were in the boat. You talked of God's intentions. You remember? Talking, sounding as if you knew what those intentions were?"

"I did say something, yes. I remember."

"Well? Did you mean it? Or was it only talk?"

"You are asking me something, and you are telling me something," said Peter. "You are telling me you have no faith or belief in God, and you are asking me to tell you of the nature of my own belief. Is that not right?"

"It is right as far as this, at least," said James Duncan, "that I have no belief or faith. That I believe in nothing. Ah Christ ... what's there to talk about? What is it all when it is over? A scribble of life on a blank page, blown into space on the wind; a meaningless nothing. You are right, I believe in nothing. That far, you have it dead to rights."

"But wouldn't it be easier for you, if you believed in God? Wouldn't you be happier?"

"I doubt you'll ever say a sillier thing than that," said James Duncan. "Of course it would be easier! Who wouldn't take on that belief, if only for his peace of mind? But; if he *could!* For something decides whether a man is able to believe or not. If he can, he does. If he can't, he doesn't. *What decides?* That is what I have been asking you."

"Perhaps it is decided by whether a man sees God working in

his life. In seeing that, and knowing what it is. Look at us . . . we're saved. We were in dreadful danger, and we have come ashore. Isn't that a sign of God? That He cares what happens to us? That He believes we should be saved?"

"Did he save my son? Did he? And my boy was innocent. Far more deserving of mercy. But *he* wasn't saved, was he? He was left to drown, left to choke out his little life with drowning lungs. So—there's an equal sign for you, that there is *no* God. Or that, if there is, He has no slightest care for what becomes of any one of us."

"I cannot help you," said Peter. "I am no good at this, and I am sorry. I need to believe that what my life is set to do, what gives it meaning as you would say, is God's intention. And so, I do believe."

"You have no doubts?"

"I have no more strength than other men," said Peter. "Yes. I have doubts."

"But you know that God has intentions, for you?"

"*I* have intentions. Perhaps they are my own. But it helps me to believe that God has put them in my mind."

"Then what are they? What *are* these intentions?"

"I do not feel ready to say."

"Is it . . . is it something that makes everything you do seem part of something far greater than yourself?"

"It is," said Peter. "How do you know?"

"I was thinking about the war. About the war as a time when, mostly, you were afraid. And yet, though I'd come to think it was, that wasn't the main thing about the war. The main thing was a feeling you didn't understand properly at the time that you were part of something larger than yourself. You were caught up utterly in that. There was a certain feeling that your life had meaning. Even with death on every side."

"It's like that," said Peter. "Something that makes you feel that death is only to be feared because it would prevent you completing what you think you have to do."

"I wish I could find a thing like that again," said James Duncan. "I can't see that you have to have a war to put meaning into people's lives. It's like burning down the house to roast the pig."

"Have you looked? Have you tried to find it?"

"I made my way in the world. I made myself better than most others at my job. Made money at it. That seemed an answer. Making your way. But when you get there, you wonder what it's all about. That's a thing that might content a man in youth, while he still believes there's time for all the things he might decide to do. I mean, there's so *much* time in front of him. He thinks he can try one thing for a few years, and then change and try another, as if it were going on forever. Well, that's for the best, I suppose. It's as well to forget about arithmetic when you measure up your life. It wouldn't do to see what a life looks like cut into ten-year slices. How few there are. Blindness to cold facts is sometimes a mercy, and it certainly is in this.

"But what happens when a man discovers suddenly that there are more slices gone than there are to come? That there isn't time to do this, and then at leisure change to another thing. There isn't *time!* That's when a man looks around for the thing that might turn the miserable riddle of his life into something that's got some sense. Even if only for him. To find a way to believe there's been some purpose in it."

"You haven't finished," said Peter, when James Duncan let his last sentence die away in silence, and rose from lying to sit up and look about him, as if, so deep in the forming and expression of these private and disturbing thoughts, he had quite forgotten where they were.

Looking about him, and remembering; now, by the uneven light of the fire's waning, seeing cold bare rocks, a narrow stretch of sand, the disturbed gleaming of the sea, a sky pale with the icy light of stars, with the faintest light of dawn emerging; feeling about him the cold breath of a dawn breeze, and hearing the sea, James Duncan, with a sinking of the heart, lost in a pang of bitter recollection the comfort of having been so rapt in thought and speech as to forget their present plight.

"I have," he said, disheartened. "Yes. I've finished."

10 He watched Peter climb the cliff and turn away. Peter reached the scrub. The trees claimed him. He was gone.

At once the close roar of the sea beat in his ears with sullen menace; the place where he was lying lost that elusive familiarity which their sleeping and their talk and their sharing of food and fire had built around them. It became bare, exposed, and bleak; revealed in all its primal harshness; a place eroded by the storms of countless ages, otherwise unchanged, never known by man or marked by the hand of man in any way, washed now, perhaps, by the very seas which came across the empty world to meet this coast in the moment of creation.

In the blue of the sky James Duncan saw the color of infinite space, the vast unpeopled space which, with his companion's sudden disappearance, now exposed him to the consciousness of intolerable dimensions in which the puny sound of his voice would be less than nothing, the fact of his existence of no greater import than that of any ant or microbe.

"Peter . . . !" he cried, and, as he had known, his voice was less than nothing.

Supporting himself against the nearest rock he gained his feet and looked along the clifftop, trembling, and in a moment, by some strange chance, Peter appeared in a clearing at the edge of the cliff and halted, and looked back.

Wildly, James Duncan waved his arm, and Peter saw him and waved in answer before he moved on and disappeared.

He didn't give me time to prepare myself for being alone, James Duncan complained. He was ashamed now of his bad moment of panic, of weakness and cowardice and childishness. But it didn't matter very much.

I am the only one who knows about it, he thought, and I know worse things than that about myself.

Still, it was true. He hadn't been given time to prepare himself for solitude.

Dawn had been spreading in the sky as they had finished talking, and James Duncan had fallen into a sleep so heavy that he had known nothing of Peter's efforts to ensure that he would have what he needed in the coming day.

Awakened, he had found firewood piled beside him, the four shells full of water, another pile of mussels; even dry grass, gathered to make a bed.

He had awakened to the touch of Peter's hand. He had opened his eyes to the sight of Peter's dark face close above him. He had blinked sleep from his eyes and, better sighted, had stared into that dark face so strangely unchanged by hardship, a face with a kind of alien and gentle handsomeness.

"I'm going now," Peter had said.

"No," he had pleaded. "Can't you wait for me? Wait until I'm stronger? So we can go together?"

Patient and firm, Peter had explained why he must go alone. He pointed to the preparations he had made. He gave James Duncan the task of keeping the fire alight all day, and made this seem important.

And then he had gone.

"He should have waited," James Duncan muttered. "I'm not as weak as he thinks I am."

He left the supporting rock, to prove he wasn't as weak as Peter thought. It wasn't really difficult ... a little practice ...

He was down on his knees in the sand, unconscious of the stages of his fall. One moment he had been standing, and the next, down on his knees.

Stiffness, that was all it was. He'd have been all right if he'd waited a little longer.

He crawled to his bed of grass. He lay face down, across the pile of grass.

Inches from his nose a tiny, speckled beetle climbed the tangled stalks. He studied the beetle in its small-scale universe, where stems of grass were relatively as thick as giant trees. The beetle was unaware of him.

I could be your God. He cast his thoughts at the beetle in silent conversation. I am so close to you. All-wise. All-seeing. I see every step you take, every movement of your crooked little limbs. Seeing the way you go, I can see what is ahead of you. I could tell you of your future, of things hidden from you that I can see. I could pluck you from your pleasant grassy world and cast you into Hell. Into the everlasting fires. If a wasp attacked you, I could save you. Or I could let you die.

But you do not credit my existence, do you; you have no faith, you irreligious insect! Here I am, breathing on you, too big for you to see.

Look at you, cocksure and confident in your minute universe; look at you, you atheist, microscopic bastard! You think you don't need me, your God, to watch and cherish you?

Why, were I not a kindly and loving God, I'd strike you dead for your willful lack of faith.

But I'll turn my head away. Now I've gone, and there is no God. How does that feel? What? You feel no difference?

Smiling at his fancies, he rested his head on an arm. As he fell asleep, he seemed to sink into the beetle's world of stalks of grass as big as trees and grains of sand as big as rocks, and when he awoke he was wonderfully refreshed.

For the first time, sleep had worked for its natural purpose of renewal, and he could not remember when that had happened last. He had come to expect nothing from sleep, and from the process of waking nothing but the revival of fears taken with him into sleep.

Was he recovering at last? Had these trials of fear been no more than the consequence of that accident, that concussion which stole his wits and robbed his memory? Had he been but sickened into craven thoughts by a crude disorientation of the conscious will; of that conscious purpose which, in normal men, held fears in check? Was he, in fact, a man of stronger spirit than he had come to think himself?

It seemed so. Waking refreshed, he recognized the birth of strength and hope within his heart.

He looked around him, not exactly with approval, but with the beginnings of acceptance.

The fire still burned, almost smokeless, flaming invisibly in the sun's full brightness. The blue sea was at peace. The rocks were of many colors, of every size and shape.

Flies had found him, and he brushed at his face, cursing, feeling the wiry stubble of his cheeks, aware of sensibilities cast aside in the stressful needs of sheer survival. He felt a sharp distaste for physical uncleanness. He studied the nearest gutter of the cool, clear sea, and thought of swimming and washing. He would. The imagined feeling of that pure water laving his heated, brutishly filthy, irritable flesh seduced him.

He drank one of the shells of water, and stoked the fire, and felt hungry. Raking out coals as Peter had done, he cooked mussels and ate them slowly, without enjoyment. It amused him to realize how little above the level of barest subsistence lay the point where desire for luxury appeared, even if that desire showed but in an appetite for more variety. You began to think of other foods, of choice, of other tastes and flavors. Discontent, starting at the very lowest level. Discontent, the leading attribute of man; lowly spur of man's peculiar evolution.

He removed his clothes and lay naked in the sun, digesting, baking in the heat, the bland coolness of the sea washing through his sleepy thoughts.

The heat that had first seemed lessened by nudity increased, and he stirred himself, and crawled to the edge of the gutter, where the last ripples of breakers diminished to nothing through reefs of rock.

The sea's fresh chill surprised him. He took a breath and let his head go under, scrubbing sand from his hair, rubbing his face and chest. He splashed around, feeling stronger and fresher. Encouraged, he tested his strength by standing, and supported by water went further out, waist deep, a little worried at what might happen if, without warning, his legs should let him down.

Movement in the water caught his eye, and he jumped nervously as a neat brown shape passed close beside his legs. The unidentified shape, a foot or so in length, bulbous of head and slim of tail, came to a rock and opened out like a weird flower of the sea. It spread buttoned tentacles, and changed its mottled skin to the darker color of the rock.

Octopus. His first thought came with a slight, instinctive shudder.

Food! That was his second thought.

He stood there wondering how to catch it, whether it would be easier than a fish to catch; a fish would be impossible. He stepped closer. The octopus stayed spread on the rock, as if it had taken root. He moved a stealthy hand almost within reach, thinking he could snatch it up before the thing could move. A quick grab. Tentacles wrapping their suckered hold about his arm. No. He couldn't do that. Peter would. Peter would do it and laugh.

James Duncan shuddered. He skirted around the octopus and went ashore. He crawled to the fire, conserving his strength with definite purpose. In the pile of wood beside the fire he selected a forked stick and tidied it of twigs.

He crawled back to the gutter and drifted himself across the pool.

The octopus had changed color so well that he thought it gone, but it was there, spread on the rock, as immobile as before.

He moved between octopus and open sea. He went closer and poked it with the stick. The thing writhed, and with a smooth movement formed itself into its fishlike, swimming shape.

It drifted a moment, jetted ahead with instant acceleration, turned from a warning movement of the stick, went the other way, tried to break to sea again, was foiled by the stick, and drifted uncertainly in the shallow ending of the gutter. James Duncan followed, eager, stumbling, and becoming very tired.

The octopus broke away, but the ready stick was there, and it drifted back. Boldly, beside it, the stick slapped water, and it leaped and turned, fled from the splashing stick, and darted to the sandy end of the gutter, to run aground.

In water too shallow for swimming, the octopus changed at once to a tangle of writhing tentacles with a horrid pulpy dome raised in evil swaying at its center.

With a gulp of something more than mere distaste, James Duncan put the end of the stick under the thing and flipped it to its back. He jerked it up the beach with the stick until he was sure it could not get away. He beat the octopus furiously about the head with the stick, until it lay still, dribbling dark ink and slimed with a paste of sand.

He dropped to his knees, and lay on the sand beside his victim.

He lay there until warnings of sunburn prickled his skin, and he knew he must put on his clothes.

The octopus seemed dead, even though its skin still twitched and moved with a kind of sliding and turning, as nerves and muscles released the tensions that hold flesh in the forms of life.

Carelessly, James Duncan picked it up, and instantly tentacles flowed around his arm, the slack bag of the head bulbed into shape, eyes dreadful in their lambent stillness held him in their glare.

"Aaaah ..." he cried, hurling his arm violently to throw the thing away. But now it was on his arm and couldn't be shaken off, he was able to face it for what it was, instead of what it seemed.

It was a helpless creature, perhaps a twentieth of his own dimensions. It seemed a monster to every instinctive sense, but to the eye of reason, as by abrupt cognition he saw it now, it was small and harmless. Removed from its proper element it became a weak thing, somehow pitiful.

But it was food, and it must be killed.

He carried it to the nearest rock and arranged his arm so that the rock became an anvil for the ugly head. With a smaller stone he beat the octopus to death, surely and thoroughly this time, with no room for doubt. He kept his eyes averted from those other eyes, which now that his fear was gone were found to shine with limpid, golden beauty, to have inside them depths of consciousness—at the very least, awareness of life, and, as he could well imagine, some part of that universal fear of death, and of those things that threatened life's continuance.

Sure he had killed it, he stripped its suckered death-grips from his arm.

He went to the fire and raked it over, and spread the octopus to cook. He put on his shirt and trousers.

Clothed, he felt the real heat of the day burning and dazzling from sand and striking around him in radiant reflection from bare rocks. He looked for shade, feeling breathless and exhausted.

Peter should have thought of this. A few green branches carried from the hill. That would have been enough. It wouldn't have taken any time; Peter could have brought the branches when he brought the wood.

He found himself ashamed to be thinking of Peter in this blaming way. Peter had done so much. Finding water was Peter's vital job, yet he had stayed his search until he had done all he could to ensure his weaker companion's security and comfort. It wasn't fair to blame him for overlooking one small thing.

From the strong, the weak could only demand just so much in help, James Duncan realized. Otherwise weakness would take on the practical values of a virtue, a perverted kind of strength which levied blackmailed advantage of the strong.

He gave up thinking about it in this way for he could see paradox appearing ... weakness as a kind of strength, something absurd like that ... and nothing was more irritating, or less true generally, than paradox.

There would be shade in the scrub on the hill. In his mind's eye he saw a mountain gully deep in forest, where humus lay moist on the shaded ground, where tree ferns spread their arching fronds, and water as cold as ice chuckled a hollow song in pebbled runs.

How stupid. It wouldn't be at all like that, up there. He corrected his mental image to more likely truth . . . a tangle of shabby trees letting sunlight through; spiked undergrowth; starved, bare ground; a debris of dry branches. The webs of spiders, the nests and hills of ants. But even so, there would be shade; it would be a cooler place than this.

Peter's journeys up and down the cliff had left a scuffled track. James Duncan made his way there, and tried to climb up Peter's track, standing at first with a stick to help him, throwing the stick away, and crawling. Lying in the end, less than a third of the way to the top, panting, concerned only to get down safe again.

He rested, and crawling backward, sliding sometimes, made his way back to where he had begun.

Now that there was no escape, the heat of the beach was ominous.

It might not be possible to endure the day that lay ahead.

What is left of my confidence, James Duncan asked doubtfully. Where has it gone? What has become of that spark of hope I woke with?

Have I become a creature who will frighten himself with imagined things if no real dangers are around? Am I frightened of myself? Do I scare myself with things that can't much hurt me—loneliness, and heat, even such a thing as the length of a normal day?

He argued with himself, muttering aloud. Losing his memory, the loss of that lifetime of experienced knowledge and certitude, had taken with it that degree of trust which men have in their powers and qualities.

He told himself that. He was not frightened of himself. No. Not at all. But he had little reason to trust himself.

But it's come back, you fool, he muttered. Your memory has returned. You have survived. Hasn't everything been thrown at you, and haven't you survived? Can't you renew some of that trust in the stamina that let you live?

At last he found a useful thought. Standing there, leaning on a rock, arguing with himself like a madman, he found a thought not framed in words that gave back a small degree of sanity and self-assurance.

It had something in it of the forgotten sweetness of optimism that had come from his last sleep—a sturdy expectation, a kind of habit of thought, that said that life might as well be given the benefit of the doubt; that after all, in spite of everything, there might be more in life of good than bad.

However true or false this thought, the feeling of it brought a stiffening of the spine.

He pushed himself away from the rock and forced himself to stand erect. Like a man. There should be an end to crawling like a dog. He thought about himself in such dramatic terms as these.

He walked with stubborn steps, conscious of this sudden pride of manhood, to the fire. He drank from a shell of water. He raked the octopus from the fire with a stick, and turned it over. It had started to cook, but not enough. He turned it over and put it on the fire again.

The octopus was smaller; shrunken, ugly. Harmless. Dead.

I killed it with a stone. I hunted it and killed it.

Yet, while it was alive it frightened me.

Not me as I am now.

Not this octopus as it is now.

Me, as I was. And it, as it was then.

It is different now. Not because it is wrinkled, charred, and dead. Because I am different. I have made the decision to take hold of myself.

And about time.

A narrow line of shade spread beside the table rock. It would be gone in an hour, when the sun reached noon, but after noon there would be shadow somewhere else. He lay in the shade, lying outstretched to make the most of it. It was a fraction cooler there than any other place. He closed his eyes, but did not sleep.

He wondered about Peter. How was he getting on? Had he found water yet? Might he not, at this very moment, be returning? Was he coming along the cliff, looking down on their rockbound beach, wondering whether to announce the good news with a shout?

He opened his eyes and began to raise himself, and caught himself at this. Showing again how complete his dependence was on Peter, on Peter's strength and cleverness.

How had this happened? How, for God's sake, had it happened?

Peter and that other chap, that aboriginal, how much they had depended on him! Who had the strength, and influence; who had the cleverness then! Hey? Who had it then?

When it began. And it was one of those things that had a clear beginning. The exact moment when it started could be recalled, and drowsing, yet clear in mind, he let recollection form itself.

11

"If you have a moment, Mr. Duncan," Wendy said. "Two gentlemen would like to see you."

She stood there, his office door ajar behind her. Glancing over her shoulder, tiptoeing to his desk, leaning to whisper.

"They're black." Batting her eyelids to show how comical that was. "Black as tar. Aborigines, I think."

"What do they want?"

"They wouldn't say." So close, bending, the neck of her blouse coming away from her breasts.

"Selling tickets or something? What is it?"

"No, really. They didn't say."

"Stop grinning. Stop that nonsense. Send them in. Get that grin off your face. They'll think you're laughing at them."

"Sweetheart," whispering, "I *am*."

Walking away, how conscious of her sex. How conscious of her power. How she moved.

"Do come in," said Wendy. "Mr. Duncan will see you."

"Sir," said one of them, graciously, expansively. "Sir, good after*noon!*" His smile might have been intended more for the widest possible display of perfect teeth than for any other purpose. Or perhaps, in truth, he was as happy as that. Happy as a lunatic.

"Isn't it a *lovely* day!" Speech left the smile quite undiminished.

"Yes."

It was an ordinary day. Was every day a lovely day to this smiling man, or had habit led him to pretend it was? He had seen him somewhere, though not in person. Photographs, TV

112

perhaps. Knew about him, should be able to recall his name. Hercules, Apollo, something unlikely of that sort. To do with strength. He looked strong. Powerful body and strong neck, on this neck a fine head, nicely set. Thick gray hair, cropped short.

"I'm Eddie Samson," he said.

"Of course." Walking around the desk to shake hands. "How do you do."

"And this is our legal man, Mr. Jirapon. Mr. Peter Jirapon. Our solicitor."

How had Peter really seemed at that first glance? Slim and quiet. Shy, certainly, in the shadow of Samson's bright assurance.

"And what can I do for you, Mr. Samson?" They were waved to chairs.

"Mr. Duncan. Sir, I will come straight to the point. You are a busy man. Don't want me wasting any time beating all around the bush. Mr. Duncan. There is a young man, one of our people. They are going to hang him. Maybe you know about it?"

"The Droverdale affair, you mean? Only what I've seen in the papers. This Lucky Jimmy fellow, or whatever he calls himself? The one that killed the girl?"

"That is the one," said Samson. "Yes, Mr. Duncan. That is the boy. He is called Lucky Jimmy. Though his real name's Jinben, Jimmy Jinben. A Ben-gingin boy; they all have names like that. Like a big family, you know. Jimmy came from way up north, you know."

"I see. Well now, what is it you want from me? You want me to sign a petition or something? I don't know about that. I suppose I would. I'm against hanging, generally speaking. Yes, I suppose I'd sign it. Though it was a dreadful thing, Mr. Samson. Rape and murder. A dreadful crime. Maybe they'd be doing the best thing to hang this chap. Sorry to be so blunt."

"It isn't that," said Eddie Samson, smiling no longer. "Boss, there's no petition. You never save the boy that way. No. We didn't come here to waste your time like that. That boy never had fair trial, Mr. Duncan. Didn't hardly know what it was they done to him."

"I'm afraid I don't know enough about it. Really. I'm not

dodging an argument. I just don't know. The odd glance at what was in the papers. No doubt you're right. But I can't see that there's anything I can do about it."

"We hoped to engage your services, sir," said Eddie Samson, with a smile of such humility, and seeming so nervous and unsure, that the first impression he gave of overcheerfulness and confidence was revealed as false. "We hoped you might work with us. This is why we come to you."

"I don't quite . . . what do you mean?"

"We thought . . . you know, with the papers and TV, and all like that? What you do for your business, boss. Mr. Duncan, there must be no hanging for this boy. They said we should come to you. You could do it, they said. It would cost money, but you could do it."

"Who said?"

"One of our people, in the league."

"Who?"

"Father Holliwell."

"Gilbert Holliwell? *He* sent you?"

"Yes. He said we must move with the times. These days, he said, it is all public relations. You can do anything at all, so long as you go about it in the proper way. And he said we should come to you, Mr. Duncan."

"Now wait on, Mr. Samson. Just a minute. I'm afraid you're under a misapprehension. People have this silly idea about what you can do with a P.R. operation. Most of it's complete and utter balls. Most of it's nonsense. I've never heard of such a thing. Frankly, I've had a few propositions at one time or another but, so help me, never one like this. Better forget it, Mr. Samson. I wouldn't touch this with a forty-foot pole."

He had spoken sharply and contemptuously because he was thinking of Gilbert Holliwell, that pompous, bumbling saint. He was attacking this fellow because Holliwell had sent him. And he saw that Eddie Samson, accepting immediate defeat, was ready to stand and go, and he saw too, the real sadness of the aborigine's first flashing smile, his simulated confidence, his commercial traveler's manner. Surely, what Samson tried to sell with this manner was an idea about the aboriginal. If you, a white man, could be cheerful, he could be as cheerful, even more so.

He could be anything you wanted him to be. He could fit in.

And now, with ordinary bluntness, not even rudeness, Eddie Samson had been reduced to accept, abjectly, that again—and such things had surely happened often—again, he couldn't match the white men's ways.

Had Eddie Samson been white, would he have been treated differently?

More than likely.

Therefore, as with a child, one must lean right over backward to be fair.

"Mr. Samson, don't go yet. I might have been a little hasty. Offhand, I can see no way to help you. But, if you think I can . . . if you have any ideas . . . I'd like to hear them."

It was Peter then who stood and spoke, while Eddie Samson turned to watch him, looking to the young man's face with something of a father's pride, and with relief so obvious that it permitted him to show his perfect teeth in the beginning of that smile.

"Something could be done, I'm sure," said Peter. "Mr. Duncan, are you worried we couldn't pay? Should that be dealt with first?"

He faced the cool anger of Peter's eyes with understanding.

"Naturally, it would be sensible to consider that. Though, believe me, there are other considerations. It's not really a matter where money is the most important thing. Better if it were, perhaps. Very well, Mr. Jirapon. I'm an expensive man. As you have noticed, I have no staff. Only a secretary. That's because I do it all myself. My time is all I have to sell. Usually I put a solid value on it."

"We have a thousand pounds," said Peter.

Eddie Samson blinked, and looked uncomfortable. That shouldn't have come out so soon. You didn't say how much you had to spend until you knew what the other man was going to charge. That was common sense.

"It needn't necessarily be that much, Mr. Jirapon. It would depend on whether I merely advised you, or whether I had to do it all myself."

God damn it, he was committing himself. He hastened to correct this impression.

"You understand I'm only talking in a general way. I'm still not . . ."

"But *could* it be done that way?" Peter interrupted. "With you advising what we had to do?"

"If I thought that was a good thing. Yes. You could do it that way. But I must say I don't like the sound of this at all. Ethics come into this. Let's get it clear: you're suggesting I should manipulate public opinion to reverse a matter which has gone through every legal process. Here's the thing: it's all been settled legally, and you want me to do that?"

"Mr. Duncan. It's what we *have* to do. There isn't any choice. Every appeal has been exhausted. Public opinion is our last resort. If that fails us, then this innocent man will hang."

"Innocent? Aren't you letting your heart run away with your head? Didn't this man sign a confession? Didn't I read that somewhere?"

"They beat it out of him!" cried Eddie Samson theatrically. "Eight of them were there! Eight big police in that little room, and they took it in turns to beat him. They scared that boy so much he would have put his name to anything, to make it stop. The hand of every man was raised against him."

"I don't know whether that kind of thing helps us very much. Don't they all say that?" His distaste was rudely obvious. He heard it himself in the dryness of his voice. It had been such an act of drama, Samson's fruity voice raised high in resonant virtue, his staring eyes uplifted.

"It is a strange confession," said Peter in apology, using a slight lift of one hand to quiet his companion. "In it there are many things not easy to account for. Words a man like Jimmy Jinben could not have known or used. At the very least, it's a very dubious thing on which to hang a man. Mr. Duncan, please believe me about that."

"I believe it is what *you* believe."

"Should we have sent a white man to talk with you?" asked Peter quietly, certainly without any appearance of resentment, looking as if he hoped that without resentment, perhaps honestly, his question would be answered.

"It crossed my mind. But I hoped you wouldn't feel it made things different." He had been caught off balance. "I mean . . . it really would have made no difference. I'd like it if you accepted that."

"You're not sure about it?"

"Now I am."

"I believe kindness, more than anything else, makes you say that. Mr. Duncan, let me tell you why we came. We talked a lot about it. Oh yes, we did. Yes, we talked and talked. Father Holliwell was against it. He wanted to send a white man to see you. But Eddie and I, we knew better. Oh yes, we knew it was better for us to come."

Peter, seeming to analyze his suddenly excited, almost stammering way of talking for the impression it might give, stopped.

"Sometimes I find myself talking like a blackfellow," he said, with a smile that sketched both pride and bitterness. "You must forgive me. But can't you imagine how Jinben found himself talking, too . . . with all those big police around him? This is why it was best for Eddie and me to come. Father Holliwell knows many things. But Eddie and me, we know things Father Holliwell only pretends to understand. We know what it can be like to go round with a black skin all the time. You see, Mr. Duncan, this is why we came.

"This Jimmy, he came from way up north. We told you that. He was only a youngster. Just a kid. He made up little songs, and people liked them. He was a big success, you see.

"I guess you must have heard his songs. He wrote that song that made him famous. You heard that song? I guess you must have. That song called *Walkin' in the Sunshine?*

"Jimmy, he was on that mission up there at Ben-gingin, and

they heard him singing these little songs of his, and someone thought he was good, you know. They taught him to play on the piano. Then, after a while, a man came visiting the mission, and he heard Jimmy. I never heard that song before, he said; and they told him; Jimmy here, he made that song all by himself. And this man said, I'd like to take this boy down south to the city; we'll put him on the radio; we'll make him famous.

"And that is what they did. They did make Jimmy famous. He came to live in the city, and he had money and everything he wanted.

"Now I tell you why we came to you, me and Eddie Samson, and not somebody else. Eddie knows all about this, and so do I. We know what it was like for Jimmy to be taken up out of his bush country as if a great bird had dived down in the bush with open claws and swept him away and dropped him down right in a white man's city. Don't we, Eddie? We know, don't we?"

"Yes," said Eddie Samson. "We certainly know all about *that.*"

"It happened to Eddie, the same way," said Peter. "He was a fighter, and it happened to him like that. He was a big boy. Strong. He was on this station where the shearers used to come around each year, and these shearers had these boxing gloves. And at night they'd fight each other, not wild at each other, just playing. Come on Eddie, they would say, put them on, boy, you look real strong, put them on. See how you go. But it wasn't like they thought it was going to be. Was it, Eddie?

"No. Eddie was too strong. Too quick for them. They taught him. They made a fighter out of Eddie. They told a man about him, and this was a man who went around from town to town when the shows were on, with a tent and a string of fighters. Five pounds there'd be for any man who lasted out a round. This man came around and off Eddie went with him. Only Eddie was too good. They all got to know how good Eddie was, and nobody would come up to take him on.

"So he came to the city, like Jimmy Jinben. Yes, Eddie was famous. Eddie had money and all the other things. He was two fights away from being Australian champion. And then what happened, Eddie? Did you get yourself in trouble? Tell it. Did you go to jail?"

"Ah yes," said Eddie Samson. "Trouble?" He had been staring into some far extent of memory, listening to Peter telling his story, a smile on his face that told of past pleasures fleetingly relived.

"Mr. Duncan," he said, still theatrically, but now with his story being told, able, perhaps fairly, to claim a few dramatic rights.

"What else but trouble does a poor bush abo in the city find? First I was drinking, you know, plonk and beer and anything I could get, and then I wasn't fighting so good. Not so good, you see. They got wild with me; I wasn't winning any more. They'd back me with their money, and I wouldn't win. Then, one day, fighting in the street, me and all the dark boys I been drinking with. Then the policeman. I never seen him, who he was, you see. Too drunk, I was. I laid him out. So I went to jail. Now that was when Father Gilbert came along. I been a good man ever since. I found someone, you see, to help me in my troubles. Here's Peter been talkin' all this time . . . Mr. Duncan, we do appreciate it how you sit and listen . . . that's what Peter been trying to say. They never teach us anything about the trouble it is to come all of a sudden from way outback to be a city man. We don't know nothin', you see. Innocent as little children. Things a white man knows is wrong, we don't know anything about. To us, these things just happen. Without thinking to do nothing wrong. Someone says, come on, boy, have a drink. Well, what is it? Lemonade? You don't know. You drink it. Ah, Mr. Duncan . . . then the trouble start. I was lucky. I found my friend when trouble came; without my friend I would have been lost in all that trouble. Always in trouble. Until something real bad been bound to happen. Ah, Mr. Duncan . . . who'll be Jimmy Jinben's friend in all his troubles? Will it be you? Won't you tell us that?"

"I'd have to think about it." He knew he would have to say more. He was annoyed to find himself somewhat more moved than he should have been by such arguments as these, argu-

ments loaded with the sanctimonious overtones he most dis-
trusted, couched in such oversimplification that logic was swept
aside in floods of sentiment.

And yet, the effect of this flagrant appeal to sentiment was
rather moving.

"I must have time to think it over." He sounded defensive,
and knew they would seize on that.

"I do wish I could say there's time," said Peter. "But I can't. I
can't say there's time we haven't got."

"When will he hang?"

"Three weeks. From yesterday."

"It must be possible to delay it? Surely?"

"We've applied for special leave to appeal. To the High
Court. If that is granted there'll be a stay of execution."

"Will it be granted?"

"It seems unlikely. We must act as if they'll hang him in
three weeks. We must find a way of using every hour that's left.
Mr. Duncan, please, won't you tell us what to do? Even if you
decide you cannot work for us, won't you give us your advice?"

"A moment. I'd like a moment to think it over."

But, idly, while they had been talking, his mind had been at
its quiet work on another level—the cool, objective level of as-
sessment, weighing this thing for problems of technique. What
would you do? How best to go about it? Factors like emotion,
ethics, intention—all those ignored, how should it be handled?

Some of the answers came. Therefore he paused, but for no
more than the bare moment he had asked.

"Listen then. First. You've gone through every normal process. What are the steps? Preliminary hearing, jury trial, appeal . . . that right?"

"Yes."

"It's been reported all the way. It's had the usual cover in the
press. Now you have to start that up again. All right? You need
a hook to hang a real hot story on. That's your problem . . . see?
To start it up again. Right now it's dead. Until they hang him.
They'll report that, and that's the end of it. Right? Now here is
what I'd do. You have to have a public meeting, get the press

along in force. You'll have to find someone who doesn't mind sticking his neck out, someone who can give them something they'll put there on the front page. Not only here, but in the other states. It has to be big enough to get on the wire. I don't know what you've got, but I don't suppose you'd be talking the way you are unless you thought you had something."

It had run away with him. All it was wise to say had been said, unless he wanted to find himself really hooked on this rat-bag operation. But the process of practical thought once begun, the flow of ideas falling over themselves once started, was not stopped so easily.

"You have to decide whether you're going to insist on this man's innocence. I wouldn't do that myself. Not outright. You know your biggest danger? Looking like a bunch of cranks. That's how you'll look if you start making claims you can't back up. Suppose you leave his innocence for now. Leave it in the background. Yes, that's what I'd do. No more than hints.

"He didn't get a fair trial. That's the hook for your story. Maybe it would have been a fair enough trial for a white man, but for a stone-age black, who didn't have the least clue what was going on, it was legal murder. Naturally, you'd have to polish that a bit. That's just a quick look at the operation. First thoughts. But how do they sound?"

"The front page of all the papers," said Eddie Samson. "Sure thing, boss. That's what we want, all right. To get it in the papers."

"This public meeting," said Peter. "I thought about that, but it seemed such a futile thing to do. I didn't think about it as a means to something else. But, of course. I believe it is the answer."

"How soon can you fix it?"

"This week?"

"Christ yes! Quick as you can. Is it clear what this meeting's for?"

"Publicity," said Peter. "To get publicity."

"No, Mr. Jirapon. It's more than that. It's no good holding a meeting just to tell the same old story. You must have a clear objective. Something a lot more active than protest. Something to bring it sharp in focus. You have to *demand* something . . . well? An inquiry of some sort? Yes. Now here it is. Listen. You have to demand a royal commission. What do you think of that?"

"Yes . . . I . . ."

"The mere fact you demand a commission will help to start them wondering. That's your job. You have to stir up so much doubt they won't dare hang him. That's your only job for the next three weeks. Never mind whether he's innocent or guilty. You have three weeks, all but a day, to raise enough doubts to save this feller's neck. When you've done that you can go to the next step. If there is one. I mean, then you can start arguing whether he's innocent. You understand that?"

"Oh yes. I agree . . ."

"Well, get on with it. Don't waste any more time."

"But, Mr. Duncan, I don't understand. About you . . . have you decided? Are you working with us?"

"I suppose I'll have to do some of it. Who's going to handle the press? Are you? Do you know anything about that side of it?"

"No. I . . ."

"Then I'll have to do it, won't I? Don't waste time. You get busy teeing up that meeting. Give me a call tomorrow and let me know how you're progressing."

"Can we talk about what you'll charge?" asked Peter awkwardly. "Your fee . . ."

"There'll be no fee. I shouldn't be doing it at all. I'm certainly not doing it for money."

Rising to stand behind his desk, he had felt tired and angry. As he listened to their stumbling attempts to express their gratitude, he had wished they would give it up, and go.

They had gone, and Wendy had come in. Wendy in a skittish mood.

"He was quite good-looking, wasn't he? I mean the young one. Did you think he was good-looking?"

What had he answered?

To hell with Wendy. That was finished.

He opened his eyes a fraction against the sun's white glare. He could see the lashes of his eyes against the glinting sky. Defects of vision, speckled patterns on the surface of an eyeball, slid across the sky. He tried to hold them still, as he had tried a thousand times before, but in the act of being held and closely watched they skimmed away.

Some time back the shade of the rock had gone, leaving him exposed. He felt dried out and burned. He opened his eyes and sat up, stupefied by giddiness. He crawled into the sea, and lay there cooling, as the realities of this prisoned place returned. A drift of smoke, and the smell of cooking flesh, reminded him of hunger. He walked to the fire.

The octopus was a charred, shapeless thing and he was sure he had left it to spoil but as he raked it out, and the skin broke, it showed a core of clean white flesh.

He squatted by the fire, picking the crust of charcoal from a tentacle. The skin came free and he held the tapered strip of pale meat in his hand, inspecting it.

I killed my own food, he told himself. I caught it and I cooked it, and it's real food. I did it all myself. He grinned with satisfaction and wished that Peter would come back now, to see.

In a cloud around his head, flies tried to join the meal. He brushed at the flies, and chewed off a bite of meat. It was rubbery and tough, but it was sweet, it had flavor and juice and substance . . . proper food. It really was.

As he chewed, as his jaws clamped with fierce enjoyment on each bite of this real, chewable food, he wondered how much he should leave for Peter. Half, at least, he supposed reluctantly, still on the first tentacle, still enjoying it so much that it seemed it would be easy to eat it all and then want more.

But with the second tentacle almost eaten generosity came more easily.

How we do fool ourselves, he thought sadly. I can't eat much more. That's where my generosity comes from. When I began I grudged the thought of each mouthful I decided I would have to set aside for Peter. Now, one more piece, and he can have the rest. Oh, I'm a bighearted fellow, all right!

He ate the third piece and covered the rest with ashes to keep the flies away. He had a drink of water and that left one full shell. There wasn't much water in a shell, two or three small swallows. It wasn't enough. He finished the last one.

How much was left on the rock? He took the empty shells and went across.

The rock was dry. The sun had taken what was left, leaving muddy stains to show where the temporary pool had been. He put his hand there, as if, without this confirmation it needn't be believed, and the rock felt hot enough to raise a blister.

There must be more. This can't be the only . . .

Oh Peter, hurry for the love of Christ. Bring water. I'm frightened.

He didn't know whether he had said this aloud or not.

"I am *not* frightened," he said sternly, aloud this time for sure, for he heard his voice telling him to believe in his courage.

Had he not killed and eaten the octopus? Didn't that mean something? Didn't it mean his own efforts could have some value in survival? That he didn't depend entirely on Peter?

He dragged himself up on the rock, and stood looking along the coast the way Peter had gone. Looking along the coast he tried to imagine that some places would be more likely to hold water than others. But he didn't know the trick. He didn't know how it was you could look at dry rocks and cliffs and, by that, discover water.

For as far as he could see, rock fringed the broken waters of the coast.

In the distance, heat danced visibly, distant scenes changed and wavered, like scenes constructed in the mind, imperfectly imagined, the kind of picture a dream or nightmare might choose for background, or the false mental picture a mind might hold of a foreign place, heard of and never seen.

12

The worst of day had passed; the worst, shadeless, gasping hour of noon. He found a strip of shade inches wide beside another rock. He was burned and dry and lonely, but if he could be sure about more water he would not mind that overmuch.

If only that were sure. To be *sure;* that vain desire for certainty, that constant, ineffectual plea of every man that the outcome of his main concerns should be assured in certain predication! And yet, this present plea, wasn't that well justified? Didn't those concerned deserve their chance—Peter and himself, and yes, of course: young Jinben?

How strange it was that Jinben, prisoned in his cell, held in that other confinement, knowing a similar dire uncertainty, now must be weighing those doubts on which his life depended. How strange that both their lives, at this same time, might now be in the process of determination by the actions of that one same man.

Would they have told him? Would Jinben know it all went wrong . . . that they hadn't made it? Hadn't seen old Fred? Were caught in a sudden flood instead and swept to sea, and nearly died? Or *had* died . . . Had they told him that?

That's a funny thing, thought James Duncan, lying as straight as he could to make the most of the shade: why haven't we talked about this, Peter and I? Here's a man's life at stake, most likely to be decided by what becomes of us, and we haven't said a word about it.

But, of course, until yesterday I wasn't well. Peter wouldn't want to worry me.

Or was it this: that the fate of a stranger lost importance when your own survival was in question?

But that, too, was odd. Though never met, Jinben was, to him, no stranger.

> *Why not leave that sorrow,*
> *Leave it for tomorrow,*
> *See how the day looks fine*
> *When you sing this song of mine,*
> *Come walkin' ...*
> *Come walkin' ...*
> *Walkin' with me, in the sunshine.*

The trite words of Jinben's simple song ran in his mind. Trite, simple, and yet—something in the tune, perhaps—lifting the heart to pleasure in some uncanny way.

He heard it coming from the amplifier before the meeting, and greeted the brave, bright song with momentary unconscious pleasure.

But because he had seen at once the dreary corroborree those two smart darkies had arranged, anger soon dismissed the pleasure.

Oh God, that meeting! What a performance!

"It's wonderful!" said Peter. "Nearly full! Only those few seats empty at the back."

And I stormed at him, James Duncan recalled with shame. I was livid with frustrated temper.

"*Where'd you get 'em?* God Almighty, where'd you get 'em? Commies and cranks by the *dozen* ... Jesus! Don't you know the boys from the press will spot this commie mob from half a mile away?"

"We had to fill the hall," said Peter desperately. "We only had two days. We had to leave it all to Father Holliwell ..."

"Ratbags, every single one of them! I *told* you about that. Well, that's buggered it, you wait and see ..."

"But I told him. I told him we should have members of Parliament, and people from the university, I told him all you said. I *did,* Mr. Duncan! And he said he'd try."

"I've seen 'em all before. Christ, you have to hand it to these bastards, they're really organized."

"We've got his songs playing over the amplifiers," said Peter, evading anger by a change of subject.

"Whose songs?"

"His. Jimmy Jinben's."

"Terrific. Who thought that up?"

"Eddie Samson."

"Bloody marvelous. Samson's a genius."

He pushed past knees to a vacant seat near the back. He looked around the shabby hall.

Bare as a barn. High-pitched ceiling lined with the Baltic pine they used before the first war, never painted, left to age for fifty years until it was a filthy, cobwebbed, dusty brown, stained by the leaks of an ill-plumbed roof.

Too high for anyone to have bothered to get them down, faded and collapsed, paper Christmas bells made homes for spiders. Ornately scrolled, lists of past masters of obscure lodges were ranged along a wall, gold leaf peeling.

He was not able to bring himself to look again at the people Holliwell had called to pack this awful place; one glance had been enough—that first knowing inspection of bulging-eyed psychotic faces, duffle-coats, beards, man-faced housewives, rows of prim, schoolteacher's spectacles. This, for sure—unmistakably—was the pink, suburban fringe, that fringe of irresponsibility and provocation, leaping with glee on any cause that could be stirred to the possibilities of trouble.

They'll hang that boong twice over, he thought sourly, if this is all they have to save him.

Heavily applauded, Eddie Samson appeared on the platform and walked to the end of the row of chairs behind the table. He raised a confident and authoritative hand.

"Brothers. Yes, brothers—and ladies too. We thank you for coming here tonight. Such numbers too. So many. We are not alone in our fight. Yes, I can see that, standing here. Yes, we are proud and glad tonight."

Standing like that, alone before them, he had astonishing presence. His teeth flashed bright and wonderful. The aboriginal softness of his voice, raised for public speech, had a deep, full quality of warm sincerity.

Eddie Samson turned, looking to the side of the platform, gesturing with a hand of welcome, and Father Gilbert Holliwell walked on, blinking, gloomy and serious, bowing slightly to applause, to sit in the chairman's place while others followed; the union leader Wally Brennan; the Reverend Albert Shelley; the Reverend Gordon Ferguson.

He watched this, deeper than ever in pessimism. He knew these names. Were these rabid charlatans all they had? Would not someone else come forward?

Had it been easy to escape unseen he would have sneaked away.

Holliwell's Oxford voice quietened the murmuring audience.

He wouldn't have very much to say, said Holliwell; his function was to introduce the speakers and do his best to preserve a semblance of order.

Kindly laughter. How splendid to have a man with such a cultured voice as Father Gilbert on our side.

Peace was indivisible, said Holliwell. No man an island. The winds of change. The color of a man's skin. Carried away by enthusiasm. Mustn't allow himself. Recent visit to China. Saw no yellow men in China. Skins of a different color. Yes. All men the same. Not black men, white men, yellow men. Black skins, white skins, yellow skins. Underneath, all men the same. Communes in China. Extr'ord'n'ry thing. Like early Christians. Living Christianity. Communes . . .

Given the right accent, it seemed, you could say anything. Accent of the right kind was a universal license to do anything you liked with words. You could fuss and bumble, say any damfool thing you liked, and it would all go down, for a ripe Pommy accent was an oil that made even stupidity acceptable. Provided always that the accent was on your side. Used against you,

you would howl it down. Class distinction. Yes. Extr'ord'n'ry
was the word for it.

Holliwell finished, and failed to mention Jimmy Jinben. Did
I come to the wrong meeting, James Duncan wondered wildly
for a moment.

Wally Brennan had no neck. His round chin joined his gross
body in folds of flesh wider than the chin itself. He jammed a
thumb in a waistcoat pocket and waddled to the edge of the
platform.

"Comrades . . ." he began roughly, growling, as if this were a
word of insult. Holliwell cleared his throat in mild reproof, and
Brennan turned and grinned.

"Mr. Chairman," he said, beginning again. "Ladies and gentlemen." He paused. "And comrades," he added softly, leering.

"One of our brother workers lies tonight in a cold cell, looking at the bars and counting his remaining days. Now I want
you all to look around you and see who it is that cares about it
when the spite of capitalism tries to claim another victim.
Yes . . . look around you, that's right. Do you see the upper
classes? Do they care? Come on now, who cares? Is it the buzwuz
of the middle classes? Look around. Who do you see?

"Yair. That's right. You see the workers. That's right. You see
the working classes. Well, who the hell did you *expect* to see?
Who else would bother to raise their voices when the racist pol-
icy of the bosses looks around for another victim whose only
crime is he has a dark skin?

"You listen to me. In the fight against the new colonialism
. . . and that's a fight we're winning all along the line, by God,
yes . . . you mark my words, we're winning, don't you worry
about that . . ."

A man in the front row rose, and stood while he buttoned his
coat, watching the speaker with a kind of cool amusement that
was almost sympathetic. The man made his way to the aisle and
came toward the back and James Duncan saw who he was.

Well, at least they'd sent Horrie. They hadn't sent one of the
kids. He couldn't let Horrie walk out like that.

He stumbled past legs, legs settled for comfort, stretched out, or crossed, that had to be pulled in or unwound to let him pass, so that faces looked up at him with pursed lips and angry eyes, craning to see around him so as not to miss a word of Brennan's harsh rhetoric.

"Hey Horace," he called loudly, as the reporter pushed at the door and went to walk through.

"Ah . . . Jimmy," said Horace. "You little beauty. Man, have you excelled yourself tonight!"

"Are you going?"

"You're bloody right I'm going."

"I'll come outside."

Brennan's voice, which had been rising steadily in pitch and volume, now shouted. The door swung closed behind them, amputating the ranting voice.

"Boy . . ." said Horace. "Oh Jimmy boy. What you trying to do? Put yourself right out of business?"

"Wait on, Horrie. You haven't . . ."

"Haven't what? Haven't given it a fair go? Who do you think you're talking to? Christ, you got your share of nerve, sport, I have to give you that."

"What are you going to write?"

"Jim . . . I'm giving you a break. The break of your life, man. I ain't going to write a frigging word."

So far the reporter had preserved that aloof, worldly air of cool amusement that seemed like sympathy. But suddenly cast aside, the trappings of this superior manner exposed an underlying spite.

"Listen, Duncan," Horace said. "Take some good advice. Watch your bloody step. Yair. You better watch it. Wake up one morning, you're going to find your name spiked on the shithook. Hey? How would you like that? And don't think it can't happen. You buggers get to think you're fireproof, that's what happens to you, think you can get away with anything. You get me along here to listen to the same old frigging pack of reds. Well, you better take a note. Don't try that again.

"Yair. Doing pretty well for yourself, aren't you? Hacking yourself a sweet bloody slice off the good old cake. Well, you listen to me, dad, other people bake that cake. Get my meaning? Know what I'm talking about?"

Difficult to recall exactly what answer you would make to stuff like that, but the feelings involved came readily to mind. The anger and disgust, both of necessity to be disguised, the fervent wish to be out of it, that it had never happened, the revived thought that the sooner they hanged the boong and got it over with, the better. They had talked on. Somehow, a little reconciled by further talk, Horace Shipton had gone.

Heard through the closed door, Brennan's coarse voice concluded in phrases repeated several times and the thud of feet guided applauding hands and voices to a volume and duration of sound judged right for this occasion. The dull booming of another voice began.

Albert Shelley. He could not have borne the pious clichés of Albert Shelley.

He turned away and started walking, past dark shops, under oak trees ridging the pavement with their thrusting roots.

He must not be long. Norm Streeter must be somewhere there. Norm had promised. Seeing Horace go, Norm might decide to follow suit. And if Norman Streeter went, that would be the end.

Once around the block, more oak trees, more dark shops. When he opened the door into the hall, heads turned in annoyance.

"Justice?" Albert Shelley was shouting, red of face, both hands raised above his head. "What do *They* know of justice? Vengeance, that's what it is. And Vengeance is Mine, saith the Lord! And Jesus Christ said, judge not . . . judge not, that ye be not judged. Aren't we warned by this? Aren't we therefore warned? Warned that it is not for us to take into our sinful hands powers that are God's? For our puny vengeance, mark you, is the vengeance of a racist white society. Are we going to stand by while they turn that vengeance on an innocent child of nature? Yes! One of God's children . . ."

Thank Christ Norman Streeter's long bald head was found at last, raised by the height of half a head above the others in his

row. He let Albert Shelley's platitudes boom past his ears un-
heard while he worked out the best way to handle Norm.

Shelley resumed his seat, mopping his brow, looking as tired
as a man who had run hard in a race for younger men; looking
as satisfied as if he had been the winner of that race.

Holliwell rose for a moment, to say that the Reverend Gordon Ferguson would introduce the resolution.

Ferguson arranged a folder of papers on the table beside him,
and polished a pair of glasses with his handkerchief. He had
seemed a man of early middle age, but the thin gold frames of
the spectacles changed his appearance, so that he appeared quite
old, almost as old as Holliwell. He gave the impression that he
was in no hurry to begin, and something in his hesitation, his
air of being troubled about something, and not knowing quite
how to go about this matter that troubled him, was oddly reassuring.

"I don't feel," he began, and hesitated. "I don't . . . ah . . . feel
that perhaps enough has been said tonight about the background to this very sad affair. I know it is not usual for people
moving such things as resolutions to speak at length. I believe it
is my duty to take somewhat longer than some of you may wish.
You must forgive me.

"Not that I know this man. I don't. But I have known young
men who could have been his brothers. I have been to that mission from which he came. I have seen the young men of that
tribe, and of other tribes. I have seen these men, these souls who
find a kind of vacuum in which they must discover the way to
live their lives.

"But more important, I believe, I have been privileged over
the past few days to examine every detail of this sad affair, and I
believe there is a story you must hear. If you are to consider a
resolution, which demands a full inquiry, then you should know
something of what you are considering. I would have thought
we might have heard more of this tonight than we have. It
seems it is left to me to tell the story, then, of Jimmy Jinben."

The young man, Ferguson said, had come from his wild

country, a child among clever men. This boy had the gift of making songs; he had a sense of rhythm, and a pleasant voice; he had, perhaps, a kind of talent. And this talent had been his ruin. He had been brought to the city because of it. He had found money and success. He had been guided, surely by bad men, toward the evils of strong drink, and to these people, even more than to others, strong drink was a strong poison. It had deprived this boy of his wits.

And that was no figure of speech. The boy had been driven mad by drink. Certified. Put away in a mental hospital. Forgotten. For the incredible thing was that when he found his senses again, when he became himself again, none would claim him. He stayed in that place because they knew not what to do with him. For two years, a sane man, he lived with lunatics. Because there was nowhere else for him to go.

And someone, at last, wrote a letter for him. One must assume that. Whether by this means, or by some other, the fact was that an old man of his own tribe searched him out, and rescued him.

"I have covered this part of the story quickly," said Ferguson. "But now we come to the part where details are important. The young man was given into the keeping of this old man of his tribe. Together, without money or other resources, these two set out to cross a continent from one end to the other. To find their long way home."

The voice of the Reverend Ferguson trembled. He seemed somewhat moved. He rubbed at the lenses of his spectacles, and replaced them, and stooped to study his notes. His audience waited quietly, watching his movements, for this was the real thing. This was the truth of a man who cared for truth. As far as could be seen from the back of the hall, Norman Streeter was as absorbed as anyone. In this pause, he seemed to be writing notes.

The adventures of the two men, Ferguson continued, could be imagined. Begging rides, begging food, begging work. Sleeping under the scant shelter of bushes in the cold nights of the south. Sometimes working for a few days. Day by day, mile by mile, slowly moving north, toward the wilder country, toward the sun, toward the land of their own people.

After weeks of this, months perhaps, they came to the small inland town of Droverdale. They camped beside the river, with other aborigines who lived there in tin shanties, and in old tents made of bags. And that night, beside the campfires, these unfortunate people drowned their sorrows in a veritable orgy of drunkenness.

"We must not blame them for this," said Ferguson sternly. "The fault is ours. These are a displaced people, wanderers in their own land, and surely it is not for us to point at them the finger of righteous scorn."

Sadly he shook his head. Yes. These men became drunk. They put into their mouths the devil who would steal away their wits. And the two wanderers, the old man and the youth, joined in. So the stage was set for all that was to follow.

At some time after midnight, the old man, variously referred to in the records as Fred, or Old Fred, or Binben Freddie, noticed that his young companion had disappeared. He was concerned at this, but he was far too drunk himself to do anything about it. He fell asleep beside the ashes of the fire.

Not surprisingly perhaps, when he awoke in the morning he was ill, and it was not until afternoon that he found himself recovered enough to begin the search for his companion. Even with the failing eyesight of his advanced years, Old Fred appeared to have little difficulty in following the young man's tracks, which led at first beside a kind of track or road that ran past the aboriginal encampment and went for several miles along the river.

"Now it is not to be denied," said Ferguson, "that if, in fact, the tracks of Jimmy Jinben followed this road they would have taken him within sight of a campfire which burned, almost surely, until late that night in a grassy glade beside the river. And it is tragic to say that in this glade, hidden under branches torn from trees, was to be found, several days later, the violated and murdered body of an unfortunate young lady. But this is to anticipate other events which I should now describe.

"The old man followed the tracks until darkness fell. It would seem that the tracks continued past the end of the road into the scrub in which the marks were difficult to follow. When he could no longer follow them the old man roamed the bush, calling out the young man's name. And this it seems is what he did for most of that night, and at some late hour, hearing a voice singing in the darkness, he called again. The young man answered, and was found. They lit a fire and spent the rest of the night beside it.

"According to Old Fred, the young man had gone silly again. He had cast away his clothing. He had been wandering naked in alcoholic madness singing his pathetic songs. Living again, perhaps, his brief experience of fame."

Ferguson cleared his throat and slowly raised a wrist close to his eyes to examine his watch.

"I fear it is becoming later than I intended. I am sorry to be taking so much of your time. I am very conscious of that. I will do this as quickly as I can."

A rustling sound filled the hall as many people, moving as one with a kind of stealthy unanimous movement, changed their posture. This was the only sound.

They went back to the encampment, said Ferguson, pausing only long enough for the old man to beg clothing to cover the young man's nakedness. They set out again on the road to the north. By some odd turn of fate, their traveling, which had been slow and painful for so many weeks, became fast and easy. On that first day, a traveler took them almost three hundred miles in his car. On the second day they covered another two hundred miles and came to the crossroads town of Coonarundah, bounced among the drums and crates of a transport truck, and it is possible that this very speed of movement, in truth so accidental, at some stage of the inquiries into the murder at Droverdale, might have been seen as a sign of guilt . . . as if the guilty fled their crime.

Then, at Coonarundah, the fate which had brought them there turned right against them. The driver of the transport truck, perhaps taking pity on them in his rough way, bought them liquor. It mattered not that these men, surely, needed food. Probably they were not asked whether they wanted food. They may have been. But they were given liquor. They wandered the streets of the little town in a drunken condition. They were a public nuisance, and they were locked up. And, at that stage, news of the murder at Droverdale arrived. They were not suspected. Who would imagine logical connection between a murder committed five hundred miles away and these decrepit waifs?

They were due to be released. Where were they going, they were asked. And where had they come from? Droverdale, the old man said. When were they in Droverdale? Two three days ago, the old man said. They were not released. And that night they were driven back to Droverdale.

"I'm afraid it's very late," said Ferguson, studying his watch again in that short-sighted manner. "I hope you will bear with me. I must finish. Then I will move the resolution. Believe me, you could not vote honestly on that unless you heard me first."

He went on to describe the young woman who had been murdered. An unusual person, an artist, and a writer. Sometimes a teacher. Having been in the Centre for some months, she was returning to the south by motorcycle, alone, camping by herself at nights. Her name was Christina Hader. Boys from the town found her body, where it lay hidden under branches.

The police came. Others followed. The scene of the crime was trampled by many feet. To such an extent that a black-tracker from the town, One-Eye Bobby by name, whose services the Droverdale police had used on previous occasions, could not give, at first, any useful information.

Old Fred and Jimmy Jinben were returned with great haste, overnight, five hundred miles in a fast car, from Coonarundah to Droverdale. Might this alone not make it seem to One-Eye Bobby, and to other witnesses, that the police had found their man? Be that as it may. It was on the following day, and only then, that the black-tracker claimed to identify tracks leading from the road to the scene of the crime, and back to the road again, as the tracks of Jimmy Jinben. No casts were made of these footprints. It was said they were too faint for a white man's eye, certainly too indistinct for plaster.

Jinben was questioned all that night, and in the morning he was charged with the murder of Christina Hader. It had been said that no less than eight policemen were present throughout the interrogation. The presence of six of these officers had been admitted in subsequent proceedings. It was claimed that a statement was dictated by Jinben and taken down by an officer. It was claimed that this was signed quite willingly by the young man. That statement was a virtual confession to the crime.

It had been claimed that many of the words and the constructions in that statement would not have been used by such a person as Jinben. It had been claimed that these words had been, as it were, put into his mouth, and that he put his mark to the statement unaware of what it might contain. It had been alleged that violence had occurred during the interrogation and that threats of further violence were used to make him sign.

Statements were taken from Old Fred, and from aborigines present at the drinking orgy on the night of the murder but, once his statement had been taken, the old man vanished. He simply wandered out of the town and wasn't seen again. He did not appear in any subsequent proceedings. The evidence of that man, crucial evidence, as one might well consider it, was not available when Jinben went on trial.

Yes, Jinben had been tried. At the preliminary hearing at Droverdale his defense was reserved. The case was set down for criminal sessions of the Supreme Court. He was tried there and found guilty. He was sentenced to death. His legal advisers had appealed to the Full Court, and the appeal dismissed, without reservation.

Ferguson removed his spectacles, and polished the lenses. He looked tired, younger without the spectacles, but very tired. He looked up quickly with the emotional expression of a man about to weep.

"That boy will be hanged in sixteen days," he said, and his voice was clear in the silent hall. "He will hang. Unless something is done. You have come here in generous number tonight in the cause of justice and mercy. To save, if you can, the life of a man who may well be innocent of the dreadful act with which he has been charged . . . for which he is to pay with his life, in a few short days.

"But have we considered the enormity of our own crime if we let society avenge itself, on him, for the deed of another man? If innocent he is, in fact? We would commit a second murder. If the first murder is terrible, how much worse would be the second? *Our* act of murder. How much worse is that?

"So we must ask ourselves this question . . . does any reasonable doubt exist that Christina Hader was murdered by this young man? Has it been shown beyond reasonable doubt that this crime could have been committed only by him, and by no other person?

"That confession, now repudiated by him on the grounds that it was extorted by threats and by violence, and signed in fear . . . is *that* to be given such credence that it can be used as the main instrument of his execution?

"And those tracks. Do those tracks seen only by the tracker, One-Eye Bobby . . . and by no other person . . . do they prove beyond doubt that Jinben did leave the road, and did murder the girl? Do they prove he was in that grassy glade? Did those tracks, beyond doubt, exist? We must believe they did, if we are to hang this boy, for there is little other proof.

"Answer these questions how we will, but one other vital question still remains unanswered. Where is the old man? Where is this Binben Freddie? He followed the young man's tracks along that road. He went with those tracks into the bush, past where that road came to an end.

"If Jinben *did* turn off the road at the scene of the murder, did the old man simply blunder past, with his eyes closed, missing the tracks leaving the road, and the tracks coming back? Or did he follow those tracks to where the girl was murdered? And if he did do that, why did not the tracker see the tracks of the old man? Why did he not say to his masters . . . here are the tracks of Jinben, and here are the tracks of the old man who followed him?

"Could it be that there *were* no tracks off the road for the old man to follow? Must we not ask . . . what light can Old Fred throw on this affair, and why hasn't that light been cast?

"Should I continue? I believe not. I do not aspire to the skills of the criminologist, I am not qualified to play the lawyer. I might confuse you, and confound myself.

"The resolution which it is my privilege to put before this meeting of citizens refers to doubts, such as I have mentioned, which persist in the minds of ordinary men even after the process of law has been concluded.

"The resolution requires that further inquiries be pursued and further evidence given, and a further finding made, that this be done by royal commission, and that a stay of execution be granted until such time as the findings of that commission be known.

"When the normal workings of the law fail to satisfy the requirements of the ordinary man that justice is done and is seen to be done, the ordinary man must seek justice and the appearance of justice by other means. The royal commission which we ask is such a means.

"I will now read the resolution."

"Damn it, Jim," Norman Streeter said when the meeting was over. "You know as well as I do it's not what I think that counts. The chief's your man. I'll file my story. I'll make it good. I told you that. Listen, that Ferguson peanut had me bloody near in tears. I'm right behind you. I think you're on to something."

"And you're on to something, too. There's a scoop here if you want it. All on your own. Horrie Shipton didn't last the distance. Did you see him go?"

"Horrie's the boy to make sure people see him when he stacks on an act like that. Though, tell the truth I damn near walked out on you myself. I thought you'd gone right off your nut. I mean ... Wally Brennan, Jesus, getting us along to hear old Wally rave. No kidding, I damn near went."

"Lucky you didn't. You're a jump ahead. Horrie missed it. This is for the front page, Norm. You give this meeting six inches single column the bottom of page six and you're murdering the best story you've had since Hiroshima."

"For Christ's sake ... *whisper* that word around here," said Streeter, pretending panic. "Holliwell or any of those ban-the-bomb boys hears you, they'll throw us out. And now we're talking about it, just where *did* you get this mob of fancy pinkos? Suppose you'll be begging me to print their names? Like our readers should see this boong of yours is putting his neck in good hands, that what you want?"

"Sure. We want that just like young Jinben wants his neck yanked off his backbone two weeks from tomorrow."

"Yair, sorry. I guess that's what we're really talking about. All right, Jim, let's stop playing about. Could be I'm like most clapped-out old journal hacks. Hate to see you P.R. bandits getting fat on what we poor buggers do for a lousy wage. But what the hell. Wouldn't I get into the racket tomorrow if only I knew how?"

Near the platform Holliwell and Ferguson were talking earnestly, Eddie Samson standing listening. Nearby, buttonholed by the Reverend Albert Shelley, Peter seemed uncomfortable.

Streeter went, and only these were left. The hall was empty and the caretaker stood at the door waiting to turn off the lights and lock up.

It had turned out well, and it could have been the worst disaster, public-relations-wise, as some would say.

The caretaker flicked the lights off and on.

"Was it all right, Mr. Duncan?" Peter asked, coming to the door. "Will it be in all the papers?"

Shelley had followed Peter and stood, waiting for the others, who walked down the aisle slowly, deep in talk.

"Who do I see about my expenses?" asked Shelley loudly.

Peter and Eddie Samson exchanged glances. Samson hurried forward, embarrassed.

"I'm sorry, sir." he said with a shamed smile. "Sorry. You see . . . there was no collection. We decided . . . that is, we didn't think . . ."

"It's the usual arrangement," said Shelley.

"Yes, sir," said Eddie Samson. "Perhaps . . . would you tell me how much? I'm sorry . . . we . . ."

"Two pounds . . . yes. Well . . . two pounds is . . . you know? The usual thing?"

Picking at the breast pocket of his jacket with two fingers, Eddie Samson wore the fixed smile of the man who reaches for money, well aware there will not be sufficient. His fingers drew out a note, and disappeared into a trouser pocket where coins jingled.

"I'll fix this." James Duncan was aware of the angry contempt in his voice, and didn't care. Hoped, in fact, that Shelley would know exactly how he felt.

"This is Mr. Duncan . . ." said Peter.

Taking the two notes, Shelley didn't look at him. "Goodnight all," he said, and pushed through the door.

The caretaker lost patience and put out the lights.

Outside in the street Peter asked again whether it would be in the papers.

It was likely, James Duncan said. But they would have to wait and see.

COMMISSION

SOUGHT IN

JINBEN CASE

Driving to the office in the morning he had seen the posters. It had been well covered on the front page, and in Streeter's account it seemed that only Gordon Ferguson had spoken at the meeting.

In the placards, seen in passing as he drove, in that heavy, black, authoritative type, a forceful demand catching irresistibly the casual eye, he had seen again the uncanny power that skilled contrivance wielded sometimes in public matters.

That wide power, sometimes used, of making something good seem bad, something bad seem good, something small seem big. The power used now, for once, for a cause that might be good, a small thing, a lost hope, that for once might have the principle of something great.

The night before, he had come under the spell of Ferguson's sincerity. From the facts that Ferguson had gathered, and the careful presentation of those facts, he had come to believe the young man innocent. He knew himself committed; for better or for worse, involved; now, for a change, in a cause that might be more significant than most.

And what had happened next?

The midnight conference with Streeter and his editor. The first blotched pull of the morning's poster.

JINBEN CASE

MISSING WITNESS FOUND

For it was learned, late next day, that Binben Freddie, disappearing from Droverdale, had completed his interrupted journey. He had not been lost. He had not been hiding. He had been at the mission at Ben-gingin for several weeks, longer perhaps; he had been there for anyone who wished to find him. As Norman Streeter, at his first attempt, had done. It had seemed the obvious place to start.

"There was this peanut at the mission," said Streeter. "This Hardy character. Soon as he came on the phone, I said . . . you ever hear of an old man called Binben Freddie? Oh yes, says he, indeed I have.

"Wouldn't know where the old boy is right now, would you . . . said I. Well, as a matter of fact, says old Hardy, I do.

"Well . . . um . . . I said, you know, tapping my fingers . . . you know, real cool? . . . now . . . um . . . where would that be, Mr. Hardy . . . hmmmmm? He's here, says Hardy, here at the mission."

"So there I was," said Streeter. "Like a man going down the

stairs in the dark who comes to the bottom when he thinks
there's still five steps to go. Ever had that happen to you?"

MISSING WITNESS FOUND

There had been that placard, seen again on the way to the
airport through the mists of early morning, the taxi driver
reading it aloud.

"What y'reckon they're trying to pull with this abo? Reckon
he done it to the sheila?"

He didn't want to talk. "Afraid I don't know much about it."

"Yair. Well, how was her rotten form, anyhow? Camping by
that river near a mob of boongs. Asking to get done. Women on
motor bikes. Jesus, I dunno. Anyhow, they got the right bloke.
Know what I reckon? I reckon they'd a topped him by now if
he'd a been a white man. All this fuss. I reckon all that's because
the dirty shit's a boong."

"Is it possible to drive a little faster? I've cut it rather fine."

"Just for you mate, I'll kick her in the guts. You'll catch y'
plane. Where y'off to, anyhow?"

"North."

"What y' goin' for?"

He didn't answer, and the driver said, "Listen; y' don't wanta
talk, all y' gotta do is say so."

Peter was waiting at the airport. They boarded the aircraft,
were noised aloft; and now in memory he gazed on clouds below
whose gaps showed a distant view of earth, a green earth dark
with mountain and with forest.

He remembered the thousand sterile miles of the inland
deserts, an arid world of geological distortion where nature's
wildest colors danced weirdly in the sight of man, refracting violence from a blasting sun.

His thoughts raced over the surface of events with something
of the headlong speed of the aircraft . . . dropping down to the
dusty airfield at Mt. Roma, a night spent at the wooden hotel in
the shabby town. The charter Cessna in the morning. The taxi-

turn, offhand pilot, dressed in khaki shirt and shorts. The turbulent flight, Peter restless in the other seat, giving way at last and vomiting. And the tiny airstrip at the nameless town where a Land Rover waited at the gate and the wind sock lay stiff in a furious local wind, dead across the strip.

Watching the pilot's hand on the throttle on that first illjudged approach, wanting to shout . . . go 'round again! Saying nothing. Seeing the throttle hand leap with the instant impulse of delayed decision, the ground falling out of sight, the canting, slipping horizon as they went around again. Coming in, then, to a safe landing.

The rough trip to the river in the Land Rover, and not wanting to remember what happened at the river . . .

But it had to be remembered.

He must remember all of it so that he could count the days.

Sixteen days, Ferguson had said. At the meeting. The meeting had been on a Thursday night.

How many days since then? And what day now?

Flying north with Peter on Saturday. Saturday night, the hotel at Mt. Roma. The men in from the mines, hitting it up all night. Didn't get much sleep.

The next day . . . the Cessna, the Land Rover, the river . . . Sunday . . . the river, the river, the flood . . . the angry wall of water, boat rearing up, outboard motor racing jumping about falling off boatman going over and the boatman's desperate eyes. Standing up to throw the oar, the only thing to keep the poor old sod afloat. The oar landing with a splash. Then falling, falling, darkness, darkness hurting.

Another day. The sharks came. Was that day Monday?

Was it Monday night, lying listening to the sharks? Was the shark killed on Tuesday? Saw land that day. At night, rain. Dreaming of Wendy, rain fell in my mouth like tears.

Coming ashore.

Yesterday, the birds. Yesterday was Wednesday? Thursday today?

Seven days gone? A week?

Sixteen days, Ferguson had said.

Half gone tomorrow. Eight days gone and eight days left. Was that right?

Peter would know.

Peter. Gone. Looking for water.

The sequence of his thoughts had brought him to this present moment.

He opened his eyes and saw where he was without surprise.

He saw the rock beside him. Red rock, almost purple in the shadow. Rough-grained, specked with crystals of glinting quartz, like sugar on a bun.

The sounds of the sea entered his mind like a chorus of voices making poetry in a forgotten tongue, poetry rhymed by the regular, sequential stops of breaking waves. He listened to the sea.

A crashing wave declaimed and at once the following line of sound began. Rocks babbled in chorus, a blowhole spoke the word it always spoke, the verse of sound approached its end in a murmur of shallow pools.

The next wave crashed.

The sea spoke in its poem of the beginning of the world, and of the world's end.

The sea told of the solitude and desolation of a lifeless planet.

James Duncan stirred in movement, deep in the somber mood the insensate sea described, cold at the thought of the sea's eternity, at the thought of man's insignificance in the face of vast infinities of time and inconceivable magnitudes of space.

He moved from the shade of the rock and stood in the heat of the sun, and he was glad of warmth.

He raised his eyes to the cliff and wished with all his heart that Peter would appear.

Because he was lonely. Because he was thirsty. Because he was, again, afraid.

But more than this, because he wanted it confirmed, he wanted Peter to agree, that though thousands of millions of people lived on a world as old as time, the life or death of one single man might with reason be thought of some importance.

13

The long day ended and Peter had not come back.

As twilight passed and night grew more intense, James Duncan faced at last the deepest chill despair of solitude. It was too late now. Something had gone wrong. He would never see Peter again.

The dreadful consequence of being left alone and helpless shuddered in his spine. The sea coughed and rumbled, the gaunt cliffs loomed in a wilderness of night, and he was all alone. From now on, for the last slow days of life and evermore in death, alone. It must be faced. Something had happened to Peter.

Yet, he was calmer than he would have thought.

You see? I was not always a coward, he told himself, I decided that today. What will I do?

I'll wait and see. What else *can* I do?

And while I wait I'll think of it no more. I'll think of something else. No, he decided, I will think of nothing.

By some freak of mental discipline he made his mind a blank. He fixed his gaze upon the fire, intent on thoughtlessness, resisting the start of any thought, the start of the thought that on no terms should be confronted, and time passed on unmeasured.

Then Peter came, so silently that he seemed to materialize beside the fire in the crouched stance of exhaustion, his clasped arms holding to his chest a gallon can of squarish shape.

Startled, James Duncan shivered with the instant release of

fears so heavily suppressed. He stared at Peter. Fear gone, thirst raging suddenly, he saw the can.

"Is that water?"

"Tired," Peter grunted. "Don't make me talk."

He kicked a hole in the sand so that the can, put down, would stand. He dropped to his knees and looked, for a moment, like a used-up beast of burden. He subsided with a groan.

"Where did you get it?" said James Duncan.

"Found it."

"On the beach?"

"No." That word from Peter was a sound of pain. He was so beaten, so unlike himself, that James Duncan, picturing the ordeal of Peter's day, knew quick shame and deep ingratitude. He wanted to do something for Peter, and he remembered the octopus, that food, all his own, hunted and killed and cooked, the only thing he had to give.

"Are you hungry?"

"What? Hungry? Oh yes . . ."

James Duncan raked in the ashes and peeled charcoal from white meat. "Here . . . have some of this."

Peter reached blindly and found meat in his hands and opened his eyes, surprised. "What's this?"

"Octopus. Go on, eat it. I'll peel some more."

Peter chewed and swallowed with the rabid hunger of an animal and by degrees came more alive.

"How did you get it?"

"I went into the water and chased it ashore and killed it," said James Duncan, not without pride. "Didn't you find any food where you went?"

"No time," said Peter. "Long way before I came to water. Seven mile, eight maybe. Listen . . . it's a little creek. Someone's been there, camping. Tins and bottles and rubbish all around. That's where I got the tin. I saw tire tracks, a jeep or something. A track to lead us out."

"Camping?" cried James Duncan, a foretaste of salvation exciting his eyes and voice. "People?"

"Not there now," said Peter. "Maybe a year ago."

"But there's a track?"

"Yes."

"We have to hurry," said James Duncan. "I worked it out today. If we're to save Jinben we have eight days at the most."

"You remembered that? Today?"

"Yes."

"And you want to save him?"

"I do indeed."

"*I* could save him," said Peter, in a voice not used before, brutal and resenting. "If I didn't have to wait around for *you*."

James Duncan was shocked and hurt. But I must say nothing, he told himself. I have no right to anger, and anger would not be wise, for anger is what he wants. He wants a row. So he can leave me. He lived again those pains and fears of solitude banished in the moment of Peter's providential reappearance. No, he would say nothing.

"I'm going to make that creek tomorrow," said Peter. "It's rough. Seven miles of it. How do you think you'll go?"

"I don't know."

Seven miles! He saw himself. Crawling hands and knees on jagged rocks. Burning sun. Peter hurrying on, leaving him behind. He'd shout..."Help me! Please, I'm old and weak. For God's sake, wait!"...and this changed, alien Peter, malicious and resentful, would turn with a scornful laugh, and hurry on.

"All right," he said, in a beaten voice. "I *do* know. I cannot go that far. You know that as well as I. You had better tell me what is wrong."

"Is something wrong?"

"Why are you angry? Tell me what has happened."

"I'll tell you," said Peter. "I am angry because I had to come back. Because I could have been fifteen or twenty miles away by now. Because, coming back for you, I've wasted several days."

"If you hadn't come back," said James Duncan slowly, "I would have died."

"No doubt," said Peter. "And because I came back it is almost certain that the other one will die. It was you or Jinben.

That was the choice I had to make. All the time, since this began, that has been the choice I've had to make. You had forgotten him, but I've never stopped thinking about him, hardly for a minute. And always there's been that choice: you or him —right from the first, when the boat was being taken down the river and you were lying there unconscious and I couldn't leave you. And again, when we came close to land, I had to stay ...

"And then, today, I went so far. I found that camp beside the creek. I found those tracks winding far into the hills, and I stood on those tracks, and it was like standing on a road. And I never knew before what the real thing is about a road. A road is a wonderful thing, a road is a thing that shows you the way to go. You see? At last I knew the way to go ...

"That's where I stood, trying to decide. You or him? I closed my eyes and prayed for guidance; and nothing came. I had to decide it for myself. I decided for you. I turned my back on Jinben. I came back. I had to play God like that, and I'm not very good at it, and I came back angry."

But he was no longer angry when he said this. His anger had died in the telling.

Aware of this, James Duncan said aggressively, though a little tentative in his attack, "You wanted to leave me, did you? You closed your eyes and asked God for the guts that needed? Well ... I'm glad that, for once, your friend upstairs was busy somewhere else. But I'll tell you what. Suppose you left me here deserted, and I died, and then Jinben died as well, in spite of your decision. How would that have been? Eh? How would that have been? How would you like to have to live with that?"

"I thought of that," said Peter. "Didn't I come back?"

"You think I'm expendable?" said James Duncan. "Something you can use, and throw away? Look, you fool! Can't you see? You'll need me yet. Maybe you're not as smart as you might think! You'll need me yet, and bloody badly. Did you think of that?"

His anger was fired by Peter's tired silence.

"Did you?" he cried. "Did you think of that? No? Then listen, friend . . . coming back was the only thing you could have done. You had no choice, no choice at all. You've learned a little from what I did to help you but by Jesus Christ you haven't learned it all! You'll need me, and you'd better not forget it. So don't you try and take it out on me! Now I've waited long enough. I want a drink. Is that water in the tin?"

Peter did not answer.

James Duncan said harshly, "Answer me, you sulky bastard. Is that water you brought back?"

"Yes," said Peter softly, and rolled over, turning his face away.

James Duncan drank long and deep. He rebuilt his bed of grass beside the fire. He lay gazing at the sky, and the frigid brilliance of the stars seemed to cool the warmth of anger in his heart, leaving coldness there at the thought of his tough ingratitude.

"Peter?" he said somewhat later. "Thank you for coming back. I'm sorry."

But all he had for answer was the heavy breath of his companion's exhausted sleep.

He was troubled for a while, and yet, going over it, he could not see that he could have handled it in any other way. It was one of those battles which had to be fought. There had to be a winner, and a loser. All words, perhaps, but in those words his life had been at stake, and any man must speak up for his life. With Peter in that mood, tomorrow would have been impossible. Now it would be different.

How long would it take to travel seven miles, he wondered, and how much further would they have to go?

Eight days left. Would those eight days prove enough?

He thought of Jinben, and of his eight more mornings to that final trembling walk from prison cell to dreadful fate.

What must it be like to wake to such a dawn? What would a man do? Would he weep? Scream? Discover some resource of courage that would last the little time it took?

He pictured a sleeping figure bundled in rough bedclothes,

turned in sleep to face the wall. An anonymous hand touched the dormant shoulder, the face turned into view, innocent, smoothed by sleep, eyes starting suddenly in fearful recollection.

The face was Peter's.

That was wrong. It was not Peter, but a different dark man who was threatened. Another man, unknown.

Close to sleep, James Duncan smiled; in drowsy reverie he almost laughed, for he had seen the structure of a most peculiar truth.

All this time, hidden somewhere in his mind, the image of the threatened man, the unknown face of Jimmy Jinben, had been for him the face of Peter. Peter had been the one who must be saved.

He brought himself awake and the stars above shifted into sharply focused points of light, a spread of crystal fragments on a velvet cloth and, awake, it did not change. Peter remained the one.

All along, in unrecognized confusion, that strangely hidden identification of Peter with the threatened man had been working in his mind, the certain source of many of his actions. This alone had brought him to this most unlikely, inexplicable adventure.

Seen from the first, Peter's lovable and serious goodness, unconsciously confused with the unknown features of that other man, had made the fate of Jinben of most urgent and personal concern. Right from where it all began. Straight off, he had wanted to be of whatever help he could to Peter.

And now? What happened now, when this was seen? Faceless now, not really ever known, did Jinben cease to count for anything? Could he be dismissed, belatedly, because not known? Imagined, most stupidly, as someone else?

Reflecting on this, James Duncan drifted again toward the fitful images of sleep.

He slept, and his dream was a dream of sleeping. Of being wakened by a hand upon his shoulder, of opening frightened eyes and seeing barred light from the dim square of the dark cell's window. He dreamed that he had been awakened to the last dawn of his life.

He jerked his mind away from this short and awful dream, which had been a kind of parable, an image of sleep doing what no conscious thought could do.

And he knew. He knew at once that it mattered, very much, about Jinben. That it would matter very much about any man. Because any man could have been him, and he could have been any other man.

It was as simple as that, and it was strange that people didn't know this, didn't talk about it, didn't think. He did not understand it, but he knew it now for utter truth that there was no man in this time on earth that he could not, by some changed chance, have been.

He sighed. He would try to remember this.

Reaching the brink of proper sleep, he thought of Wendy. He reached for her breast with a hand not conscious of its movement and in a faint rousing of those loins so sluggish from privation found fleeting recollection of life's illusory contentments.

The dream of Wendy went with him to the deepest hours of night. When cold stirred him and, shivering, he woke, the coldness was at first the cold of the dreamed bed from which the warm, dreamed Wendy had gone.

Hearing the sea, he had to leave the dream. He had to accept the hard facts of present circumstance. Lying on a cold beach beside a burned-out fire. The fogged light of dawn across the sky. Stars which had lost their full antarctic clarity and splendor. Sullen waves of sound washing the reefs in the dawn sea's uneasy motion.

He shivered again.

"Peter," he said loudly. "Peter. Is it time to go?"

Curled in sleep, Peter sighed in protest. His breathing changed to snoring. It was light enough to see him lying, wound up like a sleeping dog, wasting no part of his body's warmth.

Going around the dead fire, James Duncan kneeled.

Waking Peter, seeing Peter turn his face, calm and expressionless from sleep, then startled, alert, fearful perhaps, he saw his hand on Peter's shoulder as that warder's hand he had imagined. In this vision he saw Peter as the man condemned, about to be told of those few, strictly counted minutes of remaining life.

"Hurry," he said, with helpless urgency. "Oh come. Wake up. We have to hurry."

"Right." Peter was calm and wide awake. "Let's go."

Peter rose and stretched and yawned. He turned to relieve himself against a rock. He offered the tin of water and they drank.

Peter took the tin in the crook of an arm and started up the cliff. Following, James Duncan wanted there to be more to abandoning this place than that. A gathering of possessions, a glance around to make sure nothing had been left that should be taken. Acknowledgment of some kind that they had lived here, were leaving, and never would be coming back.

But Peter went on, climbing steadily, never more obviously a man whose ancestry had known that most radical of freedoms, the freedom of tribes sufficient unto themselves. Nomads, coming to such a place as this with almost nothing; spears, digging sticks, nets of string knotted from human hair; they would coax to life a tiny spot of fire from the end of a pointed stick, as Peter had created that fire, now left behind, now ashes.

Bringing nothing, staying as long as the impulse to remain might last, they would move on in this way, taking nothing, without a backward glance.

We are the ones who have tied ourselves in knots, James Duncan thought, reaching with stiff legs for the steep grade of the cliff. We've been tied right up by the million things we've made. Tied by our compulsion to own so much.

But, for all that, he could not go like this. While Peter continued on, he stopped and turned. He looked at the scuffled beach, the ashes of the fire, the scattering of mussel shells. He saw the pool where he had hunted and killed the octopus, the depression in the rock that had saved them with its water.

Peter turned. "What's the trouble?"

"It wasn't a bad place," said James Duncan. "I was just . . ."

"All right as long as the water lasted. Nothing there now."

Nothing; there; now.

A dry rock where water had been waiting.

Footprints.

Ashes.

Nothing . . .

At the top of the cliff they entered scrub and the beach was lost to sight. Back on the hill, sea winds had tangled the stunted trees and for some distance this made strenuous going. On the backslope of the ridge the trees were better spaced. They had room to walk between the trees on dark sand layered deep with tiny fallen leaves.

"Time for a rest," said James Duncan when they reached this easier walking.

"We've hardly started," said Peter.

"Far enough for me." James Duncan said this firmly, and seated himself against a tree. Considering his weakness of the day before he thought he'd done astonishingly well and would have liked to be given credit for getting up the cliff and through the scrub before he needed to propose a rest.

Now on this almost level ground with the pleasant carpet of dry leaves underfoot, he would do even better.

He was consequently surprised, when he rose to his feet after resting, to discover himself as stiff and weary as when he stopped. He had been cheated.

They had hardly started. Surprise at his feebleness became panic when he realized how far they had to go. It had never happened this way before. To become stiff and tired was natural; you accepted that. You rested and slept, ate and drank. Your strength came back. You became as good as new.

"I'm no better," he said miserably. "I'm as weak and stiff as when we stopped."

Peter studied him, evidently seeing something in his appearance to soften his impatience.

"You'll be all right," he said, with his old gentleness. "Have a drink."

"Should I? Will the water last?"

"Do you want a drink?"

"I do. Yes."

"Then have one."

He drank without further question. But the water had to last two days, and at this rate it wouldn't. Was Peter hoping to make all that distance in one day? They wouldn't, no matter how much Peter hoped they would, and the water would be gone.

Peter helped him up and he swayed on those leaden props which once were legs. He commanded those legs to go on walking, but the mere command was not enough to overcome their gross reluctance. He had to raise one leg and swing it forward, place it to take its share of weight, and then direct the other leg, as studiedly. After a dozen steps a slow and awkward gait became established, he was able to walk without having to give instructions to each muscle. Seeing he could walk for a while unaided, Peter went ahead to find the easiest path along the siding of the hill.

The sun appeared in morning mildness. For a time it didn't seem too bad to be walking in these conditions of temperate sun and easy going. But this lasted only until Peter, who had been leading an increasingly devious course to avoid frequent thickets, came to the sharp fall of a gully cutting across the hill. Peter halted.

James Duncan came up, and they stood examining the solid growth that choked the gully.

"I came further inland than yesterday," said Peter. "Hoped it would be better. But it's just as bad."

"There'll be a way around," said James Duncan. He expected Peter to agree. The gully was impossible.

"There isn't. I tried that yesterday. It's like this right down to the sea, and there the cliff's too steep to get around. I tried that, and I got stuck. I didn't think I was going to get back. I had to crash through the scrub in the end, and that's what we have to do."

Peter waited for no more talk. He scrambled down the bank and hit the scrub, and James Duncan knew he had to follow.

He crouched on hands and knees, and backed down after Peter. His feet slipped away and he bumped for several yards until his feet propped on the butt of a leaning tree. He was able to stand again, and turn around.

Instead of wriggling through the undergrowth, as on his own he might have done without such effort, Peter wrenched and kicked to make a track. His loud progress roused the birds of the gully to a screeching chorus of alarm.

As they crawled deeper into the gully the continued screaming of the birds became the sound of a nightmare ordeal that could never have an end. The sun filled the trapped, breathless air with choking heat. Sweat caked the dust on their faces. Flying, crawling, stinging insects needled their itching flesh; sharp branches snagged and scratched at every step. The limbs, roots, and branches of a thousand trees gathered close, as in an ugly conspiracy to hold them there forever and when it was over have their bones.

Sobbing for breath, James Duncan crawled, while Peter threw himself ahead, turning to pull the white man after him, forcing an opening for a few scant further yards, turning to drag him on again. And all this seemed to happen in the same place as if, for all this effort, they made no progress. Then the slope of the gully changed, and it was worse. They began to fight their way uphill instead of down.

"Rest now," said Peter. "I'll go on a way to break track out."

James Duncan watched him go, a long scratch on his satin-dark, bare shoulder defined by beads of blood. He lay back and groaned, calculating that they had come, at most, a mile, thinking of the other miles ahead.

Yesterday, and he realized this for the first time, Peter had crossed this awful gully twice. And he had wondered that Peter should be angry and exhausted last night. Peter had come straight from this.

It would have been, at that time last night, quite dark. Crashing through this fearful tangle in darkness was something beyond imagination.

The water tin was standing near. He tipped it as he lay and guided water to his mouth.

He shook the tin to feel the water moving, to judge how much there was, hoping the answer would justify the drinking of a little more.

No. Peter would need a drink. He deserved it, surely.

He rolled over and set himself on both knees and a hand, holding the tin in the other arm. He set himself like a runner braced in the chocks listening for the starting signal.

"Go," he whispered. "Move."

He crawled after Peter, humiliated that Peter should have to work so hard on his behalf. The ground was very steep. He had to use both hands to drag himself against the slope. He had to place the tin as far as he could reach ahead, come to the tin, put it ahead again, drag up to it.

He came to Peter. Peter turned. Kneeling, James Duncan held up the tin.

"Thank you," said Peter gravely, squatting, tipping back his head to drink. "Thank you."

"I had some," said James Duncan. "I didn't ask you if I could."

"Do you have to ask?"

"I should. That water's yours. You went all that way and found it. Carried it back. You brought it through this awful place. In the dark. I didn't know."

"We had to have it."

"I'm terribly sorry you had to come back for me."

"What I said last night . . ." said Peter. "I didn't mean it."

"I'll keep going as long as I can move," said James Duncan. "Until I fall unconscious."

"We're in the worst part now," said Peter, pushing his shoulder into a mat of branches until it yielded. "Nearly through."

He hurled himself at the scrub, and for a long time they continued upward, until the slope became more easy. The scrub thinned, an occasional gap appeared, so that the sun came through and splashed the starving ground with golden light. Sharply trimmed by shadow, the sun's bright patches looked like patterns of holes scissored in brown paper.

But there was no sudden change from steep gully to easy hill.

Blindly crawling behind Peter, James Duncan in the end gave up hope that it would ever get much better. He would go on like this all day, eyes half closed, banging and scratching himself, pushed this way and that by twisted limbs, barbed sticks and branches, tangled roots. He would crawl with his nose inches above this ground which stank of ants and rotten wood. He would keep going as long as he could. He had promised Peter. But they would never make it through. If it were not for his promise he would give up now.

Then, at last, Peter's crashing progress came abruptly to an end. Peter was helping him to stand. His eyes had opened to a glaring sun that had no shadows.

"That's it," said Peter. "A little more and we will rest."

They were on even ground with room to walk abreast, so that James Duncan could gain support from an arm on Peter's shoulders. His legs dragged. More and more Peter seemed to carry him.

"All right," said Peter. "We'll rest."

They lay on stiff grass in the shadow of a tree. They drank again, and the tin was almost empty. James Duncan dozed. When he awoke the almost empty tin was the first thing he remembered.

Peter was lying with clasped hands behind his head looking into the branches overhead, or perhaps beyond the branches, through the tree, to pure sculptured domes of cloud which had piled to enormous heights above.

Peter was gazing at these things above him with a peaceful and relaxed expression, and when he heard James Duncan stir and saw he was awake, he smiled.

"Ready to go?" said Peter. "Have a drink."

"It's almost finished," said James Duncan, licking lips

parched from sleep and wishing this didn't have to be said. "We should keep what's left."

"Drink it. The tin will be easier to carry empty."

"No. We'll need it. Listen, we're not going to get there today. We must have water tonight, and tomorrow. We can't just take a drink every time we want it."

Peter had the unconscious smile of a man with a secret, of someone withholding information.

James Duncan studied him uneasily. "What is it? What is it you aren't telling me?"

"I think we can make it today," said Peter. "We have to try. But, even if we don't, I'll see you have sufficient water."

"Where will you get it?"

"Stop worrying," said Peter. "Drink what's left."

When James Duncan drank he found so little water in the tin that it seemed childish to have fussed.

Moving into afternoon, the sun blazed down with an intensity of heat. Low shrubs between the trees began to crack with dryness. Pods on vines snapped open with faint, clear reports and scattered seed. Sweat dried on skin as soon as it was formed.

They came to the edge of another gully and James Duncan looked across the knitted trees with dread, but Peter turned toward the coast.

They walked in the loose gray sand of a windscour, trees growing thick on one side, the gully scrub on the other, so that their steps were channeled to a narrow track of windblown sand, so formal, neat, and narrow that human traffic might have made it. Almost, it seemed, the prints of human feet could be expected.

Pulled back sharply by Peter, James Duncan, lurching forward half a step, felt a queer resistance fall across his brow.

Head down, he caught the movement of a spider of phenomenal size scuttling from the shoulder of his ripped shirt to his chest.

The spider paused at the opening of the shirt. It was inches across, bloated and hairy of body, posed on legs as pointed, tensile, and glistening as drawn steel wire. James Duncan gave a cry of loathing. The spider flickered around the opening of the shirt and disappeared inside. He felt the fur of the horrid body brushing on his skin, the vibrant scrambling of those evil legs.

Before he could scream, or beat at his chest to kill the thing, or tear the shirt from his body; before any quivering reflex could be followed, Peter had swung an open hand in a powerful swing that knocked him breathless. He staggered under the blow, and fell, feeling on his skin the spider squashed to cold, damp mush. Shuddering, he looked at the brown stain spreading on his shirt.

"A big one," said Peter calmly.

James Duncan brushed at the stickiness of the web on his forehead, trying to make the feeling of the web, the awful feeling of the spider on his chest, go away.

"Poisonous?" he questioned weakly.

"Did it bite?"

"No, thank Christ."

"No," said Peter with a smile. "You'd have jumped a mile, I reckon."

James Duncan rolled his shirt and scrubbed the remnants of the spider from his chest.

Peter went aside and found a stick. "I'll knock them down," he said. "There must be hundreds. Look at the webs, all along. I suppose the insects fly down here between the trees. I've never seen so many."

"Give it to me," said James Duncan vindictively. "I'll fix the bastards!"

He slashed savagely ahead and upward as he walked, until the stick was wound with viscous web. From the broken webs, spiders of every size and shape and color dropped to the ground and scuttled away to hiding.

Giant spiders and small; black, brown, and gray; bodies hairy, or smooth in ghastly bloated nakedness; spiders tipped with yellow, tipped with orange, with red; legs furred and bent, or fiercely cocked in that wiry, glistening stance.

"I wouldn't like to walk here in the dark," said Peter.

James Duncan made a stifled sick sound in his throat. He hit out with the stick, staring at the spiders posed at the centers of their webs, spread out and pinned up there, like some monstrous entomological collection.

Peter took the stick, and James Duncan lagged behind. When they came at last to the top of sandy dunes and saw and heard the sea his legs folded beneath him of their own accord. He sank to his knees.

"Not here," said Peter. "Can't rest here. Not out in the sun."

James Duncan looked up, begging. "For a minute? Please?"

Peter moved so that his shadow fell on the prone man, who lay on his side cushioned on a bed of scorching sand, gasping in the effort to draw that one deep breath which, by some magic dimly comprehended, would reach to every corner of his lungs and bring back . . . or it seemed to him it might . . . some of his departed stamina and resolution.

But it was like trying to yawn when you wanted to yawn and couldn't; the same barrier foiled his breathing. There was a point in his breathing he couldn't pass, and at that point he had to breathe out and try again.

Peter, watching, bowing his head to the heat which came from the steely sky above in throbbing waves, was alarmed by these failing efforts James Duncan made to draw a proper breath.

He bent and lifted him. He started down the dune with plunging steps. Scraping a wavering scrawl, the white man's feet trailed out behind.

Staggering, Peter crossed the beach right into the water, until mild waves were lapping at his waist. He let James Duncan lie immersed, holding his face clear of the waves, and soon the white man gasped and drew the whole, deep breath he had been seeking. In his face Peter could see the change, the return of life and will.

"Thought you'd had a heart attack or something," he said, in great relief. "Feel better now?"

James Duncan nodded.

"We'll take it slowly," said Peter. "Give you plenty of time."

He studied the shore. He judged the soak he'd found the day before to be about a mile along the coast. He had been careful not to mention this, because, if they'd gone as well today as he had hoped, they would have gone right past. The white man would never have known the soak existed.

Peter had considered this small deceit well justified. With no more water in the can, believing the creek to be the nearest source of water, James Duncan surely would have expended every possible degree of effort to reach that water, and had he been a little stronger it could have worked.

Holding him now, watching his face, Peter had to concede that no conceivable spur would prod this sick man any further.

He must be taken out of the sun and allowed to rest, and it would be easier to move him in the water than in any other way.

"We have to get you out of the sun," Peter said, pointing. "Along there. Under the trees."

But James Duncan didn't look ashore to see trees merged with scrub where another gully met the sea, cliffs beyond the gully, a short beach stopped by rocks at the steep cliff's base. He tried to smile at Peter.

"Out of the sun. Yes. I'll be all right."

Peter towed him through the water, resting when a wave ran out and left it shallow, hurrying when the next wave made it deep.

They came ashore opposite the gully, and James Duncan bore some of his own weight as they crossed the beach to shade.

Might he not, then, recover as suddenly as he had failed? Peter decided to say nothing yet about the soak.

"Will we be staying here?" James Duncan, stretched out, looked gratefully to the branches which provided blessed shade.

"For a little while."

"No. I mean . . . will we stay? Camp? Until tomorrow?"

"No water here," said Peter, looking away.

"You said . . ."

"We have to go as far as we can," said Peter sternly. "You

know that. You can rest here for a time while I go away and hunt."

"Hunt?"

"Look for food."

"Far?"

"No. I'll be back quite soon."

"You're going to leave me," James Duncan cried in a weak voice, pushing at the ground and trying to sit up. "Oh please ... please Peter, wait. I beg you to wait. I'll come too."

"Lie down. You have to rest."

"What is it you're hiding? What are you ashamed of? You're going to leave me. That's why you will not meet my eyes. You'll leave me here to die. And save him."

"No."

"I beg you. Listen. You won't be able to save him without my help. You *must* believe me. You'll need me. Take me with you. I can walk, I tell you! Lift me up and you will see."

"You have to rest."

"Help me up. I beg you."

"That's enough. I'll stay. But you must stop this talking. You must be quiet. You must trust me."

"You swear you'll stay? Beside me all the time?"

"I swear it."

James Duncan closed his eyes but, even after Peter thought he slept, one eye opened cautiously and sought him, and closed again.

I could tell him about the soak, thought Peter, and that would ease his mind. He'd understand what it is that I've been hiding. I could tell him why. It seemed so harmless, and it seems so childishly deceitful now. But the mere existence of this secret, which he has sensed, has destroyed the growing trust between us. And that's of great importance to him. Yes, and so it is to me. As important for me as it is for him. This little thing has turned out to be bigger than I thought.

Yet, was it such a little thing? Could there ever be a little lie; a small deceit? Perhaps deception was an all-or-nothing thing?

It was. Either you trusted a man, or you didn't.

If you trusted him, you trusted him completely.

If you didn't, then you trusted him with nothing.

It seemed likely, as he considered it, that there might be no degrees—no measuring scale—of trust. If a man would tell one lie, he would tell another. If that man would engage in a single small deceit, how could you ever be sure that he had stopped at that? And what else was trusting but, simply, being sure?

When next the sleepy eye of James Duncan peeped open, it was as if his voice had said aloud . . . "I am sorry, Peter. You have deceived me. Therefore I can never trust you. Never, never again."

"Listen," cried Peter. "Open your eyes and listen."

Startled, James Duncan stared wide-eyed.

"Listen," said Peter in a calmer voice. "I didn't tell you what I discovered yesterday. Just past here I was going along the rocks, and there's a green, slippery kind of weed that grows where fresh water runs on rocks into the sea. Stuff that looks like seaweed, only it's not. Even if the water isn't running, if it's a soak or something, this weed will grow like that. And that's what I was watching for. That green weed. And I found some there. A bit past here. About a mile. You understand?"

James Duncan's eyes, now fixed on his, were wide. Like the eyes of a child hearing a bedtime story.

"I followed the weed back across the rocks, and it stopped. Water from a soak . . . well, it often runs beneath the sand. I knew there was water there. Knew I could find it. So I went back to the foot of the cliff and I saw a clump of grass that was greener than it should have been, and I pulled it up. And there was dirt there, black dirt, and the dirt was wet. So I scooped down in the dirt with my hands, and soon my hands were muddy, the dirt was as wet as that. I knew there would be some water gathered in this hole I made. I knew we would be all right.

"But I thought I'd go some distance more. I'd only come this little way, and I thought I should go along there and see what it was like. So I did. I went along the rocks. After I'd been going a long time I saw a different kind of tree away ahead. The top of it. Shiny leaves. A different color from the rest. I wanted to see it closer. I wanted to know why it wasn't like the others. Perhaps it was a kind of tree that only grows near water.

"I went on longer than I meant. That's why I came back late. I went on until I came to the creek and the place where the camp had been. That's where that dark green tree was growing, with its shiny leaves, and its top sticking out above the others.

"I brought water from the creek in that tin because I didn't know how much would have come up in the soak. But the soak had two or three inches of good water when I looked when I was coming back. It's good water; I tasted it. Only about a mile from here. We can camp there."

"You didn't tell me."

"No," said Peter, wanting to look away but sure that if he failed to meet those doubting eyes their lost trust would be lost forever. "I didn't tell you."

"Why?"

"That's the trouble. That's why I am telling you. I didn't think it mattered. I supposed that if we finished the water and you thought we had to go all the way to the creek to get more, then . . . well, I thought this would help you to get there."

"And if I knew there was water halfway, you thought that's as far as I would go?"

"Not exactly. I . . ."

"You think I'm malingering? You think I'm lying here because I'm lazy?"

"You're sick. I know that now."

"Sick?" cried James Duncan. "I'm not *sick*. I'm *old*. I've twenty years on you. I'm damn near twice your age. God damn you, if I was your age I'd have walked you off your bloody feet! Didn't I get through that death march in Germany, through the snow, when the Russians were breaking through? Didn't I see men who thought they were better men than me drop out . . . weeping, lying there . . . dying in the snow? Didn't I come through? All right. That was twenty years ago. I'm old. That's all that's wrong with me."

"You thought I was hiding something," said Peter. "Now I've told you. That's what I was hiding. I'm properly ashamed of myself. I'll never do such a rotten thing again."

"Damn you!" James Duncan shouted weakly, not listening. "Get me on my feet. I'll go to your creek! I'll show you there's no need for you to trick me. Come on, get me on my feet. I'll get to your fucking creek!"

"I said I was sorry. What else can I say?"

"Well, God damn and blast you . . . I'll do it by myself." James Duncan rolled over so he could reach the nearest tree. At his first attempt to grip the weathered trunk, bark came away like strips of paper in his hands. He tried again, and grasped the tree. He raised himself and stood there swaying, confronting Peter with glaring eyes.

"Come on," he said thickly. "Bugger you, let's get going."

He staggered to the beach, and Peter tried to help, only to have the assistance of his arm brushed clear.

He followed close, ready to catch James Duncan if he fell, but he didn't fall. He walked unsteadily along the beach right to the rocks, with his hands bunched tight in fists beside him, as if the grip of his hands would move him on.

They reached the rocks, and James Duncan turned. He examined Peter scornfully.

"What have you done with the tin?"

Peter raised his empty hands. "I . . . I left it. Back on the beach. When I was helping you. I needed my hands."

"Go and get it. How do you know we won't need that tin again?"

Peter hurried away obediently.

He's acting like a child, Peter thought, as his feet made urgent slappings on the hard, wet sand. Like a child. Angry. Showing me what he can do. Yet, in acting that way, doing exactly what I hoped to achieve with my stupid, mean deception. Prompted as effectively by temper as he would have been driven by the fear of thirst. I didn't think to make use of his temper, thought Peter, but I didn't hesitate to take advantage of his fears.

He suspected he had attempted a worse thing against the white man than merely to deceive him.

James Duncan had gone on by himself a hundred yards, using the larger rocks to help him along, using his hands to support himself while his feet stepped slow among the boulders. He had come to a shelf of rock too high to climb. When Peter came back he was standing there, facing the rock, leaning on his hands against it.

"Help me up, bugger you," he said testily. "You want me to get through this stuff you're going to have to help me. Give me a leg up."

Bending, Peter gripped a leg and lifted with all his strength, so that James Duncan came several inches off the ground. His weak arms folded, and he fell quite heavily against the rock. Quickly, Peter let him down, and both stood, breathing heavily, James Duncan glaring, Peter flinching as he awaited the curses he saw were coming.

"God damn you!" said James Duncan, weak but furious. "Not that way, you bloody halfwit boong. Get up there and pull me up."

"Yes, Mr. Duncan," said Peter submissively. "I'm very sorry. I hope you didn't hurt yourself."

"Hurt myself?" James Duncan had ready another burst of wrath but, rubbing his shoulder where he had fallen, and feeling the first sharp pain receding, he realized that his rage was gone. Unbelievingly, he suspected that he might be going to laugh. Peter's absurd expression of consternation must be causing this peculiar reaction. For there was nothing funny about this, surely.

"Go on, boy," he said mildly. "Get up there and give me a hand."

Peter scrambled up, and reached down with a hand. His eyeballs bulged as he heaved, and using his free hand to help, digging at the rough rock with his feet, James Duncan came up, balanced on his belly, and crawled on top.

"You'll have to wait," he said, lying there. "I can't go on just yet."

"No hurry," said Peter.

"No *hurry?* Well, that's a bloody switch. What made you change your mind?"

"I wish this hadn't got so complicated," said Peter. "I suppose you'll get wild again if I say what I think would now be best?"

"Yes. I might get wild. But then again I mightn't."

"I don't think we should try to make the creek today. Even going slowly we could reach the soak quite soon. Camp there tonight. I'd have time to hunt some food and light a fire. We could rest properly, start off fresh tomorrow."

"Food? What sort of food?"

"Lizards. I don't know. Maybe a snake. Might find some mussels on the rocks."

"You've given up wanting to make the creek?"

"I'm not saying you couldn't get there," said Peter. "But if you did you might have to rest all day tomorrow. Now what would be the sense of that?"

"All right," said James Duncan. "We'll do this the way you want it."

He turned his head to hide another unexpected smile.

14

They left the soak at dawn. Once more, Peter picked up the tin and started walking. Placing sore feet carefully, James Duncan followed. The hard prospect of the day ahead left no room in his thoughts for sentiment. He did not look back to their camping place, and he did not want to. He looked ahead, and was sadly discouraged by what he saw.

Defined in distance by receding planes of mist and light, brutal cliffs as dark as rusted iron charted the bluffs and indentations of the coast.

The loom of the bullying cliffs, reducing choice to a single path which must be followed wherever it might lead, pressed on his mind. Following this only path, dwarfed by the height and scale of this rockbound coast, they could do nothing to prevent it if those stony crags should push them off the land into the sea.

Reason said that Peter had gone this way before and come back safely.

But if weakness grew from day to day, as in your youth strength had, if each day found you weaker, how could you keep your nerve? How could you not become the toy of every doubt that came into your mind?

Of this Peter knew nothing.

Youth granted Peter the confident anticipation of recovered strength whenever he should rest. Youth being his only experienced condition, Peter could not understand that each hard day would drain the fast-failing resources of an older man, so that he could look ahead, and count the days, and say . . . on that day, three days hence, or four, I will wake without the strength to stand up on my feet. Or two days more. Or less. As reasonably, it could be tomorrow.

Peter would suspect him of malingering. He'd try his tricks again; but this time it wouldn't work. And, eventually, Peter would decide to leave him.

Well, damn him, let him go.

Look at him now . . . well ahead already.

James Duncan shouted, and Peter stopped.

"Let's get this straight," James Duncan said, slowly catching up. "If you want to go it alone, you'd better say so. Bloody well say it. Get it over."

Jesus, he muttered savagely, wishing the boot were on the other foot.

"I wasn't thinking," said Peter.

"Let's have it straight. Are you going to leave me?"

"No. I'm sorry. We'll walk together. We'll have a rest around the next point. I'll take it slowly."

While they were resting, the sun rose blazing and with the sun came aggressive swarms of flies from the scrub above the cliffs. The flies were small and black, and, swarming on bare skin, gave a purposeless and irritating sting.

What if you couldn't get away from them! James Duncan jumped to his feet and beat at the whispering insect cloud in sudden panic. They'd drive you mad!

He stumbled away, trying to run and leave the flies behind, but the swarms persisted in maddening flight around his head. He stumbled on and beat wildly at the air with flailing arms, and at last tripped on a rock, and fell.

"Leave me lie," he said, when Peter tried to lift him.

"They've gone," said Peter. "It's all right now."

"Leave me." Pillowed on stones, his feet in a pool of water, James Duncan closed his eyes. He did not care if this should be the end.

Perhaps he slept. He would never know. Some time later, his eyes came open, warily. Had Peter left him?

He could hear someone near, tapping with a rock. He raised his head. Peter was breaking mussels with a stone, beside his hands a meager pile of flesh.

"Peter?"

"Yes?"

"How far do we have to go?"

"To the creek? Three or four miles, I'd say. Not really far."

"And how far then?"

"Your guess is as good as mine on that."

"More than two days?"

"Probably," said Peter, taking up another mussel.

"What will you do? Leave me?"

"Not now. That's all been settled."

"I can't go on much longer. Two days, perhaps. No more."

"We'll see," said Peter.

"You might decide to leave me. To go for help. You might leave me in the night. While I was asleep. I *must* know where I stand."

"It's settled," said Peter. "I will not leave you."

"You promise that?"

"I promise."

"Yes," said James Duncan. "Easy enough to say it."

"I swear it, then. God can be my witness."

"That makes a difference?"

"It does to me," said Peter. "Because I know God hears me. He'll make sure I keep my promise. You don't trust me, I know, but you should believe and trust in God."

"Until yesterday I trusted *you*."

"I have learned from that," said Peter. "I have learned how delicate a thing trust is. I will never make the same mistake again. I swear it, I will never again mislead you."

But he saw by the other's rueful smile that skepticism remained and more than ever the loss of trust was a sad wound in his heart. Yet the firmness of his promise helped. Any man must, to some extent, feel himself ennobled by such a vow, by swearing to be faithful unto death. And it might be that. His promise could be, so easily, far more fateful than it seemed when these few words had need of being said.

He divided the heap of shell-meat with a finger and they ate their frugal breakfast, a few dripping lumps of viscous flesh, a few swallows of water.

They talked no more, but rose wordless and resumed their way.

Throughout the morning they walked on the ledge that formed a narrowing, difficult path between the dark green sea and the shadowed encroachment of the cliff. On this ledge, boulders and stones of every size and shape scattered themselves in rough profusion. Here and there the sea reached right across and lapped the cliff, and at such places they paused, while Peter decided the easiest way to cross. At times there would be an easy climb around the cliff, and Peter would take that way. Where the cliff was sheer, they waded, arm in arm, finding a careful way across the weeded rocks.

They had little trouble with these crossings until the last was reached. This last crossing came into sudden view as they climbed down a terraced slope of rock around a point.

"You can see now," said Peter. "There are the dunes. Less than a mile. We're almost there."

James Duncan spared a brief glance for their destination, but his eyes returned at once to the hazard that barred their way. In this dangerous gulf waves surged in and out, never still; a rough channel, shallow now and in a moment deep; dark and still, quiet in its flood; then instantly a rocky running turmoil of sound and frothing whirlpool and white rushing current.

"The cliff is steep," he said. "How do we get around?"

"There is no way around the cliff," said Peter.

"How did you do it yesterday?"

"It was high tide then," said Peter. "I swam."

Where the channel met the cliff a blowhole responded to the larger waves. It spoke now, in a booming cough, a heavy, forcefull, and eerie sound.

"You're bloody mad," said James Duncan.

"It's not as deep as it looks," said Peter.

"It wouldn't need to be."

"You'll see," said Peter. "Wait here. I'll cross over with the tin."

The white man stared at him.

"I'll come right back," said Peter. "You needn't worry." He sat on the edge of the channel, studying the sea.

"But Peter . . ."

"Don't put me off," said Peter. "I must watch the waves and time this right."

He leaped down and waded, waist deep, pulling at the water with his hand to help himself along. He waded across in ponderous slow motion. He reached the other side and held to the rock as a wave dragged past, so that only his head was left above the boiling water, but the wave subsided and Peter scrambled out, shaking his body like a dog.

When he turned and waved, his teeth flashed white.

Coming back, he glanced at the waves and dived straight in from the ledge, so that he swam most of the way across. He waded a few steps and held to the rock where James Duncan stood, while a wave pulled at his body. He climbed out. "You see?"

"All right for you," said James Duncan. "I won't be able to go as fast as that. I'll be bowled right over."

"Come on. Slide down."

"Are you *sure* there isn't another way? I'll climb the cliff. Peter . . . I'll . . ."

"This is the only way," said Peter. "Come on. Down you come."

"It isn't that I'm scared . . ." said James Duncan, sitting on the edge and letting his bottom slide. Oh God, though, aren't I scared, he muttered to himself, as he dropped into water to his chest, and a wave bellowed into the cliff, and another followed with a rushing sound and pushed him into Peter. He grabbed at Peter.

"Steady," said Peter. "Wait until I say."

"Now," said Peter, pushing him. "Fast as you can."

They were away from the dry rock at the edge, the other side still far away. His feet slipped and bruised among the boulders, the sea made confusing noises all around and held him back. He felt his legs give out.

"Don't stop," yelled Peter, applying strength to keep him moving.

The sea roared suddenly, James Duncan's feet were swept along the gutter, banging into rocks. He tried to swim but panic and weakness paralyzed his limbs. Heavily, the blowhole exploded into sound.

With one arm Peter was trying to swim for both of them.

"Swim!" cried Peter in a choking voice.

Starting to drown, James Duncan found in his mind the image of that writhing octopus seen, it seemed, so long ago. Vastly expanded, the image showed a dreadful beast of giant size waiting in deep black water somewhere near the blowhole. His limbs found frenzied strength and thrashed at the rushing sea as the falling wave sucked seaward. He bumped around a boulder larger than a man. Behind the boulder lay a magic calm. His feet found rocks. He stood, confused. Running past in violent motion, the water shallowed. His mind cleared slowly and he looked for Peter, and found him close, submerged, not swimming. He reached out but not quite far enough. He took one step, and several more, away from the safety of the boulder.

He gripped Peter, who made swimming movements, feebly. He raised Peter's head. He heard the coming of another wave. Peter shook his head and retched, and blinked his eyes. James Duncan dragged him to the boulder and held him while he waited for the wave, bracing his feet in gaps between the rocks, putting his back against the boulder, watching the wave swell up around them, peak a little, crack open, turn white, reach up to his shoulders. He saw the wave engulfing Peter.

His braced feet barely held. Had the wave been a little bigger it would have swept them both away, but it passed, so slight a wave that it hardly sounded in the blowhole, and suddenly the gutter was shallower than it had been since first he saw it.

The tops of dripping reefs emerged, calmer waters ran out with quiet sounds, so that the perilous channel in this interval between two waves took on the aspect of a mild rock pool. How easy it would be now to wade across.

"Peter!" he cried.

With dazed eyes, Peter stared about him.

Out to sea, another big wave tumbled into sound. Dragged by the arm, Peter followed blindly. Gagging and stumbling, he seemed to move by instinct. As the advancing wave pushed water into swelling depth they reached the rough, sharp-cornered face of the gutter's other edge. The surging mass of the deep green wave was only yards away, and watching it with rage and fear James Duncan wondered in anguish whether those seconds wasted in indecision beside the boulder were a fair price for fate to put on two men's lives.

The knobs and cracks of the wall which trapped them gave rugged handhold. He would hold on as long as he could. When he let go, he would drown. Peter would have to manage for himself. But when the wave, running wild along the narrow confinement of the channel, reached them in a smother of foam and angry sea, Peter had done nothing. Like a stunned ox he stood there, awaiting slaughter. He was swept right off his feet. Flung against James Duncan, he fumbled with instinctive hands for any hold that offered rescue. He flung his arms around the white man, who now felt this double load come on those hand-grips he had hardly dared to hope would be enough for one. But he decided he would not let go. The wave would have to break his hands, or break the rock. He closed his eyes and every fraction of his strength seemed to flow into his clutching fingers.

The channel filled. He was lifted so high that the grip of his hands was now below him. His arms reached underwater to the handhold in the rock. He took a gasping breath as his head went under. He freed one hand for a blind grab higher on the rock. His fingers scraped bare rock, touched a crack, lost it, searched, found the crack again. He moved the other hand to join this chancy grip. His mouth found air. His opened eyes, finding day-light, fixed in an instant glance a limpet plastered to the rock. With fantastic irrelevance he noted an unsuspected beauty in the graded colors of the limpet's shell. Or was it the beauty of seeing the light of day again, of seeing a chance of safety, the top of the ledge within his reach?

As the blowhole boomed, the tide of the channel stilled for a moment at its deepest flood. In this interval of calm James Duncan changed his grip again. His reaching fingers touched a crack beyond the channel's edge and, as the wave subsided, he pulled himself as high as he could go. Feeling Peter's grip sliding with the falling wave, down his legs, past his ankles, at last let go, he dragged himself to safety.

He rolled over, face-down, to see what had become of Peter. Peter was there, in shallow water, crawling on hands and knees.

"Peter," he shouted. "Reach up!"

The next wave was coming in. Peter was not listening. Peter would crawl until the wave came in, and that would be the end.

Unless someone . . .

Someone?

No, not someone. Me!

Unless I . . .

Jump down there and . . .

"Peter!" he cried again, hearing the rough commotion of the new wave coming.

Peter was shaking his head from side to side, looking up.

"Take my hand! Reach up!"

Peter was against the ledge, leaning against it, trying to stand.

He raised a flopping arm. Their fingers met. The wave came racing in. James Duncan's hand closed hard on Peter's wrist. The wave lifted Peter and, seeming almost weightless, he came right up. Miraculously, the dangerous wave did all the work. Peter was lifted so high that even an exhausted man could drag him on the rock to safety.

In safety, laid on the dry rock in the stinging heat of midday sun, Peter made a recovery of surprising speed while beside him James Duncan sought the answer to a question which seemed as momentous as any question in his life.

If Peter had not looked up in time, if Peter had not moved to save himself, would I have tried to save him? Would I have jumped down, certain to be drowned?

I will never know, James Duncan had to tell himself at last. I will never know, if under these fears of mine a spark of genuine braveness burns.

Perversely, he wished he had taken this chance to test his courage.

He pictured the worst happening. Jumping down, finding the bigger wave quite overwhelming. Their drowning bodies tossed among the rocks, hurled into the roaring blowhole, utterly destroyed in one way or another by the remorseless powers of the sea.

And still he wished . . . yes, that he had leaped down, ready to be drowned, if that had been the price to pay to know, for sure, this thing about himself.

Beside him, Peter stirred and raised his head.

"I dunno," said Peter tiredly, like a child. "What happened?"

"We're over," said James Duncan.

"I was swimming. Began to swallow water. Hit something with my head . . . that's all I know. Now I'm not feeling very good."

"Plenty of time. It's barely afternoon."

"It's all right if I rest here for a while?"

"Yes," said James Duncan. "That's certainly the wisest thing to do."

So now the boot *is* on the other foot, he thought, just as I wished this morning. For a little while I'm the strong one, who decides. Though, for sure, I don't feel very strong. But I'm no longer sorry for myself, and that is quite a thing, it seems.

To be the strong one, the one who can't afford self-pity.

How strange, when thought about, was this relationship that formed between two men in adjustment to the relative strength of each.

Peter doesn't feel so good. He's sorry for himself. And because of that I feel new forces running in my blood.

Yes, he assured himself in his musings, I *would* have jumped down to save him had that been really needed; I would, I'm almost sure of that.

But Peter, indeed, recovered quickly. Minutes later, when he rose to his feet, he did so with the wonderful agility of youth. "I guess we can go on now," he said, taking command so naturally that it couldn't be resented. James Duncan, measuring his degree of exhaustion, stifled a groan and silently agreed to be the weaker man again.

"Not far now," said Peter.

No, James Duncan thought, not far now. Not very far for me.

Around the bluff beyond the channel a wider scene revealed dramatic changes. The cliff became an easier slope, leaning from the sea, turning inland, shouldered by a massive ridge of sand. A crescent of sparkling beach received the curved, concentric lines of breakers, neat white lines scribed and distanced gracefully on a dark blue sea. They could see the fold in the dunes that hid the creek, the verdant heads of proper trees, the shining top of Peter's tree, that dark tree standing beyond all others, like no tree he knew, which had led Peter to the creek.

Peter displayed this wordlessly, with the sweeping movement of a hand, like a host offering his house and all it held to an honored guest, and stood there smiling.

"It looks ... yes, it's beautiful," said James Duncan. It seemed expected.

Peter led him away from the sea, up the loose slope of the windblown dune, and the soft sand, giving at each step, robbing each step of half its length, became as endless as a treadmill. When he reached the top, and saw the valley of the creek, even fancied he saw the glint of water from a pool, James Duncan decided that the most welcome feature of this scene was that the last steps to their goal would all be on a downward slope. At first he was conscious only of this physical relief. It was not far now, and all downhill. A few more steps, easier than any other effort the day had needed, and they'd be there. They would reach the place where they would rest.

But there was more to it than that, he saw, something quietly dramatic. A moment in life that was distinguished, as few of life's moments were, by an element of style and drama. You had toiled and suffered on the long slow ascent of one of life's steepest pitches. You came to the top; you stood on the brow of that last steep hill, gazing on the promised land.

Something like that, something symbolic that dignified an ordinary event. You caught something of that elusive mystery behind the physical acts of man, that secret force that could make sense, of a kind, of the manifold randomness of man's physical experience.

Spirit, will, emotion ... you could give that force a dozen

different names. Seeing now from the last hill this place that had been promised him, this promised land of Peter's, he felt hope rising in his heart.

Seeing those trees, those real trees which Peter had described, raising their noble heads above the common drabness of the scrub; seeing the level grass beside the creek, the creek itself, the fleeting shine of light on the waters of a pool; knowing this to be a place where other men had lived, even able to imagine as he looked, the paths they would take in their goings and their comings; James Duncan found will, as well as hope, renewed.

For the moment feeling almost strong enough to run, he hurried down the hill.

"Where is their camp?" he cried, as they came to level ground. He followed Peter to the place beside the creek, and gazed in simple wonderment at scattered rubbish. Stiffly, he knelt, to touch these abandoned artifacts as if they were as rare as those of a fabled culture thought lost in time's impenetrable shade, now found again.

"Fosters Lager," he whispered, reading from a rusted can. "Fosters *Lager!*"

He wandered bemused among the tins, the cigarette packets, the cardboard cartons beaten flat by storms. He found the tracks of the jeep, and followed them. Without volition, he began to walk along the tracks as though a supernatural voice was calling . . . a siren, a piper, the fancied sounds of fairy music. His yearning to be among those men, those people, cities, safeties, certainties, to which these tracks would lead, almost made him weep.

He heard Peter shouting, and the sound of Peter's voice was like the breaking of a spell. As if a mirage, seen for what it was, had turned invisible. He returned to the creek.

Peter was rubbing a short, dry stick on a stone beside the creek to make a point.

"Don't go away," he said mildly. "We have to light a fire."

"Ah, Peter," said James Duncan. "I'm so grateful that you found this place. You could have turned back so easily before you reached it."

"Sooner or later we'd have come here."

"Would we? I wonder . . ." He was so happy that he wanted to find more praise for Peter, but Peter went looking for the stuff he needed for his fire.

Peter came back and squatted on the ground with the fire's first leaves and twigs arranged beside him. He took from his pocket the shell they had used to give the top of their firestick a smoother bearing.

"You thought to bring it with you?" said James Duncan. "Ah, Peter. You're a bloody genius. You think of everything."

Recognizing in these jovial words the precarious nature of this present mood of happiness, he at once mislaid his optimism.

He wondered at this foolishness. Tomorrow they must suffer again, and the day after that, and the next. Looking ahead, how faint was any chance of happiness.

He bore down on the firestick which Peter rubbed between his hands with movements of inhuman speed. The first spark was a long time coming, but there could be no pause. Resting for the briefest instant they must start again, right from the very start. Even if his arms should ache beyond endurance, with no sign seen of smoke or spark, there could be no rest.

He wanted to tell Peter to give up. They could do without a fire.

But Peter would hunt in the few hours left of daylight. Peter might find a snake. The lizards had been very good last night, but snake was better, Peter said. Snake was white and sweet, like chicken. But who would want to eat *raw* snake? This effort could be borne a little longer.

Sweat ran on Peter's face; he panted for breath. Now they could smell the coming fire that couldn't yet be seen, and there at last it was, thin smoke wisping at the bottom of the stick, Peter hurling the stick away and blowing like a madman on the spark; and there was flame, licking in fibers of teased-out bark, there was flame gone, only smoke; there was flame again, Peter laying twigs with utmost care. More twigs, thicker. Smoke and flame. There was fire.

Peter waved a tired arm, and rested. James Duncan fed the fire with sticks placed gingerly. Branches went on. Soon they had to move back from the heat.

"I'm off," said Peter. "See what I can find to eat. Might be a good idea, when you've rested for a while, collect some of those beer cans, put water in them. Break off sticks and hit them in to plug the holes. Be a good idea tomorrow to take all the water we can carry. The big tin, and maybe three or four little ones. Keep us going for several days."

Several days? Who did he think he was fooling?

15

They had to leave the creek; he did not question that. But it was a place he would not forget.

Resting a few days there, James Duncan told himself, a few days with the water and the food and the blessed peaceful shelter of that place and I would have been my old self once more, able to walk with Peter step for step. We couldn't stay, I know. I might as well forget that place, remembering only the pressing need for haste, the life that might be decided by how fast we go. Though I would like Jinben to know, somehow, how much this haste is costing me, how much I've suffered, and how much more I'll maybe suffer yet, on his behalf.

He had been drinking from one of the cans filled at the creek the day before, the simple pleasures of that useful task vividly remembered. He had enjoyed again, in recollection, the coolness of that pool shaded and colored by the changing light of overhanging trees, the big trees above that whispered in the breeze while the gulping cans blew streams of bubbles that had the rainbowed, changing gleam of pearls.

And now the can was empty; he held it in his hand.

Now they had left that pleasure of coolness and sweetness, that haven, far behind. It was gone forever now, by a distance difficult to measure; a distance not to be determined by the scant miles they had come but by the hundreds—no, thousands surely—of forced reluctant steps; by the long cruel hours of day, by the slow changes of the dreary desert the tracks of the jeep had tempted them to challenge.

The track had run in the valley, for a while, with the creek, and that had been quite good, to have the creek beside them. But the track turned sharply, up a ridge, out across the top, to a desert of mean bushes, harsh tussocks, grasstrees and naked stones, mile after mile unchanged.

The track had led them to where he was now, resting in the miserly shade of a rare tree, or more exactly a bush a little larger than the others, while Peter, holding little hope of finding anything worth killing, had gone off hunting.

Sure enough, James Duncan thought, throwing the empty can away, tomorrow will be my last day. Tomorrow, and then a question mark. God knows what will happen. And even tomorrow he won't get much out of me. Not as far as today. I'll walk as far as I can and I'll pitch it in. Let Peter press on, alone. I'll tell him. I'll release him from his promise. Perhaps I will wander alone, downhill, back to the creek. I mightn't mind so much, dying there.

Peter came back, emptyhanded. Without a word he sprawled on the ground, resting, before they went on, side by side, stumbling across the tussocks of that cursed, stabbing grass, James Duncan with a heavy arm on Peter's shoulder.

Several times again they rested, and then the sun went down and they stopped for the night. Without food or fire, without even the shelter of a tree, they made their camp. Though how could that be called a camp?

They stopped in the dusk, lay in a patch of sand marked faintly by the jeep; night fell, and this was the end of that day.

In darkness, unable to tell whether it was late night or early morning, James Duncan was called awake.

"Wake up," Peter was saying. "Listen."

It was cold. So cold it would be difficult to sleep again.

"Why did you wake me?" James Duncan grumbled.

"Listen," said Peter. "It will start again."

James Duncan strained to hear the sound which had aroused Peter to such excitement and, faintly, at last it came. Somewhere in this arid waste a calf was calling, a sound forlorn as any a beast could make.

"What does it mean?" whispered James Duncan, knowing

that the elusive hope leaping in his heart was the hope that excited Peter. What did it mean? It was almost as good as hearing
the echoes of a human voice. The first human sound we've
heard, he thought, though that was wrong, of course. But the
sound was firmly related in experience to the presence of men.
Men, somewhere.

"It's a calf, calling to his mother," said Peter. "She hasn't answered. He must be on his own, and if he doesn't stop that noise
the dogs will have him."

"Dogs?"

"Dingoes, I mean. Perhaps that's why he's calling. He might
have heard a dingo, seen one, maybe. When I was hunting I saw
their droppings. The ground scratched up. The way dogs
scratch the ground to hide their droppings."

"You don't get cattle in the bush without men being somewhere near. That's what you're thinking, isn't it?"

"It could be lost. It could have wandered. But yes, I did think
that."

"Tomorrow . . . listen, Peter. Tomorrow, do you want to
leave me? And go on? Do you think that would be better?"

"I promised you I wouldn't."

"But I can change my mind, can't I? Now we're almost
there?"

"It isn't as sure as that," said Peter gently. "Just to hear a calf
calling in the night . . . that isn't enough to be sure. We'll stay
together for a while. Tomorrow, anyway."

"Tomorrow is my last day. After that . . ."

"No," said Peter. "You will find you can go on as long as you
have to. You will see."

"Tomorrow is all I can promise. I'll stand it for another day."

"Yes. See how we go tomorrow."

James Duncan moved the stiffness of his body to an easier position and patiently, but without much confidence, waited for
sleep to take away this night, and this cold desert, and put his
thoughts and senses somewhere else. Anywhere would do.

Despite the omen of the calf's forsaken call, his heart and his
hopes were as cold as the frosty breath of night, as dark as the

night from which even the light of stars was taken by a haze of clouds.

To lie there awake was to have every sense abraded by the desolation of this land.

The fitful wind brought the wail of a dreary bird of night, sepulchral as a ghost. The wind grieved and sighed in the spiny grass. Decay came faintly on the wind, the smell of ancient death, dry wood rotting, leached earth, dry bones. The wind chilled flesh and spirit. And he had wanted Peter to leave him here; alone!

"No!" he cried. "Peter? I will go with you. Listen . . . I'll go with you all the way. You mustn't leave me! You hear? No matter what I say."

"Eh?" said Peter. "What? No. Go to sleep. I will not leave you."

Hearing Peter's voice was like seeing a bright star banish the darkness of the night with reassuring light. Like waking from a dream in which he was the last and the only man left living in the world. Holding in his mind the fading sounds of Peter's voice, he fell asleep.

They awoke too early, and had to wait for sufficient light to show the track. Waiting, they huddled, clutching arms about their knees, wishing for the warmth of the sun that all too soon would change, as in the space of an hour it always did, from welcomed friend to hated enemy.

They listened for the calf, but it had given those few imploring bellows in the night, and then had stopped. They talked about the meaning the calf might have, and wondered why, if settled country wasn't far, no other cattle had been heard.

"It's light enough," said Peter, rising at last, helping James Duncan to his feet.

Seen now, the track that had seemed quite level in last night's dusk followed an easy grade to the top of a hill some distance yet ahead.

As the sun came up they were close enough to this modest crest to see disclosed a welcome change of country.

Looking back, they saw a wedge of sea, a last view, a strip of the sea's horizon where the sea is always dark and straight and blue, and never green; they could measure the progress of the day before and in the short distance they had come, which the eye could leap in a wink of changing focus, they found not the vast waste of desert in which their legs and their thoughts had labored, but a mere stretch of open country between coast and inland scrub.

Beyond the hill this inland country lay; a broken forest of scraggy trees began, filling gullies, covering the mounded hills with deceptive, verdant life. They were cheered to see this different country, and moved their legs more willingly.

The track wound over the top of the hill and turned along the siding of a gully.

They were nearly to the timber.

From the gully, four emus came at headlong, frightened run.

"What's that?" James Duncan cried, and smiled, seeing what this blur of movement was, standing to watch the outlandish comedy of the four enormous birds riding their thudding legs. They held their bodies in a straight line of motion, as if their legs were steeds and their ungainly bodies jockeys riding them, as if at any moment the legs might decide to do one thing while the bodies did another.

He noticed it as nothing strange that the emus should falter when their mad run brought them close, but Peter did.

"Something frightened them," said Peter. "They hadn't seen us. They were running from something else."

But this meant nothing to James Duncan. He watched the foolish birds running this way and that, undecided, leaping in the air, ducking their long untidy necks, before they decided on the safest course to follow and dashed away in single file across the hill.

"Oh, look!" said Peter in a trembling voice, and as Peter's fierce grip took his arm, James Duncan was afraid.

Peter looked as if about to cry. James Duncan, following the direction of Peter's wide-eyed stare, saw a man on a horse, riding from the scrub.

"Oh God, I thank you," whispered Peter.

He ran toward the man, shouting and waving his arms.

"Wait," James Duncan cried. "Wait for me!" As if it mattered now. He tried to run after Peter, but found he couldn't run, that now he couldn't even walk.

He dropped to the ground and sat there, watching Peter running. The man on the horse had his head down and seemed to be asleep, or drowsing.

At Peter's shouts, the man on the horse jerked straight in startlement and leaned back on the reins. The horse reared, so that it looked for a moment as if horse and rider were about to wheel around and bolt away.

"Wait!" shouted James Duncan again, but now to the man on the horse. "No! Wait!"

But Peter, reaching the man, was talking up to him. The man was getting off the horse and pushing back his wide-brimmed hat to scratch his head as Peter talked. They were coming along the track, the man pulling at the horse, which didn't want to come.

They came right up. The horse shuffled and lashed its tail at flies, blew snorting breaths.

" 'Day, boss," said the horseman, white teeth gleaming in a dark face. "How she goin'?"

"All right," said James Duncan absently. Tied with the man's blanket roll, behind the saddle, was a bulging sugar bag. "What's in that bag?"

"Been campin', boss. All me things in there."

"Food?"

"Yair. Bread an' stuff. Me billy and me tea. You hungry?"

Had he been able, James Duncan would have answered, but his mouth ran with saliva at the thought of bread. He swallowed and nodded.

"I'll light a fire," said Peter.

"No fire," muttered James Duncan, finding his voice, not conscious of moving to the horse better to see the horseman's every move as he teased undone the lashings of the bag, not raising his eyes from the brown supple fingers. "Take too long to light a fire."

Peter laughed. "He'll have *matches*. No more firesticks, Mr. Duncan."

The man turned. "You been Mr. Duncan? In that boat, that where you been?"

"I tried to tell you," said Peter. "We were taken out to sea in the flood. We've been walking along the coast."

"I been there that day watching you. See old Ben start crossin'. See that flood come down. I been ride this ol' horse in that flood to save old Ben, you know. But you feller gone. That when I seen you. Only, not like you been lookin' now. Would'n' know you feller anyway. Mr. Hardy, he want ebery-one look for you. Try and fin' you. Two day we look for you."

"Not now," said James Duncan. "Talk later."

Hunger lumped in his throat like swallowed grief as the bag came away from the saddle, as the last knot was undone, the bag opened, and the contents spread there on the ground.

"How much you want?" The aborigine held a knife above a battered loaf.

They did not answer.

The aborigine met their eyes. He put the knife through the middle of the loaf and in each hand held out half.

James Duncan knew he was eating like a beast, but he could not stop his fingers from tearing the loaf and stuffing the pieces into his mouth until his cheeks were bulging.

"You been prop'ly hungry all right," said the aborigine with marked approval.

He kicked leaves and grass together on a patch of sand and broke a few sticks, and bent, flicking a match in his fingers, and there was the immediate blaze of fire. With childish surprise, James Duncan watched this dimly remembered miracle and its accompanying acts; water poured from a plastic flagon into a blackened billy, tins of tea and sugar opened and set ready, a chipped enamel mug wiped with a dubious finger.

"Yair, boss," said the aborigine, standing up. "Seen you drive down the river in ol' Connor's Lan' Rover that day. I been across that river lookin' to fin' Mr. Hardy little black calf. Now

I still been lookin'. Lookin' for that little calf right now. Campin' out. All to fin' that little poddy calf."

"We heard your calf," said Peter, swallowing to clear his mouth. "Last night."

"Maybe I fin' him today."

"Not today," said James Duncan. "You'll be taking us back to the mission. Is that where you come from?"

"Yair, boss. Mr. Hardy place. Ben-gingin mission. That my place, boss."

"How long will it take?"

"How far," Peter explained. "Mr. Duncan means how far to the mission. Mr. Duncan will go on the horse and you and I will walk beside. How long will it take?"

"What you think Mr. Hardy say when I not fin' he's calf?"

"Stop talking like an idiot!" said James Duncan violently. "The calf doesn't matter, do you understand? Doesn't matter at all."

In his sudden rage he found a kind of recovery, an illusion that the vigor and decisiveness of anger would extend quite naturally to the powers of his body, so that, if he had to, he could walk all the way to the mission.

Rising to his feet for greater emphasis, he found how false this was. He could stand, but the very thought of walking another step, now that he didn't have to walk to save himself, was enough to make every sinew of his body ache in protest. But he wasn't going to have this great moment of salvation, coming so sudden and unexpected, treated as a passing incident in this stupid darky's idiotic day.

"What's your name, boy?" he said severely.

"Matthew, boss."

"All right. This man here, Matthew, this man and I, we were taken out to sea in that boat. No water or anything. We had to fight sharks, and we were wrecked in a storm. We've been walking along the coast with hardly any food or water. We're lucky to be alive . . . do you understand? I'm a sick man. You have to get us back to the mission. Quick as you can."

"That water she been boilin'," said Matthew, kneeling to put a handful of tea into the billy. He left it on the fire, watching as it foamed up brown; tea leaves flying in the water like dust in a sudden wind.

"And there's another thing," said James Duncan. "We have to see a man at the mission. There isn't any time to lose. We must hurry, understand?"

"I been hear it you come to see ol' Fred," said Matthew, swinging the billy from the fire with a stick, rapping the side to make the tea leaves settle. "Few days ago, ol' Fred, he die. Might be, you been too late."

"No," said James Duncan, brushing this news aside impatiently. This confused moron was talking about someone else. It didn't enter his mind it might be true. It was out of the question. They had come so far, suffered so much. Absurd. "No," he said again. "The man I'm talking about had another name. Peter, what did they call him?"

"Binben Freddie," said Peter quietly. "Matthew? Is that the man who died?"

Turning to see what Peter meant by this solemn question, to see why Peter was so serious, James Duncan saw that, incredibly, Peter believed this fool.

In a shock of comprehension that was a surge of pain behind his brow, he knew at once what answer would be given.

"Yair," said Matthew. "Binben Freddie. Sometime they been call him that. We jus' call him ol' Fred. But that one. He the one. He come back here to die. This here his baby place, you know. He been very ol'. This where he have to die."

"Oh Christ," said James Duncan. "Oh Peter, what do we do?"

"Get back. As quickly as we can. But which is the quickest way to do it?"

"Boss," said Matthew. "Better I been go. See Mr. Hardy. Leave you feller here. Mr. Hardy come an' get you."

"No," said James Duncan. "You wouldn't . . . you'd get . . ."

This fool would get it wrong. Get lost or something. Forget about them and not come back. They'd be as badly off as ever.

But Peter said, "It might be best. Does Mr. Hardy have a

truck? Something that could come along this track and get us out?"

"This track? Oil feller been make this track. Larry an' Joe ... they been 'merican feller, with that green jeep. They been make hole all over, put dy'mite down. Bang. They been listen with wi'less set. They been camp creek 'long near sea. Boss, maybe a jeep be better for this track."

"What kind of truck does Mr. Hardy have?" Peter insisted patiently.

"He got Lan' Rover."

"You're sure?"

"What you been askin' me?"

"A Land Rover? Mr. Hardy owns a Land Rover?"

"That Lan' Rover prop'ly belong mission, I think," said Matthew, scratching his head while he wondered about this. "We always been call it Mr. Hardy Lan' Rover. Mission Lan' Rover, maybe. You want I should, I ask Mr. Hardy. He say who it belong."

"Listen, for Christ's sake go and get the bloody thing!" shouted James Duncan. "Get back there as fast as you can and tell him to come and get us."

"Yair, boss," said Matthew nervously, gathering the horse's bridle and making as if to mount immediately.

"Not yet," said Peter. "Wait a minute. Can you get back there tonight?"

"This ol' bony-back horse, he don' go so fas'," said Matthew. "If I been go long way round it maybe take all night. That other way, we have to swim that san'bar. Never been swim that san'bar when it been dark. I been go long way roun', I think."

"Go the safest way," said Peter. "Go the long way. But go as fast as you can. Have a drink before you go and leave us your food and water. Blankets. Leave us everything. That all right?"

Matthew didn't answer. He watched James Duncan, and waited.

"Tell him," said Peter. "He wants to hear it from you."

"He knows what to do," said James Duncan.

"It would be better if you told him"

"Do what Peter has told you," said James Duncan quietly, feeling weary and ashamed. He sat on the ground without looking at Matthew.

"Have your drink," said Peter to Matthew. "I'll get the blankets."

Matthew poured a mug of tea, and blew on it, and drank it scalding hot.

"Do you understand what to do?" asked James Duncan.

"Tell Mr. Hardy he been come quick as he can, an' get you."

"Yes. And kick that horse along."

"Yair, boss."

"We'll camp beside the track under those trees down there," said Peter.

Matthew nodded. He mounted the horse and kicked hard with his heels.

They watched him ride away.

They watched for a long time after he had disappeared, and for a long time they did not have the heart to speak.

16

"Minutes would have done it," Peter said. "Ten minutes saved and we'd have been across before the flood came down. We'd have been there before the old man died. When I think of all the time we could have saved . . ."

James Duncan watched the devouring glow of flame etch instant patterns on the backlog of the fire. Stirred by thermal zephyrs, flame grew and spurted bright, and lapsed. And you might as well, he thought, try to predict a fire's next sketch as think you could know the real thoughts of another man.

Flame might lick into transient life a picture that reminded you of something. Being reminded, you saw that thing: that face, that animal, that ship, that landscape tiny and remote. Did another man see that same thing? You never knew. Try as you might to get behind the talk of another man and know his thoughts, you never could.

What was Peter getting at? What did he *want?*

Whatever it was, it had gone on long enough. Throughout the day he had been silent, bearing the pointless repetition of Peter's complaining voice, a weary listener, too tired to look for argument, knowing argument would follow if Peter were answered in the way he should be answered. But it had gone on long enough. Let Peter speak again, just let him say one sentence . . .

"And so it was all for nothing," Peter said. "All of it. That's what I can't believe."

"Have you finished?" said James Duncan, with the aggrieved restraint that gives warning that moderation will not last. "Is that the lot? All right. I've been listening to that crap all day." His voice was rising. "I've put up with it. You've been bitching like a disappointed spinster all the bloody day. Going round in circles. And I have had *enough!*"

Had he ever used this voice on Peter? Peter's eyes were wide. Peter did not speak.

"All *right!*" James Duncan shouted. "I've got your message! You can stop now before you oversell it. You're not happy? Things went wrong? You've dropped your bundle? You don't know what comes next, and you want someone to tell you what to do? Well, I will! I'll tell you."

Though he had known that anger would feed on speech in that self-dramatizing habit anger had, it surprised him when it came. It seemed too much, an ersatz anger, rising not from reason but from unresolved emotion. He calmed himself, because he had to think. Anger had committed him, and thinking must come to his assistance.

And thinking would, for there it was, that old machine of other times, switched on inside his head, warming up, ticking over, looking at ideas, selecting, rejecting, coming up with answers.

"Though you could have asked me," he said, not quite ready, but calmer and assured because he could feel the answers coming. "You could have been man enough to admit you didn't know, and wanted to be told. Too much pride, perhaps? I'm disappointed. Never mind. I'll tell you. We start from this . . . We've had a setback. The old man's dead. Okay, that has to be accepted. It means we can't do it like we had it planned. We have to find another way. We have to *use* what's happened. Yes, by Christ, and here it is! What a terrific angle, the old man dying like that. Terrific! Should have seen it before. Couldn't have turned out better. We can really put the heat on."

Moved by quick excitement, he rose to his feet. He saw it all.

"Christ, yes!" he said, kneeling, facing Peter across the fire, wild eyes shining from his bearded face. "Here's how it goes. Tomorrow, we'll be out. We'll meet the press. They'll know by now, for sure; it could be they'll be there to meet us. And we're the hottest piece of news since federation. Back from the bloody dead! We've been lost, drowned, written off... and here we are! We're back. Jesus, every word we say they'll want to print. Press, radio, TV... for a few days it will be as if we owned them. We can write our own ticket, say what we like. It will all go in. Look, you couldn't buy it for a hundred grand."

"And will that bring the old man back to life?" cried Peter in a choked voice that might have come from the frustration of a puzzling rage. "Have you planned some way to resurrect him?"

"Back to *life?* Shit no!" cried James Duncan, his own anger flaring crudely in a rougher voice. "Who'd want that? For us, he's better dead. Because we can blame *them,* now. We can accuse, point the finger, we can call up the screaming pack. Now we can say... *who let him die?* There's not a soul in the country who, in two days' time, won't be shouting out that question."

"And what about Jinben? What will that do for him?"

"Well bugger me, who's the lawyer around here?" said James Duncan. "How far do I have to take it? *This* is what it does for Jinben... he was accused of murder, and there was one witness, and one witness only, who could establish whether he was on the scene or not. One witness who could clear him. And that witness wasn't questioned. He wasn't held. They let him go away. Didn't get his story. Let him die! *Why?* That's the word we have to hammer! Why, why, *why?* Why didn't the coppers get his story? Did it spoil their case? Did they *want* him to go away? *Why?* I tell you, boy, that little word is the toughest in the language when you use it right. In a few days we'll have everyone believing that the old man's story would have established Jinben's innocence."

"And that is why you're glad the old man died?"

"I wouldn't say that, exactly. But I'll tell you this: if he had to die he might have picked a useful time to do it. Let's face it... who knows what the Christ the doddering old bugger would have said? And we'd have been stuck with it, whether it was for us or against us. Now he's dead we can play it any way we like. Now are you with it?"

"I suppose so," said Peter.

"Speak up," said James Duncan sharply. "You don't seem much impressed. Well, that's okay. Kick it around. Maybe you have a better angle?"

"I haven't any angle. I think it's likely that your plan will work."

"Work? You're bloody right it will! But it's not that, is it? It's something else. I've spoken, and now it's up to you. What's on your mind?"

With a discreet movement, Peter put his face in shadow. He did not answer.

"Something's been bugging you all day." Why did Peter hide himself in shadow and in silence? The white man's mind hunted with its old professional sharpness for withheld motives. "Go on," he said. "What is it?"

"Nothing."

"Then I'll tell *you*," said James Duncan. "All this time I've been dependent. You've been the strong one, and I the weak. You told me what to do, had all the answers. Saved me several times. And now that's over. Our lives are changing back to what they were. And you resent it."

"That is not true."

"Be honest. You've been getting on my back all day. But indirectly. Wanting my help, but too bloody stiff and proud to ask for it direct. Knowing you would have to follow my lead once more, and hating it."

"It isn't that at *all!*" cried Peter, letting his expressive eyes be seen again. "Where we have been . . . that was a life and a world I know, and it was proper I should lead. Now we have left my world and we are coming back to yours, and it is right that there should be a change. In some things, you should lead now, and I'll be glad to follow."

"Glad? Why should you be glad?"

"Because there are so many things in your world that I cannot do. Some that I wouldn't want to do."

"Your world is a dreadful, barren place," said James Duncan. "We could have died there. And yet, the way you talk, I get the impression you prefer it."

"I do not know. I did not know how lost I was, between these worlds; for I had almost forgotten that real world in which my life began."

"Beside the creek, do you remember?" said James Duncan. "That was a good place. We could have lived there. And, yes . . . it was another world, a good one. I'd have given anything to stay. Is that the kind of thing you mean?"

"All of it," said Peter. "All my world. I had forgotten. That whole wide world of natural things in which there is nothing that the hand of man put there. That world just as it was when it was made, where life doesn't depend on cities and machines and ships and on the work of other men but on the simple things your own two hands can do."

"It is a hard world," said James Duncan. "Hard and cruel, and sometimes frightening."

"Uncivilized, yes," said Peter. "Untamed, unchanged. But it is the real world."

"Not for me."

"No, not a world for many white men. Perhaps that is why the white man has done his best to make himself another world, so that it sometimes seems that the sole object of his every effort is to construct an artificial world to replace the world of natural things. Could it be that this is the white man's real religion—to make the whole world over? So that when it's done the whole world will be his, with no place left for any other way of living?"

"You're in good form," said James Duncan appreciatively. "Though one might venture to point out that most of the world seems keen enough to have those things for which you blame the white man. Keen? The wildest tribes of Timbuktoo are screaming bloody murder because matters aren't being altered fast enough to suit them. But let that go. I was getting at something else. What's been bugging you all day? That's what I really want to know. Let's leave the philosophic talk and deal with that."

"You never let up, do you?" said Peter. "I guess I have to tell you. Though you might wish you hadn't worked so hard on me to know. This is what troubled me . . . I knew I must ask your help in saving Jinben in another way. You would know what to do, now that the old man is gone. You would know, and you would tell me. And it would be some kind of trickery. It would have to be. I could not bring myself to encourage you in that. And yet, in the end, I must."

"And now? Now you've heard what I propose?"

"Now I am only sad. It was just as I expected. Trickery without the slightest scruple. Once more I've seen your mind at work, and this time I caught some of the feeling of what it must be like."

"The feeling? What do you mean by that?"

"How it must be to be a white man, in a job like yours. To do the work you have to do. To twist things, and to use things, and to make things seem not what they are. I felt what it must be like not to be able to worry about the truth."

"You're bloody hard to please," said James Duncan. "And what you say, I'm surprised it doesn't make me angry. It should, and I've every right to lose my temper. You've been bloody devious, and you're bloody unreasonable, and you must know it, and I wouldn't advise you to say a thing like that again."

"I say it because you would not let me rest until I'd told you," said Peter. "And I say it because it is true."

"That's quite enough," said James Duncan. "Listen to an order. When we get out you'll go along with what I say. You will not argue. You can take those high-falutin' principles of yours and you can shove them. Because it's not *your* neck that hangs on this. That's what you've forgotten. And let me say this . . . nothing is so easy as to revel in your virtue at another man's expense. And nothing is more despicable."

"You need not worry," said Peter. "I agree it must be done the way you say. I know that has to be accepted. I am sorry that I came into your life. I am sorry I became one of those who used you."

"I can do without that," said James Duncan. "Nobody's using

me on this. Nobody's paying me. Nobody made me take this on. I came into this of my own decision."

"But I think of all those others who will use you. I think of your going back to that life of yours, letting yourself be used and used, and used again. Like a tool that has no wishes of its own."

"Used? Well, yes. I suppose one is. Most men are. Used at times for bad things, but now and then for good. But you've a very naive habit of exaggeration. Aren't all men used like that? Is that so bad?"

"It is to me. I believe a man should use himself. He should seek out the right work for his life and use himself in that. Not let himself be bought, and used, by others."

"Ah, but who's up who in this crazy world?" said James Duncan in a brooding voice. "Who uses who? It's bloody hard to tell. I've done things, I admit, that I'm not proud of, things that were evil in their end result. But that was nothing more than— work. A job of work. A man can take great pride in doing even a bad thing very well. And so, you do your best. Sometimes you might have doubts, but there's always something to excuse you. If you don't do it, they won't find it hard to get another man who will. Or so you tell yourself. And so you do it, and it mightn't be so good, but when you look around at what the others in your game are doing, it doesn't seem that bad."

"Why must it go on like that?" said Peter. "When you go back, can't you choose? Work on the good things only, and leave the bad?"

"Why, sure! That's if I was smart enough to judge good from bad before a thing was started and carried out."

"But you can! Always. I am sure you can!"

"Listen to me," said James Duncan with some sadness. "I'll make the oldest wish of an older man. I wish I was young again and knew what I know now. That way a man might be sure enough that all he did was good. For such a man would have the young man's feeling for goodness, and the older man's cynical experience of evil. The catch is, that you don't get that experience without losing most of the goodness on the way. It seems that goodness is founded most on hope, and hope is a young man's plaything, soon worn out."

"Not mine," said Peter, with utter certainty. "My hopes will never weaken."

"Easy enough to say! But you're like a man listening to a traveler telling of another country. You doubt the traveler's tales. How can you know about that other country until you've discovered it yourself? Wait twenty years. Twenty-five. You'll be as old as I am now. And then you'll see!"

"It will not happen. Not to me. Do not measure me by other men. Perhaps I am not as other men; perhaps my hopes are greater."

"What are you driving at?" said James Duncan, curious suddenly, and perhaps uneasy. "This is not the first time you've hinted at a mystery. As if you thought some great future lay ahead of you. What are you saying?"

"Nothing," said Peter, seeking shadow for his face again. "I say these things on impulse, and when they're out I wonder why I said them."

"No. Come on, boy," said James Duncan, in his voice a little of the gentleness a man might use to coax a wild bird to his hand. "Tell me. It's all there, isn't it? You have it all worked out. Well, sooner or later you'll have to pull it out for someone else to see; and why shouldn't it be me?"

"But I am not *ready!* And it's so impractical. I . . ."

Though Peter stopped, the rising inflection of his words suggested indecision, and James Duncan was too shrewd a man to speak. He looked into the fire, and waited.

"Laugh if you must," Peter said at last. "But I believe my life is destined to be used by God. I will be God's instrument in something great, for years I've been aware of that. He has a use for me. He will use me in the cause of truth and goodness. Does that sound smug? Oh yes, it must! But you might allow for my humility. Perhaps you will. Perhaps you'll let me say such things without an accusation of conceit?"

"Conceit? It never occurred to me. But there must be more to it than that. Much more than you have said. You must have planned this work of yours, and I'll get it out of you. Because, maybe, I need to know. Yes, you'll tell me more."

"We still have water," said Peter. "Will I make some tea?"

"You might as well."

As Peter stooped over the fire, James Duncan said, "Could it be religion? . . . no, if that was what you had in mind, you wouldn't have spent those years swotting for the law. So what did you have in mind? Could it be politics?"

"Would that be so impossible, for you to be as disbelieving as you sound?"

James Duncan smiled. "I was thinking of truth and goodness. Politics! What a place to seek such homely virtues!"

"I shouldn't have told you. I knew you'd laugh. I'm no match for that clever, restless mind of yours. Please . . . that's enough."

"Parliament? Well, why not?" said James Duncan, that smooth machine ticking over, weighing chances. "Why not? It could be done. Given the right build-up. Labour Party? I guess it would have to be. A good Labour seat, party behind you. They could be kidded into that. The mob would go along. It could be done . . . why not?"

"I see why you smiled," said Peter. "I'd laugh myself, at the idea of finding truth and goodness in party politics! Do you think I'm mad? Do you think those worn-out machines of corruption and compromise are all there are to politics?"

"You'd form another party? A new one? Is that what's in your mind?"

"I do not know."

"Truth and goodness . . . it sounds so innocent," said James Duncan. "It sounds so idealistic. But for Christ's sake, what is wrong with idealism? Why has that become old-fashioned, something to be sneered at? Couldn't it be . . . I don't know, couldn't we be coming to a time when ordinary people might like to find their innocence again? Mightn't they be getting tired of being so shrewd and smart, mightn't they be sick to death of a world where materialism becomes the only social virtue? Mightn't truth and goodness come back into fashion? God knows we've had a gutful of the opposite! Perhaps that's what people really want? Listen, *I* want it! I'm shrewd, I'm smart, but *I* want it. Peter, I could sell this! Start your party. Let them laugh!"

"And what would happen?" cried Peter, forgetting his reservations. "Isn't that how they all began? Something is thought to be good, and perhaps it is. It begins there, with some good ideal to be expressed in politics. And a machine is set up to do this good thing, a political machine, a party. But time passes, the good thing is forgotten, all that matters is to keep the old machine in operation, and no compromise is too great a price to pay for that. How do you think I could begin like that, knowing that would happen?"

"Then you never will begin. The parties have the game sewn up."

"Ah yes. But time is on my side," said Peter, with a young man's utter confidence in the powers of youth and time, the confidence which sometimes seems like arrogance. "I can wait twenty years. Thirty, if I must. I'll still be young enough."

"No. You cannot wait that long."

"Why not?"

"The water's boiling," said James Duncan.

Peter threw tea into the billy and swung it from the fire.

"Why can't I wait?"

"Because I'll be too old to help you," said James Duncan grimly. "Or dead. I cannot wait that long."

"*You?*"

"You'll need a man like me. One who knows which way is up. Someone who has mastered all the tricks."

"Tricks? Is this to be a thing that's done by tricks?"

"A figure of speech. Not the way you make it sound; as if the tricks were everything. It's simple common sense. A matter of having a good case and presenting that case to the best advantage. And I'm entitled to make a claim or two on this, because I'm something of an expert. I know my job, you should know that! Dealing with the public, that's my job. Helping them to form the right ideas. And what else but the public are you dealing with in politics? You'd better be sure that your relations with the public are managed by an expert hand. You'll find that out. You're going to need a man like me."

"I've had a chance to form a few ideas about the way you work," said Peter.

"You're bloody right you have! And, if I recall correctly, you were keen enough on persuading me to use my wits on your behalf!"

"That was for a different thing, a man's life. Perhaps not a case where one can afford to be too particular about the means one uses."

Stung, James Duncan said, with intended crudeness, "Perhaps you'd better go away and pray. Ask your friend upstairs what *He* thinks about it. You'll make a proper balls of this if you try it on your own. Listen, maybe I want to get into the act. Maybe God wants to call me in. How's that for a novel thought?"

"Would you make a cruel joke of this?"

"I might. But not for laughs. From being hurt, perhaps. No, God damn you, I'm not joking! You'll need a man like me . . . that's the first thought I had when you were talking. Well, was that *my* thought? I wouldn't know. But one thing's for sure, by God, that thought didn't come from my own interests, or from common sense. You use big words. Truth and goodness! How the hell do I know what those words would mean to you in practice? Something I wouldn't like, that's quite conceivable. Yet . . . something . . . God knows what, something that puzzles me, that even frightens me, tells me I have to do whatever I can to help you."

"You're serious?"

"As serious as I'll ever be. I've swallowed your snide insults with hardly a word of protest. Well, good Christ! That alone is evidence of *something!* Senility, perhaps. The softening of my poor old brain. But it shows I'm serious."

"I suppose, if I say, as I must, that I need time to think this over, you'd take that for another insult?"

"I would, but I don't expect to see you stopped by that. Believe me, my temper tells me to let you muck along in your own pious way. You have a lot to learn. You're a good man, but you are also something of a prick. Yet, for all that, something tells me I must help you. Whether you are willing to accept my help, or not."

"I have doubts," said Peter. "I am sorry and ashamed to say it. But I must be honest."

"Honesty can be a rather hurtful thing," said James Duncan resentfully.

Peter said no more. They drank the tea in silence, and Peter stoked the fire. They settled down beside the fire to sleep.

It won't work out with him, James Duncan thought, shifting his weary body on the unreceptive ground, knowing by the liveness of his mind that sleep was far away. But I can't go back to my old life.

What a fool I was. We'd be talking still if I hadn't frightened him with that crazy offer to help him in his screwy plans. We'd have passed away this long, long night of waiting, talking by the fire. And that would have been much better.

Crazy. Could that be me, who offered himself to be used in the fanatical dreams of this obsessed young man? Who let myself say anything at all, no matter what was in my mind, until I had measured him against the background of my normal life?

For that could be the explanation. In his world, as Peter calls it, in these days of suffering that we've shared, I've lost the sober balance I've always tried to keep in my affairs and my beliefs.

But I will not waste that suffering! I'll not take up my previous life the way it was. I can't. I must find that splendid cause that is greater than myself. I must find the meaning that my life has lacked. That something I have never found to which I can give myself, with pride and with joy, and without reserve.

He could imagine the enormous relief of spirit; he felt it in his heart—that release of tension, that joyous peace of mind that would come from being merged again in something great. Giving himself! No reservations! Knowing all he did was good. No doubts! No need to hide his actions from his conscience.

And then he saw himself again as others might . . . a developed man of some maturity, intelligent, well versed in the world's sophistication; these claims seemed fair enough to make. That's how some would see him. And this shrewd man, this worldly skeptic, had pleaded . . . yes, begged almost, as far as he was able . . . to be allowed to place his skills and his life at the disposal of a callow ignoramus, an egotist of wondrous immaturity, an innocent, a young blackfellow convinced he was a chosen man of God. Good *Christ!*

Chosen of God! If that wasn't the lunacy of egotism, what could it be?

Well . . . ?

Well, what *could* it be?

A simple truth, perhaps. A truth so simple that it seemed like lunacy. Even if not whole truth, still a belief of such power that with it anything might be achieved. A belief that could do great things.

And I need to believe in great things, he cried to himself again. I must! Life must never be the same! Peter was right! I despise so terribly so many of the clever things I've done. I *did* work to make things that were good seem dubious, and I did contrive, for bad things, a respectable appearance. For that was my work, the paltry work to which I gave myself. And Peter was so right that I couldn't raise my anger above its first hot thought.

I *will* find peace! I'll turn all my skill of hand and brain to some great work, and if it is not Peter's work—if he does not want me—then it will be something else. For this is the secret, and I have sought it all my painful life. Through all that emptiness of discontentment, that sadness and that grief, I have made my way. And this is at the end. This secret that will carry me to the very end of life with reason for contentment, knowing that I wasted most of it, my years, my work, my life, but in the end I used myself for something good.

Yes, he told himself, in the calm certainty of fixed decision, that is what I'll do.

Sleep began to reach across his thoughts.

"Goodnight," he said, and Peter stirred in sleep and muttered drowsily in answer.

Light played in the shadowed branches overhead as the fire reached with crackling flame for heated twigs. In the changing light the trees above seemed taller and more richly foliaged than they really were.

The air of night was cool and still, as passive as water in a sheltered mountain pool. Without effort, bodiless, he seemed to float in the substance of the night, and fell asleep.

Night neared its end and the hints of day's first sounds aroused him. Birds called themselves awake and tuned their voices for the chorus they would sing to greet the dawn. He heard in the trees the stirring of their wings. The fire was dead, and dawn was on the way. And so was help, he reminded himself with heartfelt gladness. They were safe, and help was coming.

He drowsed in the warmth of this luxurious thought and drifted into the tranquil depths of another sleep.

He opened his eyes to the glaring light and heat of morning sun. Flies made a busy airfield of his face.

Peter was kneeling beside the fire, nesting sticks around the billy. Hearing him yawn, Peter turned. "Breakfast in bed if you wait a minute."

"Breakfast?"

"Well, a mug of tea. That's all there is. And it's the end of the water. I reckon this Hardy chap had better hurry."

"Shouldn't he be here by now? You don't think he could have gone past in the night?"

"With us right on the track? Oh no. I guess it must be further to the mission than we thought. But, all the same, I'd be surprised if we don't see him in the next few hours."

But they waited all through morning while trees drew in their skirts of shade, and noon went past, new shadows found increasing length, and all the time their restless ears strained for the first sounds of an engine, until they could no longer deny the fear that something had gone amiss.

"What if that fool of a boy went arse-over-turkey off his horse?" said James Duncan. "We could die of thirst before he walked out to the mission. Suppose he lost himself, or got off the horse to have a leak, and the horse bolted? Anything could have happened. Jesus, why didn't we keep some water? We should have known it wouldn't happen right."

"Maybe it's time we started walking," said Peter. "But walking will dry us out. We'd soon get thirsty."

"I'm thirsty now."

"You've been resting. Far worse walking. How do you feel about it?"

"I can walk. How far, I wouldn't know. But I'd feel better walking. Oh, that *bloody* boy! We were mad to let him go!"

"Well then," said Peter, "let's go."

"Aren't we taking anything?"

"What is there to take? Nothing left to eat or drink. It's only weight to carry."

They kicked sand over the smoldering fire.

Walking away, their steps were slow and aimless. Walking was slightly better than waiting around, and that was all. It wasn't like starting on a journey with a promised destination.

Because it seemed so pointless, they rested often. Because it seemed unfair to be made to suffer thirst, when they had been given every right to believe themselves finished with such hardships, their thirst seemed worse than at any other time.

With weary legs, James Duncan walked beside Peter, cursing fervently that blackhearted, black-faced moron, Matthew, who, he was now convinced, had gone off on his search for the lost calf, forgetting them, and leaving them to die.

The sun set and the faint tire marks in the sand disappeared in failing light. They dared not go on in case they wandered from the track.

"Will I light a fire?" said Peter.

"What the hell's the use," said James Duncan. "Oh, that bloody boy! We could have been . . ."

"Quiet," said Peter. "Please let me listen."

"No," he said in a moment. "I thought I heard . . ."

"Give it up. He won't come now. Turn off your wonderful imagination."

James Duncan dropped to the sandy track, and lay there. I will not walk another step, he told himself. Not ever. It isn't fair. I will not walk a single step. This is the way it finishes.

Oh God, he thought, with sudden realization, with fear and shock that tiredness blunted but still left felt acutely: this could be the beginning of the end. How easily it could come like this. After those bold thoughts last night, my new life could finish here. We're such a perfect set-up for one of life's ironic jokes. I can see God laughing. Not Peter's God. No. Not his God of truth and goodness, an evil god of my very own. The devil god whose cruel smile has spoiled my life.

"I did hear something!" cried Peter. "I did!"

"Ah, for God's sake, no more. No more, Peter. Not unless you're sure."

"But I *am* sure. Please be quiet so I can listen."

Peter leaped to his feet and stared into the dark, turning his head this way and that so his ears could sift the stubborn silence of the night for the faintest sound.

But no sound came. Instead of sound his eyes caught a moment's flash of light on a distant ridge, and then imagined, or sensed, or even saw, the glow of headlights moving in the scrub.

"I saw it!" he cried, though he wondered how much had been the illusion of a sight his eyes so greatly wished to see. And then the sound of an engine came, thin and clear, so clear that even a white man's ears could hear it.

"I heard it!" James Duncan shouted. "Heard it! Peter, quick! Do something. We must do something! Light a fire!"

Peter was infected by this frenzied demand that something must be done, whether it was needed or not, for, if the truck came on this track, as it must, it would need no beacon. But regardless of sense, their excitement demanded action.

"Quickly," cried Peter. "Help me."

James Duncan raked dry grass into a heap with shaking hands. "Where are the matches? Light it. Light it so we can see what we are doing."

The grass hissed into flame. They hurried with sticks and

branches, and the fire crackled and flared, and danced their shadows wildly through the trees. Readily established in this frantic lighting, the fire launched into raging life, bright enough to blind them to the darkness all around.

Knowing now that they must be found, they fell into a calmer mood. They stood with the fierce heat of the fire behind them, staring into the night, tracking with their ears the sound of the approaching engine, screwing their eyes to miss no single treetop flash of the coming lights.

The lights at last beamed skyward from the nearest rise and glared directly in their eyes. The lights leaped in the roughness of the track, coming ever closer. They came right up. Stopped. Incredibly, the lights had reached them.

"God bless you," said James Duncan brokenly, standing by the driver's door, reaching with both hands to the window.

"Oh dear," said an uncertain voice, as his hands were clasped in a fervent grip. "I'm so terribly sorry to have been so long."

The door opened and a man stepped down. He was seen in the reflected headlights to be small and thin and spectacled.

"And the other one!" he said, turning to Peter with outstretched hand. "My dear fellow!"

"Do you have water?" James Duncan said, hearing in his voice a thirsty growl, not caring how rude it sounded. "Something to drink?"

"How dreadfully stupid of me. Water. Yes, of course. Oh water, yes, poor chaps."

Talking to himself the man dived into the cabin of the truck and appeared again with a plastic flagon, which he handed to James Duncan, who unscrewed the cap, and was about to drink, and paused.

He held out the flagon. "Peter?"

Rescue had been so swift and certain, and so final. It had been so sudden that he had not realized that never again would he have this chance to make a gesture of such meaning and sincerity. In ordinary life such gestures came from mere politeness. Not now. This was the real thing behind politeness. Not my need, but yours.

Peter looked at the flagon, and smiled.

"No," he said. "You first."

The small man watched them taking turns to drink. As the flagon passed between them, back and forth, until they'd had enough, he clicked his tongue in sympathy.

"I'm Clarence Hardy," he said. "The boy said you're the two men who were coming to see me when the flood took out our boat? Mr. Duncan? . . . and Mr. Jirapon? You really are those men?"

"Yes."

"The old man died, you know," said Hardy. "The one you came to see. Old Fred. Quite sad, really. Fine old man. A wanderer, alas, as many of these people are. He came back to his childhood home to die. He knew he was dying, but wasn't at all afraid. Remarkable, really."

"Sorry," said James Duncan. "Sorry to interrupt. Is there anything to eat?"

"Food, of course! Good heavens, what's wrong with me! You must be starving."

He produced a parcel from the cabin. "Only sandwiches, I'm afraid. I was in such a confounded hurry to be off. Pretty rough, you'll find; made them myself. Meat and pickle, all I had."

Watching him tear away the wrappings of newspaper, James Duncan moistened cracked lips with his tongue. He saw that the sight of food had the same effect on Peter and, with a third man there, the sharing of this childish reaction emphasized a previous thought. Yes. For all time now, something rare and most important had reached its end. For these few days, endless seeming now in retrospect, they had shared everything. Life's needs had been divided naturally in equal shares. How absurd that this last shared thing—lips licked at the sight of food—should be so comical.

"I believe that what the old man had to say was most important," said Hardy as they ate. "It was of considerable significance."

James Duncan chewed hastily, and gulped, to free his mouth for speech. It wasn't reasonable to be angry with this man who had come to save them, but he was.

"Of course it was," he said. "A schoolboy would have known that. Couldn't you have asked him questions, and written what he said? For God's sake, did it never occur to you to take a statement, when you saw that he was dying? You knew he was dying? You had warning?"

"Oh yes. I . . ."

James Duncan was in no mood to listen to excuses.

"Then it was your duty, wasn't it, surely, to . . ."

"Take a statement. Yes," said Hardy, interrupting in turn. "Of course it was. Please. If you'll only listen. I knew I should take a written statement, but a better plan occurred to me. A splendid plan. You see, I have a tape machine. Not mine, really. Wouldn't want you to think we have such luxuries. No. It belongs to Professor Fisher. Perhaps you know him. Prof. Fisher? Anthropologist? No? I've recorded some things for him. Our myths and legends and so forth. They're dying out. We must get them recorded before they vanish."

"What did he say?" James Duncan broke in urgently.

"Fisher?"

"No, damn it. The old man. Did you . . ."

"Yes, I did. That's what I meant. I asked him questions. I recorded our conversation. I am afraid I don't know whether it has any legal value. I supposed it was a kind of dying deposition. I've an idea there's a certain fixed procedure. But I'm most ignorant of legal matters. However, I did my best. I . . ."

"What did he say? Tell us what he said!"

"He rambled on, you know. I wouldn't like to . . . well, he was coming north with that young fellow, Jinben, that's clear enough. They were coming back here to Ben-gingin. I had him talk about the night when the girl was murdered. But you know all this."

"They were drunk that night," said James Duncan, forgetting food, choosing his words with care. "Jinben wandered away from the camp. The next day the old man tracked him. Now please, Mr. Hardy, listen carefully. This is the point of most importance. Did Jinben's tracks leave the path and go toward the river to where the girl was murdered? Or did his tracks continue on? That is extremely important, and it is virtually all that matters. What did the old man say? You must be able to tell me."

"I wouldn't dare," said Hardy earnestly. "I wouldn't take the risk of saying something which could so easily mislead you. You see, I had no idea of what was important and what was not. Away up here we are so remote from news. It is best for you to wait until we reach the mission and you can hear it for yourself."

"Who else knows?"

"Does it matter?" asked Peter, his curiosity aroused by a subtle change in James Duncan's voice.

"It might," said James Duncan curtly. "Who knows, Mr. Hardy?"

"About the tape? I told nobody. Though Fred's death is known, of course. That man ... Mr. Streeter, is it? The man from the newspaper? He was going to fly up when it was known that you were ... well, drowned, we thought. He telephoned. I told him that Fred had passed away, but I did not tell him about the tape. I don't know why ... a man from a newspaper, perhaps I felt ... well, I didn't tell him. Only yesterday I was wondering what I should do about it. But there we are. I need wonder no more. You came all this way to hear him, you suffered so much. And you shall hear him. It does seem right."

"Mr. Duncan told you what was important," said Peter. "Surely you must remember that small part of it?"

"Really," said Hardy, with prim but clearly adamant firmness. "Really, I assure you it is best to wait."

"You realize how badly we want to know?"

"Indeed I do. And I do admire you. You've had a dreadful time, as I can well imagine ... this is a cruel land, here in the north ... and yet you are so concerned about this young man's fate. Instead of thinking of yourselves, you are thinking only of what might help him. Yes, I do admire your constancy. But, my dear fellows, I would not dare to say a word. I've such a shocking memory. I might mislead you."

"He's hiding something," said James Duncan to Peter. "It might not be good, what's on the tape."

"Oh please. No," said Hardy. "Don't make me feel that I've upset you. I'm such a fool, that's all it is. I *know* I'd tell you something that was wrong."

"This is absurd," said James Duncan. "Why can't we go?"

"Of course," said Hardy.

"How long will it take?"

"It isn't really far. Indeed, if we could go the shortest way, it would be quite close. No more than fifteen miles. But we can't go that way; we cannot cross the river. We encountered a great misfortune with the boat we keep to cross the river. Oh but, good heavens! You know that, don't you?"

"We quite understand about the boat," said James Duncan with weighted politeness, amazed at the things people managed to forget. "Perhaps you could say how far it is the other way. I quite understand we have to go around to the bridge, but how long will it *take?*"

"I suppose it's near enough to forty miles."

"A couple of hours?"

"I should very much hope so. But one must allow for . . . well, mechanical difficulties, you know? Our poor old conveyance has seen much better days."

"Perhaps we could start, and hope for the best?"

"I think so. Yes, I think so. Look, you chaps climb in the back. I put a mattress there. Thought you might be . . . well, you know it's quite astonishing to find you in such good shape. I'll put out the fire. I was very relieved to see it."

"Jesus . . ." said James Duncan, as he and Peter relaxed on the mattress in the back of the Land Rover.

"He's very excited," said Peter. "I shouldn't think he'd be like that all the time."

"He wouldn't want to be. I shudder to think what's on that tape. Something isn't right."

"Here he comes," said Peter.

"Fine. That's fixed," said Hardy, climbing in. He speeded up the engine, which had all this time been left to run, and for a few moments it ran with a healthy sound of power. It then coughed several times and stopped.

"*Pest* of a thing!" cried Hardy. "It's been doing that the whole dashed day. Took me hours and hours to get here. I had that dratted carburetor to bits a dozen times." He reached into the back for a box of tools, flashing a torch on and off several times, so that, lit from below, his thin face looked satanical.

"Can I help?" said Peter.

"No, my dear chap. You must rest. I've done this so often I could do it blindfold. The blessed petrol, you know. It's absolutely full of water. And I haven't the least idea of how it gets there."

"I don't give a bugger what he does or how long it takes," said James Duncan, as tinkering noises came from the direction of the engine. "I'm going to sleep."

He closed his eyes and wriggled in the comfort of the mattress. In the troughs of waves of sleep he was fleetingly aware of sounds and motion, and sometimes of Peter and Hardy talking, but the assurance of safety backed these slight distractions with a feeling of confidence that left him undisturbed. It was safe to sleep, and he slept on until he was purposely aroused.

"Better wake up," Peter was saying, tugging at his shoulder.

He rubbed an arm across blurred eyes and raised up on an elbow.

"Are we there?"

He stared through the open back of the Land Rover. There were headlights behind, and shadowed figures.

"Mr. Duncan . . ." a shadow called urgently. "Mr. Duncan?"

"Yes?"

From darkness, a flash of lightning struck blinding in his eyes.

"One more," said someone.

The soundless lightning struck again.

He would see this photograph, coarsely screened, blurred on newsprint, and he would not believe that the stubbled face, the matted hair, the staring eyes, were his. That was yet to come. For the moment he was blinded and confused. He sat up.

"Jack Richardson, Mr. Duncan," a man said, scrambling up to sit beside him. "*Northern Mail.*"

"Please. A moment or two. I've been asleep."

"Switch up those lights," shouted Richardson. "Can't see a bloody thing in here."

The lights leaped to high beam, so that Richardson was seen more clearly, a squatting figure dressed in white with a Panama hat pushed off his brow.

"That's better," said Richardson. "Everyone thought you blokes had had the chop. Glad you made it."

"Are we there?"

"The mission? Nearly. Still a mile or so to go. We were boring it up this road to get there and we see your lights ahead. Tooted until the old boy stopped. Sorry, pop, I gotta have your story. Can't wait. Christ knows how I'm going to get it there in time. Only got the dope this morning. What a drive! Three hundred bloody miles! But worth it. This is real hot stuff. All right, what you got to say? That feller you came up here to see, that Binben Freddie, he died, several days ago. So what you going to do about it now?"

James Duncan sighed and took a heavy breath. He tried to remember what he had decided must be said, but nothing in his mind was working.

"Can't it wait?"

"Sorry, dad. Gotta have a lead. Don't need all of it. But I must have a first take to start the story. Listen, you're in the game. You know how hot it is. I gotta get it on the wire."

"Not about the old man. Not yet."

"Okay. Let's get it started the other way around. Like what happened to you and the other character?"

"We started in the boat to cross the river. Then the flood came down. A great brown wave, higher than a man. I . . ."

"Yair. All that we got. That's old stuff. One of the boongs saw it happen. Said you were drowned, otherwise there'd have been a bigger search. What happened next?"

"That first night? Well . . . I banged my head. Blacked out. Don't remember much."

"How'd you bang your head?"

"The boatman went overboard. He was swimming in the flood. I stood up. Threw him the oar. I lost my balance and fell, hit something with my head. We were taken out to sea. In the morning, couldn't see the land."

"Listen, for Christ's sake," shouted Richardson. "Will you sods keep from in front of those lights. Can't see a frigging thing in here."

"Sorry, Jack," a voice answered. "I was keeping handy in case there was another picture in it."

"All right, Mr. Duncan. You couldn't see the land. Have anything to drink? Any water?"

"A little tube of sweets. We shared it. No water. We lay still and tried to catch birds. They wouldn't come close enough. You tell him, Peter; I'm tired."

"Peter, hey? You're the other bloke? What's the name again? How do you spell it?"

Peter spelt out his name. "We tried fishing, that day," he said. "Used blood on a bit of rag for bait."

"That's good. Yair, that's the stuff. Catch anything?"

"It brought the sharks around, that's all it did."

"Sharks eh? Man-eaters? Yair . . . they're always man-eaters in the good ol' *Northern Mail*. Okay. What happens with the sharks?"

"They attacked the boat. We had a heavy weight, old piece of iron. The thing Mr. Duncan banged his head on. We hit the biggest shark with that. Knocked him out. The other sharks ate him. They didn't come back after that."

"You making this up, Nugget? You wouldn't be having a loan of me?"

"Now, cut that out," said James Duncan sharply. "You're being damned offensive. Would you talk that way to me?"

"No, sir, I guess I wouldn't."

"Then don't to him. Don't make out he's a liar."

"Okay. Well, look . . . I'm sorry. I never meant . . ."

"Listen to me . . . yes, and print it, too. This man you're being rude to is a damn sight better man than I am. You can believe me about that, mister, because I found it out the toughest way you can. He's a better man than me, and I'm bloody sure he's a better man than you, Mister . . . whatever you said your name was."

"Richardson's the name, sir. Call me Jack. Jack Richardson. *Northern Mail*. No offense meant, sir. I . . ."

"Well, fair enough. Let's get on with it. Let's for Christ's sake get it done."

"Not much more, sir. What next? After the sharks?"

"We drifted all that day. Came in sight of land and drifted out again. In the night there was a storm. Rain. We caught some water. I don't know, that was the third night in the boat, I think. We were washed ashore. Boat sank. Peter saved me."

"Okay. I'm getting the picture. Oh man, this really is a beaut. So you came ashore. What happened? Find water?"

"Peter did. Found water and lit a fire. No matches. Made fire with a stick. And that's hard. Harder than you'd think."

"That so? Jeeze, that's an angle. You know . . . this Peter, he's an abo, knows the lurks to stay alive. Looks after you. How would that be?"

"You don't have to invent it. That's exactly how it was."

"Now come on, father. Nobody's inventing anything. You know the way it is . . . you have to do the best you can with what you got. You gotta have that good ol' story. So what was next?"

"We kept walking. Came to a creek. Found an old camp, oil surveyors or something. Followed their tracks out."

"Right! I have it all from there. How the boy found you and all that stuff. Only want the leads for now, we'll get the details later. The *Mail's* got them beat on this one. We got twenty-four hours' clean start. They'll have to take it all from us. That's what we like. All right. Now listen, you chaps come up here, didn't you, to get this old Freddie's story on the Droverdale sex murder. So what you plan on doing now he's dead? Where's it leave you?"

"I'm ready to tell you about that now, Mr. Richardson," said James Duncan. "And I want you to get it exactly right. I'd like it taken word for word. Are you ready?"

"Yes, sir. If you'll go slow I'll take it just the way you say it."

"Good. Now, this is a direct quote. Don't you ball it up. Ready? Asked what effect the death of Binben Fred would have on the heavily supported campaign to gain reprieve for Jinben, Mr. J. B. Duncan said ... are you getting this? ... Duncan said, far from weakening Jinben's case, the untimely death of this key witness adds enormous weight to the case the authorities will be required to answer ..."

Richardson interrupted. "Just a moment, Mr. Duncan. I think there's something I should tell you."

"Wait. I haven't finished yet."

Richardson tried to speak, but James Duncan had clear in his mind exactly what he wanted to say, and he was determined to say it while the words were ready.

For a moment they spoke together, neither listening to the other, and suddenly Hardy was there, breaking into their tangled conversation.

"Mr. Richardson, these men are very, very tired," said Hardy. "Really! It isn't a fair thing at all. You must let me take them on, so that they can rest. Leave it until tomorrow."

Richardson jumped to the ground and stood with Hardy, talking persuasively.

"Are you going to tell him about that tape recording?" Peter whispered.

"God no! Not a word," James Duncan muttered. "Christ's sake, don't mention it. And let's hope Hardy has sense enough to keep his babbling mouth shut."

"But ... shouldn't we ..."

"No! We shouldn't. We have to hear it first. Something's not right. I'm scared of what might be on it. And if Richardson heard about it, if he got the slightest hint, he'd stop at nothing to get it in his hands. And Hardy's fool enough to let him have it."

"But what if it *is* against us? What can we do?"

"I'll fix it, that is what I'll do," said James Duncan in a savage whisper. "I'll get to that bloody tape machine and I'll wipe it off the tape."

"Oh no! You couldn't do it."

"That's enough! Stop talking like a bloody fool. Shut up about it. Leave it all to me."

"All right, five minutes," said Richardson, turning back from Hardy. "Now, Mr. Duncan, you better listen. I've been trying to tell you. There's something you have to know. You're going to get your royal commission. What do you say about that?"

"What?" said James Duncan weakly. "No. I don't . . . what did you say? Royal commission? You're sure?"

"I guess they had to do something about it," said Richardson. "When you were lost, it hit everybody. There was so much publicity it pushed all the other stuff right off the front. Believe me, Mr. Duncan, you couldn't have done it better if you'd worked it all on purpose. Would you like to make a quote or two on that?"

"It's wonderful news." His voice was strained, but as he turned to Peter his words came on a strengthening note of triumph. "Did you hear that, Peter? Did you hear it?"

"Wonderful news," said Richardson, scribbling. "What else? Any other comment?"

"Yes. It makes no difference to what I said before. Tell them this . . . it won't be Jinben who'll be under investigation . . . yes, write this down. The task of the commissioners will be to investigate the actions of those who were in authority, those who perpetrated this shocking travesty of justice. The police. The men who had the only witness who could prove that Jinben was not at the scene of the crime and let that witness go without bothering to get his story. The men who let that witness die with his story still untold. Now, this is the question . . . why? Why did they let that witness go without the slightest attempt to keep him? Why? Would his evidence have ruined the case against young Jinben? Would they have had to stir themselves, perhaps, to find the actual criminal? Was that too much trouble? Was it out of prejudice against a man of another color? Was it because Jinben was poor, a helpless aborigine without a friend to turn to? Was it . . ."

"You'd better take it easy, sir," said Richardson, for James Duncan's rising voice quavered at a pitch of indignation that threatened an emotional collapse. "You're tired, sir. You're overwrought. I should have told you about the commission before, I suppose. It was too great a shock."

"Of course it was!" cried Peter. "Can't you see? Can't you leave him alone? Can't you see he's had enough?"

"Don't make such a fuss," said James Duncan. "Perhaps I became a little too indignant, but what does it matter? I stick to what I said. And I want you to write it just the way I said it."

"There's something more to tell," said Richardson. "But now I don't know how to go about it. I guess I've made a mess of this. Thought I was being smart. I don't know. Too smart, maybe."

"Is it bad news?" asked James Duncan quietly.

"Good news, I'd say. As good as any news you'd want to hear."

"Jinben has been reprieved? Of course. They'd have to. Is it that?"

"Yes," said Richardson. "That's what it is."

"For how long?"

"Completely. His sentence has been commuted to life. He won't hang now. Attorney-General announced it last night. Quote . . . the commissioners cannot be asked to sit beneath the shadow of the gallows . . . unquote. So, that's it, Mr. Duncan."

James Duncan began to weep. He brushed at his eyes and muttered curses at his tears. Peter moved to comfort him.

The photographer leaned right in. His camera flashed.

"God damn you, Harry!" shouted Richardson. "You can pull that frigging plate and jump on it. Ain't you got no bloody manners left at all?"

17

"That's it, I think," said Hardy, and the tape recorder winked a dull red eye. He pressed a button, and at once tape coiled from a spool sent spinning at fastest speed in the wrong direction.

"Oh, bother!" said Hardy. "It will have to be rethreaded."

James Duncan yawned loudly, and sighed so rudely that Hardy looked around. Well, Christ, what did he expect? It had to be rudeness, or something worse. There had to be some outlet for nerves that were so on edge as to indicate some physical calamity approaching. And he'd had more than enough of Hardy, his stupid awkwardness, his prissiness, his fussy manner.

They had eaten a heavy meal and James Duncan would have given anything for sleep. But after such long waiting, and such unsureness now, there could be no thought that the hearing of the tape should be deferred.

Peter sat on the edge of his chair, tense with excitement, all expectation, and in a few moments, James Duncan was fairly sure, Peter was going to receive about the worst shock of his life.

Because, if Hardy's evasions had been judged correctly as coming from that form of astuteness which is made to seem like foolishness, there was something on that tape they wouldn't like at all.

The machine gave a loud squeal of feedback sound that bounced the volume needle to its limit. While Hardy leaped to make adjustments, as his recorded voice said something indistinct, the room throbbed with a most outlandish noise, a rising and falling of sonorous vibrations.

"I'd used some of this tape," said Hardy. "Not very much. But now the thing is going well I don't dare run it over to the part we want."

"What's that?" said James Duncan. "What weird stuff is that?"

"Bullroarers," Peter said.

A dark voice engaged the other sounds in dolorous chant, and Peter, listening with shining eyes, absorbed, swayed in his chair, and then the song ended in a sudden shout. The tape spun on in silence.

"Now," said Hardy, raising a finger, and from the machine his flat, recorded voice was heard. "Testing, testing, one two three testing. In a moment now, Fred. It has to be turned back first to make quite sure it's working. Ah, yes . . . that's fine. Are you ready?"

A moment of quietness, a faintly hissing silence, and then a hoarse voice spoke, a voice infirm and slow with age.

"Yair, boss. You know I been ready all this time."

Precise and light, Hardy's voice resumed. "This is Clarence Holland Hardy, manager of Ben-gingin Aboriginal Mission. And now, Fred, you had better say your name."

"Long time now that you been know me, Mr. Hardy. My name Fred . . ."

"Are you known by any other name?"

"Sometime, boss, they been call me Binben Freddie."

"Will you tell me why you came here to the mission?"

"That mission here? Well boss, she been my baby place. When I comin' close up finish . . . reckon I like it better I been finish in my baby place."

"In other words, you were born here, and you have come back here to die?"

"Yair, boss."

"Now, Fred, I'm very sorry, I believe I really am obliged to ask you this . . . Fred, *are* you dying?"

"Don' you be sad, Mr. Hardy. Prop'ly ol' feller I been, this time. Sun, he come in that sky tomorrow, reckon I been lookin' up at him for one las' time. Don' see him come aroun' no more.

That ol' sun, tomorrow, maybe he been lookin' prop'ly good to me."

"I take it that . . . what you mean is . . . you expect to die tomorrow night?"

"Ah boss, I been prop'ly ol' an' sick."

"I should think that will do. Yes. I do hope it will do like that. Well now, where do we begin? Will you tell me how it happened that you met Jinben in the city? Would you tell me that?"

"Yair well. Long time then, I been down south. Been movin' roun' all that time so I fin' work. Been pickin' fruit, mos'ly. Feller one day, he been tell me that little Jimmy been in trouble. That feller . . . he been quarter caste, he been prop'ly white, nearly. You listen a me, he been tell me, you go down that place where they been keepin' little Jimmy, an' maybe I been help you.

"He been tell me: Fred, you take that Jimmy back where he belong, you hear? So I fin' out that place they keepin' Jimmy, that nut place, Mr. Hardy, where they been lockin' up them silly feller. On'y, boss, Jimmy he not been prop'ly mad at all. Jimmy, he jus' been on that metho.

"Well, sometime, me an' this feller, we been goin' down that place, an' he been talkin' wit' them feller run that place. By golly, he been tell them feller off or'right! He been tell them I been Jimmy uncle, an' I been lookin' after Jimmy. By golly, boss, should be you been hear that cheeky feller!

"Then, sometime . . . me an' Jimmy, we been startin' out that long way comin' here. We been goin' all that way too slow, too slow. We been workin' a bit this place, workin' a bit that place, an' sometime Jimmy he been singin' outside a pub an' get a bit a money. An' sometime Jimmy he been drinkin', an' me an' Jimmy, we been prop'ly fightin' over that. Yair, boss, we been goin' too slow, too slow."

"Very good. Now, Fred, what was the name of that place where the woman was killed? Tell me about that."

"That been Droverdale they call it. They been tell me all 'bout that place when I been pickin' apricot. An' long time I been tellin' Jimmy . . . when we been comin' to Droverdale, we been lay off there a coupla week or so. I been hear it, that black-feller camp at Droverdale, she been bes' camp you ever see. So, when we been gettin' near that place, me an' Jimmy we prop'ly hurry.

"Well, boss, maybe that place or'right for all them wil' feller what like drinkin' all a time, an' fightin' all a time. Maybe I been silly, takin' little Jimmy there. Them Droverdale black-feller, they been nothin' but a mob a no-good bludger. I been seein' that too slow. When Jimmy he see that place, an' he say to me . . . we been stayin' here a while or'right, pop, she look or'right to me . . . when Jimmy he say that, maybe it bes' I take him on an' leave that place.

"But, I dunno, I been too tired that time. That nex' town, he been long way off. You be good boy, Jimmy, I been sayin', an' we been waitin' here a while. You be good boy, Jimmy.

"An' that firs' night even, they all been prop'ly wil' . . . all aroun', them feller they been gettin' plonk an' beer, an' I reckon you ain't likin' what I been sayin' nex', Mr. Hardy. That night, ol' Fred, he been gettin' drunk as anyone, an' that been true, Mr. Hardy. So much drunk that I been sleepin'. That Jimmy, he been start it, he been sayin' . . . come on, pop, you been have some too. Come on, dad, little drink don' hurt you.

"I dunno. I been prop'ly full that night. An' who been lookin' after little Jimmy when ol' Fred, he been gettin' drunk and sleepin'? Who been keepin' Jimmy out a trouble?

"Been open up my eye nex' mornin' . . . oh crikey! No time I ever been that sick. Fire, he all gone out. All a them drunk feller lyin' roun' on groun' snorin' jus' like pig. An' I been gettin' up an' lookin' for that Jimmy. An' I been sick. I been sick this way, an' I been sick that way, an' I been sick all roun'. Oh crikey!"

"Jinben wasn't there?"

"I been seein' Jimmy nowhere. I been seein' one a them cheeky feller there an' I been ask him, where my boy? Where little Jimmy? An' that feller he been sayin' . . . why you been so worry, pop, that boy he been aroun'. That boy a yours, maybe he been ol' enough so he not been needin' silly ol' man look after him. One time, ain't you been young like him, dad? Don' you remember? Don' you remember, pop? Don' you remember some time when you been nearly die when you don' fin' some girl open up her leg for you an' let you put it in? That how your Jimmy been las' night. Las' night he been like real mad feller, he been lookin' mad, an talkin' mad. Your boy been sayin' las' night ... how many girl in Droverdale, hey? How many girl? Never min', he say, never min' how many, I been goin' now, he say, maybe I been rootin' every fuckin' white girl in this fuckin' town.

"Now I been sorry, Mr. Hardy, you don' like me talk like that. On'y, that what this feller he been tell me when I been ask him."

"No, no. It doesn't matter at all. You must tell it in your own words."

"Not been my word, boss. Them word been what that cheeky feller he been sayin'."

"Quite all right. I understand that, of course I do. Tell me what happened then."

"Soon I been sick another time, after I been talkin' with that feller, and I lie down me head 'nother time an' go to sleep. Open me eye again an' look aroun' for Jimmy, an' he still been gone. Then I been sayin' that cheeky feller again ... why you don' give Jimmy one a your girl? An' he been sayin' ... you don' worry 'bout that boy a yours, pop, he don' wan' no black meat. We been sayin' our little Ruby she ready for pokin' any time. We been tellin' him: Ruby, she open up her leg for any feller, an' she pretty good, we been tell him that, she been wriggle aroun' an' jump an' make it prop'ly tight, our Ruby she been knowin' real good way to do it. Ruby, she 'bout the bes' there is.

"An' that feller been tellin' me ... that Jimmy a yours he been prop'ly finish wit' lubra, dad, that boy he reckon he been real big wheel down south, an' he don' do it no more, on'y wit' white girl. Las' night he been shoutin' out, pop, tellin' 'bout all them white girl been let him have it.

"An' Mr. Hardy boss, when I been hearin' that feller I been seein' trouble. Been open these ol' eyes, Mr. Hardy, an' I been look aroun' for Jimmy track. I been prop'ly crawlin' on that ground, sniffin' like ol' dog. Then I been see at las' he go that other way. He not been goin' to that town. He been drunk, an' he been silly, he get los' an' he go that other way.

"I been trackin' him 'longside that river, 'longside that little road, an' I been thinkin' . . . you good boy, Jimmy, you not been fin' no trouble 'way out here. I been goin' fair long way, an' I been lose that track. Not been seein' where that Jimmy track been goin'. Then I been crawlin' all aroun' till I been fin' he's track again. That track been fool me, boss. That track been leave that little road. Been goin' down that river.

"Then little little way an' I been seein' that tent beside them tree. An' little motorbike. An' somethin' been makin' ol' Fred get frighten. Ol' leg . . . they don' like goin' on. An' I been standin' there makin' my min' up prop'ly slow . . ."

Moving so swiftly that the pain of jerked muscles made him grunt, James Duncan came to his feet. He was across the room, jabbed thumb reaching for a button. The tape spools flicked and stopped.

Roughly in the heavy silence, hoarsely, he said, "I want to hear that part again."

"No," said Hardy, rising from his chair. "I must ask you not to touch it. That machine is very tricky."

"Not to worry, I've used these things for years." James Duncan, turning from Hardy, made confident adjustments. Rewinding, the tape whirred quietly.

"Mr. Duncan . . ." Peter's voice was high and strained. In his shocked face James Duncan saw alarm and hesitation, indecision. He pushed a bullying hand at Peter and snapped it open in an odd gesture which demanded silence.

When he spoke to Hardy his manner made a spurious change. He said, over his shoulder, while his hidden hands were busy, "That stuff at the beginning. Like to hear it all again sometime. Tell me . . . those bullroarers . . . I take it they were genuine?"

Though he was suspicious and uneasy, Hardy seemed forced by a compulsion of politeness to answer mildly.

"Naturally. How else would one make such sounds?"

"You're right. It was a silly question. But I know little about such things. How do they make that noise?"

"Mr. Duncan. I must . . ." Hardy moved, trying to see around James Duncan, who moved as if by accident to block his view.

"That's enough!" said Hardy, very sharply. "Really! You *must* stand away. It is my duty to insist."

"Why should you speak like that?" said James Duncan, attempting a reassuring smile, but finding his trembling mouth unwilling to obey. "Is something wrong?"

Hardy's suspicion changed to certainty.

"Stand back at once! What the devil are you doing?"

Hardy leaped forward and James Duncan felt his body sag. He had finished. It had gone on long enough. In another moment Hardy would push him aside and there would be a last absurdity; grown men wrestling like children. He moved away.

With a cry of anger, Hardy fumbled at a switch. His hands were shaking. The tape stopped running.

"Yes! It has been recording," he said. "You said you were an expert? Then you know what that means, don't you?"

"Recording? But it couldn't! I didn't . . . I simply ran it back and turned away . . . no, I . . ."

"Oh, *stop!*" cried Hardy, in bitter vexation. "Please stop this wicked nonsense. How can you not know what you've done? You've ruined it. You've erased it from the tape."

"You said you would," said Peter.

Wounded, James Duncan turned, but the pain in his eyes flashed suddenly to anger.

"Shut up!" he said viciously. "Keep out of this."

"You're making a childish fuss about nothing," he said contemptuously to Hardy. "Run it through once more. You'll see."

"Don't *touch* it! Keep right away from that machine," said Hardy, and his smallness, his fussy and seemingly ineffectual manner were seen as surface qualities, irrelevant now that his true temper was disclosed. Suddenly, he appeared as a man, iron-willed, even dangerous, when aroused. And the strength of his control was shown in the way in which he subdued himself.

"I'll do that," he said. "Very well, I'll play it through. Even though I'm perfectly aware of what you've done."

He reversed the tape and pips of high-pitched sound rippled in the speaker. The tape stopped and began to turn the other way, and once more the old man's voice was heard.

"You see?" said James Duncan, without conviction.

"Wait." Lip curling, Hardy watched the other man come close, intent on listening, bending his head to the tiny speaker.

"Then I been see at las' he go that other way," said the old man's voice. "He not been goin' to that town. He been drunk, an' he been silly, he get los' an' he go that other way. I been trackin' him 'longside that river, 'longside that little road, an' I been thinkin' . . . you good boy, Jimmy, you not been . . ."

Ludicrously, now, with gross irrelevance, James Duncan's voice cut in . . . "That stuff at the beginning. Like to hear it all again sometime. Tell me . . . those bullroarers . . . I take it they were genuine?"

Now for all time caught, his voice was glaring evidence of guilty intent as, false in every repeated note, it asked its stupid question.

As Hardy's voice answered, as that false question was met by Hardy's audible suspicion, James Duncan raised his eyes to Peter, and Peter returned his gaze in sorrow.

Not in gratitude; perhaps that would be somewhat much to ask; not in complicity, or even anger. But in sorrow.

"Turn it off," said James Duncan tiredly. "You're absolutely right. I messed it up. And I am very sorry."

"Not yet." Hardy raised his pointed, righteous chin. "We will see the full extent of the harm that you have done. With your clumsiness . . . your pretended clumsiness . . . or whatever it really was."

From the machine, his voice uttered in sharp echo and left a silence. An evasive answer from James Duncan. Another silence. Sharp words, A clash of voices, a cry of anger, a click, and the old man's voice again . . . "An' then we not been waitin' long an' that feller come pas' an' I been wavin'. Me an' Jimmy we been pick up in that fas' car, that big vee-eighter Ford that feller he been drivin'. An' that night we been mile an' mile pas' Droverdale."

I did it, James Duncan told himself. Skilled and efficient in these things, as I have always been. All gone. All that mattered, gone for ever. Now turn it off.

Please turn it off.

The words whispered in his inner ear and came again in echoed repetition, as if in his mind another voice was speaking.

Oh God, I've had enough, please turn it *off!*

Yet he did not speak, for something most disturbing was occurring in his mind. In his mind thoughts and words were whirling in confusion as if these thoughts and words, these abstract concepts of a life's realities, were being swept away like the fallen leaves of many seasons caught in a whirlwind gust.

And in his heart, something tense and potent, powerful as a tight-coiled spring, had snapped. All gone. All gone that resolution of the heart, that vanity of strength and purpose which had force enough to take him through most deeds to which his hand and mind were set—as, in this room, just now, it had. And, all that—gone.

Yet he had not changed his expression. He stood there still, as if unmoved.

Oh God.

All had collapsed in the chaos of his mind, and he could not tell them. More than anything he ever wanted, he wanted to get away—from them, and from himself. And he was confined within this room. He was held here, and he could not bear it.

He walked to the window and let his eyes escape to the sun-struck world outside.

Feathered with ocherous dust, scraggy hens jerked in listless pecking across the stony yard beside the house. Trees in a row, as bare of trunk as poles, bounded the dreary yard. The leaves of the trees—pointed, drooping, narrow, lacking the slightest breath of movement—struck metallic light from a naked morning sun.

Beneath the trees, in clouds of reddish dust, dark children played their games.

No escape out there. None anywhere. Not from himself.

And still, in the room, the hoarse voice of that dead man spoke. That poor old man.

Now, suddenly, that voice came with a different sound. Now, suddenly, that voice was real, a dead man's voice. Real his death, and real the fact that this voice was all that he had left behind him.

Before, that voice had been alive, even though you knew the man was dead. Dying, when these very words, heard now, were uttered. And from that old man these were all the words there ever would be. You could count them, a lifetime's store of words, running to their end. Running out, a life, and all that its years of life had meant.

And I, too, James Duncan thought, I too. Each word I have ever said, one less of my total store. And I have been so prodigal with words.

How many are left to *me?*

He saw that the words he had stolen from the tape had the incalculable value of all things not replaceable. He saw that what he had done could never be undone.

And that was one of the things from which he would never find escape.

The voice ended. He turned from the window, watched by the other men. He met their eyes. By seeing him they seemed to confirm the reality of a common life, to make his life—himself— a solid thing again, and real. His mind cleared.

"What are you going to do?"

"What *can* I do?" said Hardy. "What can I achieve by doing anything?"

"It was not an accident. I meant to do it all along."

"You must not tell me. I do not want to know."

"But I must explain . . . listen, I had my reasons. Good reasons. There was nothing wicked . . ."

"I have a great deal of work to do," said Hardy in a cold and bitter voice. "I will be busy. I will see you tomorrow, before you leave. But now I must ask to be excused."

"Peter! You must tell him. Peter! You know my reasons . . ."

"I know you said you would," said Peter. "But I did not believe you would do it."

"Oh Peter . . . Peter! Haven't we suffered together? Peter, I . . ."

Their eyes were turned away. The brief reality their eyes had given him was lost. His mind had lost its strength, and now his heart. And now his limbs.

As he fell to the floor the two men seemed to rise in the air and fly above him.

You do not understand, he said, as they knelt beside him. You will not let me tell you.

But he could see they did not hear him.

Peter! We did so much to reach this place and save that boy. Listen! We suffered. We came so far! And I could not stop! I could not change my course! I had to go as far as it was needed, to save his life. His life, and somehow yours. Why won't you understand?

They did not hear him.

Hardy was holding his wrist. He could feel the pulse of his heart beating on Hardy's fingers. He groaned.

"Ah," said Hardy. "He isn't . . . yes, that's better. You had me worried. Now, look at me. Yes. Move your fingers? Move the other hand. Yes. Now your feet, move your feet. Can you talk? What is your name?"

"Jim." It was a stupendous effort, but he heard the word. He had said his name. He closed his eyes.

"I don't know, really," said Hardy. "But I should think he'll be all right. We'll put him to bed. My medical knowledge is rather limited, I fear. A stroke was what I thought at first . . . or, heart . . . but he doesn't seem to have those signs. Has he a history of any sort?"

"He has a history. Yes," said Peter. "He has been through an ordeal which could have killed many a younger man. He came through on his nerve and courage, and I think he might have used that up. Yes. Here in this room he used the last of it. He turned to me . . . he reached out his hand to me for help, as I reached mine to him the other day, when I'd have drowned without his hand to help me. And I drew my hand away. I let him fall."

"That's not much use, that kind of talk," said Hardy. "What are you trying to say? Do you think he needs a doctor?"

"No," said Peter. "I think he needs a friend. A friend who does not care whether what he does is good or bad."

"Such friends are rather hard to find," said Hardy slowly, perhaps with pity.

18

It seemed to James Duncan that the sound of shouting voices roused him, but when he opened his eyes he knew he was finished with sleeping for a while and would have awakened anyway.

He faced an unlined wall, a frame of timber studs which showed the backs of rough-sawn boards. His body ran with sweat.

Out in the yard, men shouted at some cheerful game. He heard the flat sound of a kicked ball, a hollow bouncing, the mocking, playful cries of men.

He turned in the bed to face the window from which these noises came.

"Well!" said Peter. "You're awake at last. How is it now?"

"How long have you been there?"

"An hour . . . two hours? . . . I wouldn't know." Peter had a book across his knees, but something in his attitude, the way he sat his chair, something reflective and thoughtful in the expression of his face, showed that he had not been reading.

"I'm thirsty," said James Duncan, and Peter reached for a jug beside him on the floor.

Sitting up to take the glass, James Duncan said, "I'm well aware that what I did can't ever be undone, but I'd like to say I'm sorry."

"Not now," said Peter. "It would be better not to talk about it now."

"No doubt," James Duncan agreed, handing back the glass. "No doubt, if you and I were other people, perhaps it could be left. Perhaps it wouldn't matter. But you and I have been too close for that. There was a bond between us, and it is broken. That is what appalls me. How close we were; and how distant now. How far you have turned against me. That is what I can't accept."

"You must not disturb yourself."

"There's no call for you to be so damned evasive! No need at all to spare me. I'm quite all right. I needed to sleep, and I have slept. If I want to talk, you'll listen. If I want to ask questions, you will answer. I must know exactly where I stand."

"Where you stand?"

"Yes. And don't you fool around, or else you *will* disturb me. What chance is there that I will be forgiven?"

"Forgiven? By me? Is that something I'm supposed to do? Jump on a pedestal and start to judge what others do?"

"Oh, you're bloody smart," said James Duncan, in growing irritation. "Smarter and smarter as we go along. Jesus. I don't know why I bother."

"It isn't a simple matter of forgiveness," said Peter, softening his voice, recalling, perhaps, the other's need for kindness. "There's so much to be admired in what you did . . ."

"Ah, don't give me that! You . . ."

"No. Let me say it. You showed fantastic strength of will. You had decided what you had to do, and you went ahead and did it. No man could have stopped you. And yet, you'd gone far past your limit of endurance. A moment later you collapsed from sheer exhaustion. So there's much to be admired in what you did. That force of yours, that strength of character and will . . ."

"That's enough!" cried James Duncan furiously. "Am I a *child?* You think I'll swallow stuff like that? You think you can butter me up with stupid praise, the better to tear me to pieces with that righteous tongue of yours? You *fool!* Don't you think I *know* that what I did was wrong? That you have judged me? That we are finished, you and I?"

"What do you want of me?" Peter was shaken by this outburst, and James Duncan, seeing this, felt anger die. Swept by a wave of different feeling, his own face was left exposed in naked honesty. The slightest of tremors moved his mouth.

"What do I want?" he said. "Or what do I deserve? Two different things. What I want is very simple. Not very much at all. A clean sheet. A new start. All the wrong things I've done forgotten."

"And I can give you that?"

"You could, yes. My new start, you could give me that. I offered myself, and I was sincere, as much in earnest as I've ever been. But all I ask now is that you tell me what you have decided. Will you accept me? My help, my skill? Or shall my life go on the way it always has before?"

"And you think it is possible . . . that it is wise . . . to decide this now?"

"It *must* be now. It will be now, or never."

"Right now? This minute?" said Peter, in a wondering voice. "When only hours ago you showed you'd let no scruple stop you in achieving what you'd set your mind on? When you showed how ruthless you can be? To judge it now; you think that improves your chances?"

"Ah, now it's coming out! By God, yes, this is the time for your decision. This will be the test!"

"And who is being tested?" Peter said. "Is that what you mean? Is this a test for me?"

"You can be the judge of that," said James Duncan with a grim smile. "Maybe I had *my* test. Maybe I failed it. Perhaps now, we're testing you. Your honesty, for one thing. Your sincerity. Whether you've the guts to lay it on the line."

"Why can't you wait?"

"No, damn you, I will not wait. You'll take me at my worst, and you'll decide. And I will go without complaint whichever way you say. Listen . . . a plain yes or no, and you could have this over in a moment."

Peter rose from his chair and went to the window, seeing prospects hidden from the other man. The present moment: the sky a blaze of crimson where the sun had set, men and boys with hard, bare feet kicking a ball around in the subsiding heat of evening, gleaming dark bodies wet with perspiration.

And he saw a future: with utter trust the implicit need in all things where his dependence fell on others.

"Always, I will be your friend," he said. "Remember that. But you are asking more of me than that, more than I can give you. The answer is no. If you're determined you must have it now, that is what the answer has to be. And how can that surprise you?"

"It doesn't," said James Duncan. "It merely confirms the meanness of your spirit. No, I'm not surprised. Maybe I've had a fortunate escape."

"We have both been tested now," said Peter.

"And each have failed," said James Duncan. "Though I might claim I came off a little better, in my test, than you in yours. With a little more dash, perhaps? Your test was too easy. No sweat, no risk. Only the feelings of a sick man to contend with."

"I would not have said that made it any easier."

"I shouldn't be so sorry for myself," James Duncan said. "At least I knew what I had to do, and I did it, regardless of any cost. And I did it for you. You started me on this; you set me on saving Jinben. And, in that, I was loyal to the bitter end. I could not let them hear what the old man said, and I wiped it out."

"It was the truth," said Peter. "In the end, we heard the truth."

"Of course. But not a truth that was fit for other ears. Or so I thought when I had only seconds to decide."

"But Jinben is *guilty!*" Peter cried. "That dreadful deed; he did it! It was no longer our task to save him. His guilt released us."

"But I was doing it for *you*," said James Duncan. "However absurd that sounds, it's true. It was as if, almost, in doing that, I was saving *you*. I was confused; I see that now. And I was wrong, I see that too. And for being wrong, in having those seconds to decide what I should do for you, and in deciding wrongly . . . for that you have condemned me."

"Must I say more?" said Peter unhappily. "Can't you leave it?"

"Be a good sport about it? That what you mean? Let you kick me in the teeth, and just lie here and take it? All right. Pick up your tender conscience and run away. Shove off; it's over."

"I can't. Something has to be said, though I'd have chosen any other time to say it. But the time is your choice, please remember that."

"Go on, wrap it up. Get it off your chest."

"You've offered me your help, and you could help me greatly; I have no doubt of that. And I've wondered about your offer ever since you made it. I've wondered, mostly, just what kind of help you'd give me."

"I'll answer that. It would be the best help you could get from anyone. I could get you into Parliament; few men could say that with such confidence as I. I could put you where you could *do* things, instead of sounding off about them. Where you could apply those ideals of truth and goodness that you're always preaching."

"And in the process of getting there? What might you do to truth and goodness on the way? We had the *truth* on that tape this morning, and what happened to *that*? Who destroyed it?"

"Very clever," said James Duncan in a gloomy voice, examining Peter's face in the fading light of evening. "Top marks for that one."

"And how long would it be before you decided again that you must destroy the truth to help me?"

"Couldn't it be that I might have learned my lesson?"

"Is truth a lesson? Is it something that's used because it's practical to use it? Is it something you choose because it pays off best? No! You follow the path of truth because your heart tells you it's the only way. And *your* heart has followed too wandering a path to change its habits now. No longer could you follow truth wherever it might lead; whether it was for you or against you. You would fight it, turn truth the way you thought it had to go. No matter how you feel about it now."

"Oh you saintly bastard," said James Duncan. "I could never reach your standards. I admit it. I'd never aspire to that. But I can help you! And you're a bloody fool if you refuse to see it."

"Help me?" cried Peter. "Yes, you'd help me ... You'd help me be like *them*. Like you, and all the others. For you're an expert in this subject of the truth; an expert on the other side of truth, where truth is a kind of putty that can be molded by your clever fingers to the most convenient shape. Yes! You'll be one of those I will be fighting, one of those who have reduced the truth to another paltry gimmick. One of those who have stolen truth away from that mixed-up world of yours until even the best of things is only partly true. And it can't go on like that! In the end, you'll find, men cannot live in a world that's built on lies and distortion, and cunning, and leftover fragments of the truth.

"But you professionals . . . all you P.R. men, and admen, and newsmen; your politicians and your priests; your leaders . . . you think that men will adapt themselves to such a world. That is the fatal conceit which has mucked up all that your world's supposed to stand for. That's why your lives have lost their meaning and their purpose . . . because, in everything, all is expedience and compromise. I am sorry. Do I have to tell you this?"

"Not right now," said James Duncan, with a coldness that seemed like anger, but a coldness that was only coldness, a chill motion in the empty spaces of his heart. "Not now. Wait until you've grown a little older. Wait until you learn what life is really like. Wait until you have to meet life with compromise."

"I'll never compromise," said Peter, with utter confidence. "And that might be my only strength. I'll never compromise, not even from kindness and affection as, with you, perhaps I should. Yes. Only in that do I differ from all those others who have set out with the best intentions. And I must guard this strength by any means. I will *never* compromise. Not with you, not with anything I meet. But I will never encounter a crueler test than this decision now."

"Leave me, and let me sleep," said James Duncan, in a dead, exhausted voice. "Suddenly I'm very tired. When we go back to the city, perhaps we'll talk about it then."

"I am not going," said Peter. "I am staying here. For a while, six months . . . a year, longer maybe. While you were asleep I was talking with Mr. Hardy. There's work here to be done. Something to be learned. I . . ."

"I haven't a clue what you're talking about," said James Duncan, yawning. "And I don't much care."

"Hardy is not the man he seems," said Peter. "This is no ordinary mission. He is guiding my people to a new life of cooperation and achievement. I have decided I must stay, and give my help, and learn."

"Bloody marvelous, I'm sure. I'm half asleep. Goodnight. See you tomorrow, before I leave."

Leaving the room, Peter turned and, looking at Peter as if he would never be seen again, James Duncan saw the dark hair waved from the handsome brow; the broad snub nose; the full-lipped mouth; the sadness of those dark eyes, for all their softness, steady and determined in their gaze.

Peter raised a hand, palm up, as though he felt that some final token of friendship should be offered. But the hand was empty.

After a while James Duncan left the bed and walked with slow steps to the window.

Full night had fallen on the world outside. Distant windows glowed on the hill beyond the trees. All else was dark. Flavored with eucalyptus smoke, the hot smell of dusty day still lingered. Somewhere in the house a cheerful voice was raised in tuneless song.

Was that enough to make a man so sad? Night's mood in this far corner of the world?

Suddenly, he ached for city sounds and city lights, for the noise and presence of many people close around him. For lights, and traffic sounds, and movement.

He arranged the rumpled bed, and again lay down.

Mosquitoes whined around his face.

Staring into darkness he found that in the easy sweep of a moment's recollection he could join the events of those past long days, from the moment of stepping aboard the boat to cross the river, to this moment now, this moment of being in this bed, of being safe. Safe!

That's it, he whispered. It's over. Finished. And I came through! That unexpected and terrible interval in my normal life has ended. In two more nights, sleep will find me in that other bed I know so well. And I can take my life up where I left it off.

He thought about that life, so far away that it seemed to belong to someone else.

He thought about that life, and he began to sort through its odds and ends as if it were some ragbag where a forgotten treasure might have been mislaid.

He closed his eyes. With a kind of despairing lust he summoned the thought, the fleshly image, of Wendy Bracker.

But when she came into his mind there was nothing there he wanted at this moment. Or ever again, perhaps. No spark of hopefulness that, by such a thing as that, life was justified, made more endurable, given reward and purpose.

He fell into a light and restless sleep.

He woke sharply, trapping the thought that had banished sleep.

If he is staying, then why can't I?

He returned to the window, now the source of a cooling breeze which helped to inspire a more objective mood.

But how could he bear this dismal place, so far removed from everything that habit valued?

How could he last out that long apprenticeship in truth and goodness ... without soon scorning such sharp standards of righteousness as Peter set?

And to what end? To show Peter that he could be trusted? For nothing more than that?

He stared into the night, now seeing more. The bare yard where the men had kicked the ball at dusk; the dim shapes of the rustling trees; movements of people in the soft light of those windows on the lonely hill. And darkness all around, darkness unrelieved as far as the mind could reach.

Was this for him?

Was the change in his life to be so arbitrary and absolute as this?

It wouldn't work, he decided instantly. A man my age does not overnight become a saint. And who, for Christ's sake, wants to be a saint?

Not me!

But there were other ways. He must work out how to do this without the need to be a saint; without wanting to be a saint. He must remember that shrewd intelligence of his, and use it.

He must find the way to do what he wanted with Peter ... to help Peter, or be helped by him; to make Peter into something; whatever it was ... but without giving up his own place in that other world he couldn't leave.

He must do what they said he had to do. Go home tomorrow. Yes, but after a while, come back.

He was shivering. He returned to the bed, but not to sleep. To let his active thoughts construct a brighter future.

In absorbed excitement he pictured this arid dustheap of a place made rich with the green of pasture, cattle grazing fat. That could be done. A dam higher up the river, piping and pumps, irrigation. Things like that could be done with money. And money came from the skillful designs of clever men ... publicity! And he was the man for that!

Quick with enthusiasm, his thoughts transformed this dreary place into a paradise. He could see most of the ways to go about it.

Peter would see. Peter would see what could be done.

He could sleep now.

He knew he could have his way.

About the Author

John Iggulden is an Australian, the author of three previously published novels, of which the last, *The Clouded Sky,* was the first to be produced in the United States. Much of the background for that book was drawn from the author's penchant for gliding; he won the National Gliding Championship of Australia several years ago. Mr. Iggulden, now in his forties, a successful production engineer and businessman, has for some years turned to writing as his main interest.